# WEIRD WORLDS

The three battled the universe to return to their own world and time. Veg struck out on his own, encountering a multi-colored blizzard, edible fog and giant, menacing plant life. Cal and Aquilon, joined by the creature OX, had found a way to visit any world they had ever imagined—including the dimension from which they had come.

But was there a chance of rescuing their lost friend Veg? Could their frail human bodies withstand the strange forces of OX's vast powers? And most important, could this alien be trusted to return them to the safety of their own universe and time?

"If you read OMNIVORE and ORN and were fascinated, you must read OX."
*Fantasy and Science Fiction Review*

*Other  Avon  Books  by*
**Piers  Anthony**

| | | |
|---|---|---|
| BATTLE CIRCLE | 35469 | $2.25 |
| CHAINING THE LADY | 35121 | 1.75 |
| CLUSTER | 34686 | 1.75 |
| KIRLIAN QUEST | 35113 | 1.75 |
| MACROSCOPE | 36798 | 1.95 |
| ORN | 40964 | 1.75 |
| OMNIVORE | 40527 | 1.75 |
| RINGS OF ICE | 38166 | 1.50 |

# OX

# PIERS ANTHONY

AVON
PUBLISHERS OF BARD, CAMELOT AND DISCUS BOOKS

AVON BOOKS
A division of
The Hearst Corporation
959 Eighth Avenue
New York, New York 10019

Copyright © 1976 by Piers Anthony
Published by arrangement with the author.
Library of Congress Catalog Card Number 78-70835
ISBN: 0-380-41392-2

All rights reserved, which includes the right
to reproduce this book or portions thereof in
any from whatsoever. For information address
Avon Books.

First Avon Printing, August, 1976
Second Printing

AVON TRADEMARK REG. U.S. PAT. OFF. AND
FOREIGN COUNTRIES, REGISTERED TRADEMARK—
MARCA REGISTRADA, HECHO EN CHICAGO, U.S.A.

Printed in the U.S.A.

# Chapter 1

# TRIO

. . .

It had a shiny black finish, solid caterpillar treads, a whirling blade—and it was fast. It was seemingly a machine—but hardly the servant of man.

Veg fired his blaster at it. The project charge should have heated the metal explosively and blown a chunk out of it. But the polished hide only gave off sparks and glowed momentarily. The thing spun about with dismaying mobility and came at him again, the vicious blade leading.

Veg bounded backward, grabbed the long crowbar, and jammed it end first into the whirring blade. "Try a mouthful of *that!*" he said, shielding his eyes from the anticipated fragmentation.

The iron pole bucked in his hands as the blade connected. More sparks flew. The blade lopped off sections, two inches at a time: CHOP CHOP CHOP CHOP! Six feet became five, then four, as the machine consumed the metal.

At that point Veg realized he was in a fight for his life. He had come across the machine chewing up the stacked supplies as he emerged from transfer and thought it was an armored animal or a remote-controlled device. It was more than either; it had an alarming aura of sentience.

He tried the rifle. The flash pan heated as he activated it; steam filled the firing chamber. Bullets whistled out in a rapid stream, for the steam rifle was smoother and more efficient than the explosive-powder variety. They bounced off the machine and ricocheted off the boulders on either side. He put at least one bullet directly in its eye-lens, but even this did no apparent harm.

Still, the contraption had halted its advance. *Something* must be hurting it!

The rifle ran out of bullets. Veg grabbed an explosive shell and slammed it into firing position as the machine moved forward again. He aimed at the treads and let fly.

Sand billowed out, for an instant obscuring the target. The machine wallowed—but a moment later it climbed out of the cavity formed by the explosion and emerged undamaged.

"You're a tough one!" Veg said admiringly. He was a man of barely dominant peace; he loved a good fight when he could justify it. He hurled the rifle at the enemy.

The weapon flew apart as the whirling blade swung to intercept it. One large section bounced away to the side. The machine turned to chase after it, chopping the piece up where it had fallen and scooping it into a nether-hopper. It did not, he saw now, have parallel treads, but a single broad line of cleats, individually retractable like the claws of a cat. The hopper opened just before this wheel/foot—and closed tightly when finished, like a mouth. Sophisticated . . .

Veg grinned for a moment. Wonderful technology, but the stupid thing didn't know the rifle was no longer dangerous! It had fought the weapon instead of the man.

Then he sobered. The machine wasn't *fighting* the rifle, it was *consuming* it! It ate metal.

He hadn't been battling this thing. He had been feeding it. No wonder it had halted; as long as he was willing to serve good metal by hand, why should the machine exert itself further?

This revelation didn't help much, however. It suggested that the machine was distressingly smart, not dumb. The human party would need that metal to survive. He couldn't let a ravenous machine gobble it all down.

8

Still, that gave him an idea. If metal fed it, would food hurt it?

Veg tore open a pack of food staples. Here were breadstuff and vegetables and—he paused with distaste as his hand rummaged—meat.

Then he brightened. What better use for it? He hauled out a plastic-wrapped steak and hurled it at the machine, which had just finished the rifle, burped, and turned back toward the man. The blade rose to catch the package; bits of flesh, bone, and plastic splayed into the air.

This time he observed the scoop-like orifice, the hopper, in action behind the blade. The different processes of the machine were well coordinated. The bulk of the freshly sliced meat and bone funneled directly into this mouth, just as the metal had. Veg held his breath, another steak in hand. Would the machine get sudden indigestion?

No such luck. A spout opened, and clear liquid dribbled out onto the ground: the surplus juices of the meat, apparently unneeded by the thing's metabolism. The machine assimilated the organic material as readily as it had the inorganic. And came on for more.

Would liquid short it out? External liquid, not digestive fluid. Veg found a bottle of water and heaved a full gallon at the fan. The machine was drenched.

First it shook; then it glowed all over. Death agonies for this nonliving creature? No—it was merely drying itself off efficiently by a combination of vibration and heat. It had not been incapacitated.

"Takes more brains than I got to handle this metal baby," Veg muttered as he danced nimbly aside. It was hardly the occasion for introspection, but Veg had high respect for the intelligence of his friend Cal and wished he were here at this moment. Cal could have looked at the oncoming machine and made one obvious suggestion, and the thing would be finished.

The two men had met years before, in space, introduced as a prank by idle crewmen. Veg was a vegetarian and, after too much ribbing, somewhat militant about it. Since he was also an extremely powerful man, the sniggers had soon abated. Rabbit food did not necessarily make rabbits.

Until word circulated of a man who was a pure carnivore, eating nothing but meat—man flesh, at that!—and who thought vegetarians were stupid. Veg had not reacted overtly, but his muscles had bulged under his shirt tensely.

Tiny, weak Calvin Potter—about as inoffensive as it was possible to be. Yet it was technically true: Owing to a savage episode in his past, he had been rendered unable to consume any food except human blood. And he was a genius, compared to whom all other people, including vegetarians, *were* stupid.

If Veg had suffered ridicule, it was minor compared to what Cal endured. Veg did not like being made a patsy for the torment of another man. He took the unhappy little Cal under his bone-crushing wing, and very shortly no one thought anything about him was even faintly humorous.

Yet as it turned out, Cal was the stronger man, able because of his intellect to tackle even a predator dinosaur alone and barehanded—and to survive. He had actually done it.

There was no way to summon Cal. Veg had beamed through to this alternate world first, to set things up for his companions and scout for any dangers. Aquilon was to follow in an hour, Cal in another hour, along with the mantas. All nice and neat.

Only about two hundred and fifty pounds could be transferred at one time, and the equipment had to cool off after each use. That was why things had to be spaced out. Or so the agents claimed. Veg didn't believe the male-agent, Taler; the female, Tamme, was obviously no more trustworthy, but on a woman it didn't really matter.

He retreated again. Well, he had found danger, all right! Rather, it had found him. An animate buzz saw with an omnivorous appetite. If he didn't figure out something pretty soon, it would eat him *and* the supplies and lie in wait for Aquilon . . .

That goaded him to fury. The thought of the lovely woman being consumed by the machine . . .

Veg had always been able to take or leave women, and because he was large, muscular, and handsome, he had taken a number. Until Aquilon, the girl who never smiled, came into his life. She was an artist, whose paintings were almost as beautiful as she. Though she was competent and independent, she was also deep-down *nice*. Veg had not known what real love was, but to know Aquilon was indeed to love her, though she had never solicited it. Part of that love now was to give her up without resentment; *that* was the essence she had taught him simply by being what she was. She might have split the Veg-Cal friendship apart—but she needed them both as much as they needed her. So they had become three friends, closer than before, with no competition or jealousy between them. Finally she was able to smile . . .

"I'm going to get you out of here if it kills me!" Veg cried. He hoisted the bag of food to his shoulder and began running. "Come, doggie!" he called, flipping back a package of raisins. "Soup's on—if you can catch it!"

The machine had been sampling the fabric of the tent-assembly. It angled its blade to catch the raisins. Evidently it liked them better—more iron?—because it followed after Veg.

He led it across the desert, away from the supplies. His tactic was working—but what would happen when he ran out of food?

Aquilon stood chagrined at the carnage. The supplies had been ravaged, bits of meat and metal were scattered across the sand, and Veg was nowhere in sight. What had happened?

She cradled the egg in her arms, keeping it warm. It was a large egg, like a small football, nine inches long. It was all that remained of two fine birds she had known and loved. They had died, protecting her and it. There was no way to repay them except to vindicate their trust and preserve the egg until it hatched.

She felt a sudden urge to paint. She always painted when upset; it calmed her marvelously. She had painted the phenomenal fungus landscape of Planet Nacre, where she and the two men had had their first great adventure together. She had painted the savage omnivore of that world—and seen in it the mere reflection of the worst omnivore of all, man himself. She had painted dinosaurs

11

—but how could she paint the ravening monsters that were the souls of human beings, herself included?

She could try; it might work this time. To make visible the ego of the human omnivore . . . but to do that she would have to put down the egg . . .

Then she saw the tracks. Veg's footprints led away from the camp, partly obscured by something he must have been dragging. Had he gone exploring? He should have stayed nearby, securing the camp against possible dangers, not gallivanting about the countryside. Not that there was much countryside to see; this was about as gaunt a locale as she cared to endure. Sand and boulders . . .

But what would account for the destruction of supplies? Someone or something had vandalized them, and she knew Veg would not have done that. The cuts were peculiar, almost like the marks of a rampant power-saw. Strange, strange.

She was worried now. If something had attacked, Veg would have fought. That was the omnivore in him despite his vegetarianism. That could account for the mess. If he had won, why wasn't he here? If he had lost, why were his footprints leading away? Veg was stubborn; he would have died fighting. He would never have run.

She had thought she loved Veg at one time. Physically, sexually. She had tried to be a vegetarian like him. But somehow it hadn't worked out. She still cared for him deeply, however, and his unexplained absence troubled her.

She contemplated the prints. Could he have lost—and been taken captive? If someone held a gun on him, even Veg would not have been so foolish as to resist. Yet where were the prints of his captor? There were only the treadlike marks of whatever he had been hauling . . .

No, she still didn't have it. First, there would be no one here to hold a gun or any other weapon on Veg. This was an uninhabited wilderness desert on an unexplored alternate world. They were the first human beings to set foot on it. Second, the prints diverged in places, sometimes being separated by several yards. If Veg had been dragging or hauling anything, the marks would have been near his own prints, always.

She stooped to examine the other marks more carefully, cradling the big egg in one arm. She touched the flattened sand with one finger. Substantial weight had been here—a ton or more, considering the breadth of the track and the depression of the sand. Like tire marks but wider, and there was only one line instead of parallel lines. What sort of vehicle had made that? Not a human artifact . . .

The obvious thing to do was to follow the tracks and find out. But she wasn't supposed to leave the campsite until Cal and the mantas were through the aperture, and she didn't want to walk into the clutches—treads?—of whatever had followed Veg. There was no real cover here apart from the boulders; as soon as she got close enough to see it, *it* would see her. And if it had made Veg move out, there was no way she could fight it. Veg was an extraordinarily able man physically.

So she would have to stay here, keeping a sharp lookout, and clean up the mess. If she were lucky, nothing would happen until Cal arrived. If she were luckier, Veg would return unharmed.

She turned, letting the bright sunlight fall on the egg, warming it. Ornet was inside that egg, the embryo of a bird that possessed a kind of racial memory: perhaps a better tool for survival than man's intelligence. If only the right habitat could be found. And if only a mate for the bird could be found, too. Maybe one could be fetched from Paleo, the first alternate-Earth, and the pair would start a dynasty here in some desert oasis, and she could watch the community prosper . . .

Desert oasis . . . this was Earth, or an alternate of it; the landscape matched some place and some time on the world she knew. Where—on Earth—was this? Cal was the only one who could figure that out.

The shadow of a human being fell across the sand before her, jolting her out of her reverie. Aquilon froze before she looked up; it was too soon for Cal to appear, and Veg could not have come upon her unawares. Who, then? She looked—and gave a little gasp of amazement.

A beautiful blonde girl stood before her, shaped like

a siren beneath her flowing hair. Siren in more than one way: She was nude.

The apparition's blue eyes surveyed the scene coolly. Aquilon, functionally attired in denim, felt out of sorts. "Who are you?" she demanded.

"Pointless to go into all that now," the nymph said. "Please give me the egg."

Aquilon stepped back involuntarily. "No!"

"You must. You can't preserve it any longer. Not here in the desert with the awful machines. I have found a new Garden of Eden, a paradise for birds; when it hatches there—"

"No one else can—" Aquilon broke off, realizing what her mind had balked at before. "You're *me!*"

"And you're me, close enough," the blonde said. "So you can trust me. You—"

"But you're—you're more—"

The woman's eyes dropped momentarily down to her own bosom, following Aquilon's gaze. "I bore a child; that's why. I lost mine; you'll keep yours. But you can't keep the egg."

Aquilon retreated. "A baby? I—"

"You are in danger. You can save yourself but not the egg. There is little time, and it's too complicated to explain right now. Give it to me." She reached out.

"No!" Aquilon retreated again, hugging the egg. Her mind was spinning with this inexplicable development. How had her buxom double manifested here? *Could* she trust her—or was it some weird kind of trap? To know that the egg really was safe . . .

"Give it to me!" the blonde cried, diving for her.

Aquilon straightarmed her, but the force of the woman's lunge shoved her back. Her heels caught against a bag of supplies, and she tumbled backward, the blonde on top of her. Both of them screamed.

The egg, caught between them, had been crushed. The large embryo within, released too soon, flopped blindly and died.

Cal looked about. The supplies had been savaged. Veg was gone, and Aquilon was lying on the ground near a mound of sand. He rushed to her.

She was not dead. She was sobbing. She lifted a sand-smudged face to him as he put his hand on her shoulder. In one hand was a fragment of broken shell.

Cal realized that the precious egg had been smashed. She must have fallen while holding it and then had to bury the remains. Hence the tears, the mound of sand.

He felt sharp regret. That egg had meant a lot to her, and therefore to him. He had hoped it could be preserved until it hatched, inconvenient as that process was.

But more important, now: What had this loss done to Aquilon? And where was Veg? Had Veg had something to do with the destruction of the egg? No, impossible!

He let her be. She would have to recover in her own fashion. There was no genuine comfort he could provide; the egg was irrevocably gone. He analyzed the tracks instead—and was amazed.

Veg had gone somewhere across the desert and not returned. Aquilon had apparently fought someone—a barefoot person, possibly female, for the prints were small. Those tracks staggered a short way over the sand and then vanished. And some kind of vehicle had come and gone, doing damage to the supplies enroute.

Had the agents sent in other missions? Other people, with power equipment—and bare feet? For what reason? If there were two or more missions, they should have been informed of each other's presence so they could rendezvous. Certainly they should not have raided each other. And Taler, the agent leader, had had no reason to lie about this.

Still, the rebuilt-human-androids that were the agents were smart, strong, and ruthless in the performance of their assigned missions. Cal had a sober respect for them even when he had to oppose them. One agent of the SU series, Subble, had been assigned to ascertain the truth about the Nacre adventure; he had done so. Three of the TA series had been sent to salvage the alternate-Earth Paleo for human civilization; they had made a devastatingly direct attempt to do that, also, despite all Cal's efforts. As a result, the enclave of dinosaurs had been wiped out, the Orn-bird killed, and the trio of "normal" people taken prisoner. As though a girl like

Aquilon could ever be considered typical, or a man like Veg!

"Hex! Circe!" he snapped, turning to the creatures who were sitting motionless near the aperture, their lambent eyes fastened on him. "Find Veg. Careful—danger."

The two mantas leaped into the air, flattening into their speed-form as they moved. They sailed across the desert like two low-flying kites, swift and silent.

Aquilon rose. "Cal!" she cried despairingly.

He walked toward her, wishing with one part of his mind that she were the kind to fall into a man's arms when she needed comforting. But she was not; very seldom did she break down. She was a tough, realistic girl. As long as she lived, she would function well. That was probably why he loved her; her beauty was secondary.

"What happened?" he asked gently.

"A woman came and broke the egg," she said. "And she was me."

"*You?*" Those bare, feminine prints . . .

"Me. My double. Only more so. I hit her . . ."

Something clicked in his mind. "The alternate framework!" he exclaimed. "I should have known!"

"What?" She was so pretty when she was surprised!

"We're dealing in alternates now. There must be an infinite number of alternate-Earths. Once we start crossing those boundaries, we run the risk of meeting ourselves. As you did . . ."

"Oh!" she said, comprehending. "Then she *was* me. Only she'd had a baby. But why was she here—and where did she go?"

"We can't know yet. Did she say anything?"

"Only that I could survive but not the egg. She wanted to take it to some Eden . . ."

"She must have known your future. Perhaps she was from a slightly more advanced framework. In a year she could have had her baby and lost her egg, so she knew from experience—"

"No—it was her *baby* she lost." Aquilon shook her head, unsettled. "She said I would keep mine. But I'm not pregnant!"

"There are other alternates," he pointed out. "An

infinite number of Aquilons will have had babies, and an infinite number more will be due. She could have mistaken you. She meant well."

"And I fought her," Aquilon said. "I shouldn't have done that . . ."

"How could you know? And you had a right to retain your egg no matter what she knew. You fought for it before to save it from dinosaurs."

"But now neither of us have it. She was crying as she left . . ."

"She wanted to save the egg—and instead destroyed it," Cal said. "She felt as you would feel."

Aquilon looked at him, her tear-streaked face still sandy—and lovely. "Then she is desolate. I should have given it to her."

"No. Each world must look out for its own. We fought to prevent Earth from despoiling Paleo; we must also fight to prevent other alternates from despoiling *us*. But we must understand that they are very much like us . . ."

"Omnivores!" she said bitterly.

"But there is a positive side. Orn's egg has been lost in this alternate—but there must be many alternates where it was saved. In some you kept it; in others the other Aquilon took it. But the chick isn't dead, there."

"Ornet," she said. "Offspring of Orn and Ornette . . ."

He smiled. She was coming out of it. "By any other name . . . Now we must find out what happened to Veg."

Her eyes followed the tracks across the sand. "Do you think he—?"

"I sent the mantas after him. Somehow they know; they would not have gone if he were dead."

"Yes, of course," she murmured.

They cleaned up the supplies somewhat, making packs for each person, just in case. A blaster and a rifle were missing, and one of the long crowbars, suggesting that Veg had taken them. "But we already know that we face a strange situation," Cal warned her. "Conventional weapons may be useless."

"Machine!" she said suddenly.

Cal looked up inquiringly. "We have no machines here."

"My double—she said something about machines, here in the desert. 'Awful machines.' A danger—"

Cal looked once more at the tread-tracks. "A machine," he murmured thoughtfully. "Following Veg . . ."

"Oh, let's hurry!" she cried. "And take weapons!"

They started out warily, following Veg's tracks and those of the mystery vehicle. Cal was ill at ease; if a human being could appear from another alternate, so could heavy equipment. Suppose some kind of tank had been dispatched to hunt down the visitors to this world? They just might have walked into an interalternate war . . .

Aquilon stopped abruptly, rubbing her eyes. "Cal!" she whispered.

Cal looked. At first he saw nothing; then he became aware of a kind of sparkle in the air ahead. Faint lights were blinking on and off, changing their fairy patterns constantly.

"A firefly swarm?" Aquilon asked. "Let me paint it." She was never without her brush and pad, and now, without the egg to hold, she could paint again.

She hesitated. He knew why: Her sudden freedom made her feel guilty. How much better to have given the egg to her double! The woman would have taken care of it every bit as well as Aquilon herself because she *was* Aquilon—wiser for her bitter experience. Or at least, so it would seem—to *this* Aquilon at this moment. He had to divert her thoughts.

"Fireflies? With no plants to feed the insects?" Cal asked, posing what he knew to be a fallacious question. "We have seen no indigenous life here."

"There has to be life," she replied as she quickly sketched. "Otherwise there would be no breathable atmosphere. Plants give off oxygen."

"Yes, of course . . ." he agreed, watching the swarm. "Still, there is something odd here."

The sparkle-pattern intensified. Now it was like a small galaxy of twinkling stars, the individual lights changing so rapidly that the eye could not fix on them. But Aquilon's trained perception was catching the artistry of it. Color flowed from her automatic brush, brightening the picture. This was the marvelous, crea-

18

tive person he had known, expressing herself through her art.

The flashes were not random; they moved in ripples, like the marquee of an old cinemahouse. These ripples twined and flexed like living things. But not like chains of fireflies.

"Beautiful," Aquilon breathed. Yes, now her own beauty illumined her; she was what she perceived.

Suddenly the swarm moved toward them. The lights became bright and sharp. The outline expanded enormously.

"Fascinating," Cal said, seeing three-dimensional patterns within the cloud, geometric ratios building and rebuilding in dazzling array. This was no random collection of blinkers . . .

Aquilon grabbed his arm. "It sees us!" she cried in abrupt alarm. "Run!"

It was already too late. The glowing swarm was upon them.

# Chapter 2

*Survive!*

OX assimilated the directive, knowing nothing but the need. *How, why, mode,* were absent; there was no rationale. Only the imperative. It was inherent in his being; it made him what he was. It *was* what he was: the need to survive.

He turned his attention to the external.

*Disorientation. Distress. Nonsurvival.*

OX retracted, halving his volume. What had happened?

Survival dictated that he explore despite the pain of the external. OX realized that through DISTRESS related to NONSURVIVAL, certain forms of distress might be necessary *to* survival. Judgment was required. He modified his capabilities to accommodate this concept and thereby became more intelligent.

Experiment and intelligence provided a working rationale: He had extended himself too precipitously and thereby thrown his basic organization out of balance.

The lesson: Expansion had to be organized. Four dimensions became far more complex than three, requiring a different *type* of organization.

OX extended a fleeting outer feedback shell to explore the limits of his locale. It was not large; he had room to move about but had to contain himself somewhat.

20

*Discomfort.* Minor distress but growing. $\overline{OX}$ hovered in place, but the discomfort increased. He moved, and it abated. Why?

The base on which he rested, the network of points, was fading. He was his environment; he occupied many small elements, drawing energy from them, making a sentient pattern of them. This energy was limited; he had to move off and allow it to regenerate periodically. Merely sitting in one spot would exhaust that set of elements: nonsurvival.

The larger $\overline{OX}$ expanded, the more points he encompassed and the more energy he consumed. By contracting within optimum volume he conserved survival resources. But he could not become too small, for that limited his abilities and led to dysfunction.

$\overline{OX}$ stabilized. But his minimum functional size was still too large for the territory to sustain indefinitely. He could exist at maximum size briefly or at minimum size longer—but the end was nonsurvival, either way.

*Survive!* He had to keep searching.

He searched. Unsuccess wasted resources and led to discomfort. Yet even in his distress, there was a special irritant. Certain circuits were not functioning properly. He investigated.

All was in order.

He returned to the larger problem of survival—and the interference resumed persistently.

$\overline{OX}$ concentrated on the annoyance. Still there was no perceivable dysfunction. It did not manifest when he searched for it, only when he was otherwise occupied.

He set up a spotter circuit, oriented on the troublesome section. He had not known how to do this before the need arose, but this was the way of survival: the necessary, as necessary.

$\overline{OX}$ returned to his larger quest—and the irritation manifested. This time the spotter was on it. He concentrated, pouncing, as it were, on what he had trapped.

Nothing.

Paradox. The spotter oriented on any malfunction; it was a modified feedback, simple and certain. Yet there was a malfunction—and the spotter had failed.

OX suffered disorientation. Paradox was nonsurvival. It was also annoying as hell.

He disciplined himself, simplifying his circuits. No paradox. If the spotter hadn't caught it, there was no malfunction. But there *was* something. What?

OX concentrated. He refined his perceptions. Gradually he fathomed it. It was not *his* malfunction but an interruption from an external source. Thus the spotter had had no purchase.

Something was obscuring some of his elements. Not obliterating them but damping them down so that he was aware of the loss of energy—peripherally. When he investigated, he shifted off those particular elements, and the effect abated. He could only perceive it through that damping, while his circuits were functioning. Ghostly, it avoided his direct attention, for it was an *effect,* not a *thing.*

Was it an ailment of the elements themselves? If so, his survival would be more limited than originally projected—and he was already in a nonsurvival situation.

OX cast a net of spotters to determine the precise configuration of the damping. Soon he had it: There were actually three centers set close together. A stable, persistent blight. No immediate threat to survival.

Then one of the blight spots moved.

OX fibrillated. *Distress!* How could a blight move, retaining form? Stable or recurring form with movement was an attribute of sentience, of pattern. Blight was the *lack* of pattern.

Modification. Perhaps blight could slide somewhat, forced over by some unknown compulsion. Nonsentient. All blight spots would suffer the same effect.

Another spot moved—the opposite way. Then both moved together—and apart.

*Disorientation.*

# Chapter 3

# TAMME

· · ·

Tamme emerged from the aperture, alert and wary. She had not told the three explorers that she was coming along and did not expect them to be pleased. But after the disaster on the dinosaur world, Paleo, the agents were taking few chances. These people were not to be trusted; left alone, they were too apt to concoct some other way to betray the interests of Earth.

The camp was deserted. Tamme saw at a glance that weapons and food had been removed: more than would normally have been used in the three hours since the first person had been sent through. They were up to something already!

But it was strange. Too many footprints led away. Veg, Cal, Aquilon—and a barefoot person? Plus something on a caterpillar tread. And the two mantas.

Caterpillar? Hardly standard equipment. Where had they gotten it?

Answer: There was nowhere they could have gotten it. Tamme herself had put through all the supplies in advance, checking and rechecking a detailed roster. This was the first human penetration to this new world. Sensors had reported breathable air, plant life, amphibious animals, fish—all far removed from this desert where the aperture actually debouched but certainly part of this alternate. Also advanced machines. That was what made immediate exploration imperative.

Machines did not evolve on their own. Something had to build them. Something more advanced than the machines themselves. Ergo, there was on this world something more than the sensors had indicated. Either an advanced human culture—or an alien one. Either way, a potential threat to Earth.

But windows to new worlds were hard to come by. The first such breakthrough had come only a few months ago, and Mother Earth naturally had not wanted to risk valuable personnel by sending them through a one-way aperture. So volunteers had been used—three space explorers who had gotten in trouble with the authorities and had therefore been amenable to persuasion. Expendables.

An unusual trio, actually. Vachel Smith: a huge vegetarian nicknamed Veg. Deborah Hunt, called Aquilon: named after the cold north wind because, it seemed, she seldom smiled. And Calvin Potter, a small, physically weak man with a fascinatingly complex mind. The three had been lost on a planet called Nacre—theoretically it glowed in space like a pearl because of its perpetual cloud cover—and had befriended the dominant life-form there: an animate fungus with extraordinary talents. The manta.

It had been a mistake to loose this group on the world beyond the aperture, and soon the authorities had recognized that. But by that time the trio, instead of perishing as expected, had penetrated to the nearest continent and gotten involved with the local fauna—they had a talent for that!—which turned out to be reptilian. In fact, dinosaurian. Extraction had been awkward.

Three agents of the TA series had accomplished it, however: Taner (now deceased), Taler, and Tamme herself. But when they made ready to return to Earth with the prisoners, another complication had developed. Their portable return-aperture generator had opened not on Earth but on a third world.

They had known there was risk involved—of exactly this kind. The apertures were experimental and erratic. Though Paleo was the only alternate to be reached so far from Earth, despite thousands of trials, one trial on Paleo had produced this unexpected and awkward pay-off. Perhaps it was a better initiation point.

The original Earth/Paleo aperture remained. It had been broadened so that massive supplies could be trans-ferred, and the three agents had built their own pre-fabricated ship with which to pursue the fugitives. A fourth agent had remained to guard the original aper-ture, which happened to be under the ocean near a Pacific islet a thousand miles from the western coast of Paleocene America.

It had seemed easier to transfer back directly from this spot—on the continent—rather than make a tedious trip back with the prisoners. Location seemed to make little difference to the apertures; they could start at any point and terminate anywhere—usually in the vacuum of interplanetary space. They had radioed Taol for approval, and he had contacted the Earth authorities for approval. If the supplementary aperture were suc-cessful, it would greatly facilitate the exploitation of Paleo.

Then, with the surprise development, new orders: check it out with sensors and explore it personally if necessary—but HOLD THAT CONNECTION! There was no certainty they could ever locate that world again, given the freakish nature of apertures, so it had to be held open now. Earth, enormously overpopulated, its natural re-sources approaching exhaustion, needed a viable alterna-tive to expensive commerce by space travel. This could be it. More personnel would be funneled through the main aperture in due course; meanwhile, use their present resources in case the connection became tenuous.

Thus, reprieve for the prisoners. They were free—to engage in another dangerous exploration. They had not, however, been told about the machines. This time an agent would accompany them. Just to keep them out of mischief.

Agents had been developed to handle this sort of emergency. An agent was not a person; he was an android on a human chassis, molded to precise specifica-tions. Tamme had no past beyond her briefing for this mission; all she knew was the material in the common pool of information shared by every agent of the TA type. And that overlapped considerably with the pool of SU before her series and TE after it. But it was a good pool, and all agents were superhuman both physically and mentally. She could handle this trio of humans.

She paused in her reflection. Better qualify that. She could handle them physically because her strength, reflexes, and training were considerably superior to theirs. And emotionally, because though she had feelings, they were fully disciplined. But the woman Aquilon had her points, and the man Calvin had a freakish mind that had already demonstrated its ability to fence successfully with the mind and perception of an agent. Random variation in the "normal" population had produced an abnormal intelligence. Too bad the authorities hadn't recognized it in time.

Tamme grimaced. The truth, known to every agent but never voiced, was that the authorities were not overly smart. If ever a class of agents were programmed to tackle the problems of Earth directly, they would begin by putting the incompetents out of power. What a waste, to serve a stupid master!

Meanwhile, the immediate: Was Cal behind this odd disappearance of the trio? Had he anticipated her presence or that of Taler—she had matched Taler, scissors/paper/rock, for the honor and lost—and arranged some kind of trap? Possible but improbable; there had been no hint of that in his mind before he was transferred. He *could* have done such a thing, but probably *hadn't*.

All of which meant that the obvious surmise was the most likely one. She had forced herself to run through the alternatives first as a matter of caution. The three explorers must already have encountered one of the advanced machines of this world, and it had taken them —somewhere.

Which was one reason they had not been told in advance that Tamme was coming along. What they did not know, they could not betray. In case the machines turned out to be intelligent enough to make an interrogation. An agent had to consider every ramification.

So the expendables had been expended. That accounted

for everything except the extra set of prints. The bare feet walked into the sand and stopped as though the person had been lifted away at that point. But by what? A flying machine?

She checked the origin of the bare prints. The same: They appeared in the sand from nowhere. Odd indeed. Unless someone had intentionally made those prints by walking backward, then forward in his/her own tracks to make them seem like the mystery they were . . .

Tamme carried their spare aperture projector so that she could return to Taler on Paleo regardless of the firmness of the existing connection. Assuming hers did not open onto a fourth alternate-world! For a moment she was tempted to go back immediately. This situation was eerie. Which was ridiculous; she was not afraid of isolation or death.

All right: She had a machine to deal with. A formidable one if it had so neatly managed to kill or capture all three humans and their mantas already. Best to tackle it promptly. And with extreme caution. Too bad she couldn't radio Taler across the aperture!

First she made a survey of the general premises. She ran, loping over the sand at about twenty miles an hour, watching, listening. There was nothing lurking nearby. She completed her circle and set out after the massed trail of footprints, machine tread, and manta marks. Veg and Aquilon, apparently together. A curious parade!

But soon the tracks diverged. Veg, tread, and mantas continued forward, but Cal and Aquilon turned aside—and stopped. Their prints disappeared just as the bare ones had. Two more people were gone inexplicably.

Another flying machine? Then why hadn't the others taken note? If they all were captive, why hadn't all of them walked all the way to wherever they were being taken? More mystery—and she was not enchanted by it. Her working hypothesis was taking a beating.

Tamme resumed the trail after making another scouting circle. She had good perceptions; she would have known if anything were hiding near. Nothing was.

Several miles farther on, the mantas diverged. One went to the left, the other to the right. An encircling maneuver? Encircling what if they were already captive?

Now she had to make a choice: Follow one of the mantas, or follow the main trail. Easy decision: Fast as she was, she could not face a manta. The fungoids could do a hundred miles an hour over sand or water. Veg she could overtake as long as he were afoot.

But the machine was an unknown antagonist. She did not care to risk an ambush by such a device. So she followed the trail by eye, moving some distance to the side, alert for whatever she might find.

Veg's tracks were not forthright. Now they turned right, now left, and now they faced backward—but the scuffing of his heels showed he was walking backward, not changing the direction of his motion. Facing the machine evidently but staying clear of it. Why? Overall, the trail curved slowly left as though the two were traveling in a great circle back to the base camp. Not exactly the pattern of captivity.

A manta appeared, moving swiftly over the sand. It was beautiful in its seeming flight; she had great admiration for its mechanical efficiency and artistry. Tamme was armed but held her fire; these creatures were phenomenally apt at dodging. So it was unlikely she could score on it from any distance, and she did not want to antagonize it unnecessarily.

It came to rest before her, coalescing into a dark blob, the huge single eye glowing. The mantas, she knew, projected an all-purpose beam from that eye; they both saw and communicated by means of it. Was it trying to tell her something?

"Which one are you?" she inquired experimentally. They could actually see the compressions and rarefactions of the air that made sound; thus, they could in effect hear, though they had no auditory equipment. All their major senses were tied into one—but what a sense that one was!

The thing jumped up, flattened into its traveling form, and cracked its tail like a whip. Six snaps.

"Hex," she said. "Veg's friend. Do you know where he is?"

One snap, meaning YES.

Communication was not difficult, after all. Soon she had ascertained that Veg was in good health and that the manta would conduct her to him.

Veg was resting as she came up. He was leaning against a boulder and chewing on a hunk of dark bread. "Where's the machine?" Tamme asked, as though this were routine.

"It finally got full and lost its appetite," he said. "So it left. Lucky for me; I was almost out of food."

"You were *feeding* it?"

"It was bound to eat. Better to feed it what we could spare than let it take its own choice. Like vital supplies —or people. The thing eats meat as well as metal! But when I started feeding it rocks and sand, it quit. Not too smart."

So the machine had been attacking him—and he had foiled it at last by throwing what the desert offered. Veg might not be a genius, but he had good common sense!

Veg considered her more carefully. "What the hell are *you* doing here?"

"We don't trust you."

"It figures." He wasn't even very surprised; she could read his honest minor responses in the slight tension of his muscles, the perspiration of his body, and the rate of breathing. In fact he was intrigued, for he found her sexually appealing.

Tamme was used to that in normals. She *was* sexually appealing; she had been designed to be that way. Usually she ignored her effect on men; sometimes she used it. It depended on the situation. If sex could accomplish a mission more readily than another approach, why not?

But at the moment her only mission was to keep an eye on the activities of these people. Veg was the simplest of the lot; his motives were forthright, and it was not his nature to lie. She could relax.

"Have some bread," Veg said, offering her a torn chunk.

"Thank you." It was good bread; the agents' supplies were always nutritious because their bodies required proper maintenance for best efficiency. She bit down, severing the tough crust with teeth that could as easily cut through the flesh and bone of an antagonist.

"You know, I met one of you agents," Veg said. "Name of Subble. You know him?"

"Yes and no. I am familiar with the SU class of agent but never met that particular unit."

"Unit?"

"All agents of a type are interchangeable. You would have had the same experience with any SU, and it would have been very similar with an SO, TA, or TE."

His body tensed in quick anger. Amused, Tamme read the signs. Normals found the concept of human interchangeability repulsive; they always wanted to believe that every person was unique, even those designed to be *un*-unique. If only they knew; the camaraderie of identity was the major strength of all agents. Tamme never wanted to give up any of her programmed attributes—unless every agent in her class gave them up. She only felt at ease with her own kind, and even other series of agents made her feel slightly uncomfortable.

"Decent sort of a fellow, in his way. I guess he reported all about what we said."

"No. Subble died without making a report."

"Too bad," Veg said with mixed emotion. Again Tamme analyzed him: He was sorry Subble had died but relieved that the report had not been made. Evidently their dialogue had grown personal.

"Agents don't antagonize people unnecessarily," she said. "Our job is to ascertain the facts and to take necessary action. We're all alike so that the nature of our reactions can be predetermined and so that our reports need minimal correction for subjectivity or human bias. It is easier on the computer."

"That's what he said."

"Naturally. It's what we all say."

Again that predictable annoyance. Veg looked at her. "But you *aren't* alike. He—he *understood*."

"Try me sometime."

He looked at her again, more intently, reading an invitation. Sex appeal again. He had evidently been through a traumatic experience with the girl Aquilon and was on the rebound. Here he was with another comely blonde female, and though he knew intellectually that she was a dedicated and impersonal agent of the government, his emotion saw little more than the out-ward form. Which was why female agents *were* comely —through they could turn it off at will. Normals had a marvelous capacity for willful self-delusion.

The other man, Calvin Potter, was far more intriguing as a challenge. But the expedient course was to enlist the cooperation of the most likely individual, and that was Veg. Cal would be deceived by no illusions; Veg was amenable, within limits, and more so at this time than he would be a month from now.

"We *are* alike," Tamme repeated, smiling in a fashion she knew was *un*like any expression Subble would have used. "I can do anything your SU could do. Maybe a little more because I'm part of a later series."

"But you aren't a man!"

She raised a fair eyebrow. "So?"

"So if someone socked you—"

"Go ahead," she said, raising her chin. She had to refrain from smiling at the unsubtlety of his approach.

He moved suddenly, intending to stop his fist just shy of the mark. He was, indeed, a powerful man, fit to have been a pugilist in another age. Even sitting as he was, the force of a genuine blow like this could have knocked out an ordinary person.

She caught his arm and deflected it outward while she leaned forward. His fist passed behind her head and momentum carried it around. Suddenly she was inside the crook of his arm, and their heads were close together.

She kissed him ever so lightly on the lips. "There will come a time, big man," she murmured. "But first we must find your lost friends."

That reminder electrified him. He had a triple shock: first, her demonstrated ability to foil him physically; second, the seeming incipience of an amorous liaison with a female agent—intriguing as a suppressed fancy, upsetting as an actual prospect; third, the idea of dally-ing with a stranger while his two closest friends were unaccounted for.

Of course, Veg was not as culpable as he deemed himself to be in that moment. Tamme had scripted this encounter carefully, if extemporaneously. He had never supposed seriously that she would have anything to do with him—and he had not known that Cal and Aquilon were missing. The appearance of the mantas had seemed to indicate that things were all right; he hadn't thought to query Hex or Circe closely, and the mantas, as was their custom, had not volunteered anything or intimated that something was wrong. He had supposed that Cal and Aquilon were back at the camp, their occupation made safe by his diversion of the vicious machine.

Tamme had shocked him with a kiss while informing him that this was not the case. In due course he would think all this out and realize that the agent had used him, or at least manipulated him. But by that time the significance of her remark "There will come a time" would have penetrated to a more fundamental level, and he wouldn't care.

Child's play, really. That was why Cal was so much more intriguing. She would of course make the attempt to impress Cal because he would then be less inclined to work against the interests of Earth—the interests as the Earth-Authorities saw them. But she expected to fail. The girl, too, would be a difficult one because the weapon of sex appeal would be valueless. Aquilon had sex appeal of her own in good measure—and it was natural rather than cultured. A rare quality! Also, Aquilon had already killed a male-agent, Taner; she would do the same with a female-agent if the occasion required it.

And there was a mystery: how had she killed Taner? She could not have caught the man off guard, and she could not have seduced him. Agents used sex as they used anything necessary; They were not used *by* it.

It had to have been through the agency of the mantas. The fungoids were extremely swift, and the strike of their whiplike tails could kill. But they had to be airborne to attack and within striking range, and the reflexes of an alert agent were sufficient to shoot down a manta before it could complete its act. It was a matter of split-second coordination—but the agent had the edge.

Taner had been careless, obviously. But that did not excuse the slaying of an agent. When the facts were known . . .

They were now both on their feet, ready to go. Veg's thoughts had run their channeled course. "They're not at the camp?"

"No. Their tracks follow yours, then disappear."

"That true, Hex?" he asked the manta. Distrust of agents was so ingrained that he wasn't even conscious of the implied affront. Why should he take her word?

Hex snapped his tail once. Vindication. Tamme wondered whether the creatures could read human lies as readily as the agents could. She would have to keep that in mind.

"Maybe Circe found them," Veg said.

Hex snapped twice.

"I think you should look at the tracks," Tamme said. "Something strange is going on, and we may be in danger." Understatement of the day!

"Wait," Veg said. "The mantas came across with Cal, right? They *must* know." But as he spoke, he saw that Hex was ignorant of the matter.

Tamme shrugged. "I guess that Cal found you missing, so he sent them to find *you*. While they were gone, something got *him*." She perceived his new alarm and quickly amended her statement. "He's not dead so far as I know. He's just gone. The tracks walk out into the sand and stop. I suspect a machine lifted him away."

"A flying machine?" He pondered. "Could be. I didn't see it—but that ground machine sure was tough. But if—"

"I don't think it ate them," Tamme said, again picking up his specific concern. He had strong ties to his friends! "There's no blood in the sand, no sign of struggle. The prints show they were standing there but not running or fighting."

"Maybe," he said, half relieved. "Hex—any ideas?" Three snaps.

"He doesn't know," Veg said. "Circe must be looking for them now. Maybe we'd better just go back to camp and wait—"

Tamme reached out, took his arm and hauled him to the side with a strength he had not suspected in her. They sprawled on the ground behind a boulder. Wordlessly, she pointed.

Something hovered in the air a hundred feet ahead. A network of glimmering points, like bright dust motes in sunlight. But also like the night sky. It was as though tiny stars were being born right here in the planet's atmosphere. She had never heard of anything like this; nothing in her programming approached it.

Hex jumped up, orienting on the swarm. He shot toward it.

"Watch it, Hex!" Veg cried.

But Tamme recognized a weakness in the manta. The creature had to be airborne to be combat-ready. Actually it stepped across the ground rapidly, one-footed, its cape bracing against the pressure of the atmosphere. It had to aim that big eye directly on the subject to see it at all. Thus, the manta *had* to head toward the swarm —or ignore it. Probably the creature would veer off just shy of the sparkle.

Hex did. But at that moment the pattern of lights expanded abruptly, doubling its size. The outer fringe extended beyond the manta's moving body. And Hex disappeared.

So did the light-swarm. The desert was dull again.

"What the hell *was* it?" Veg exclaimed.

"Whatever took your friends," Tamme said tersely. "An energy consumer—or a matter transmitter."

"It got Hex . . ."

"I think we'd better get out of here. In a hurry."

"I'm with you!"

They got up and ran back the way they had come.

"Circe!" Veg cried.

"There's something after us—and don't you go near it! It got Hex!"

"Oh-oh," Tamme said.

Veg glanced back apprehensively. The pattern was there again, moving toward them rapidly. Circe came to rest beside them, facing it.

"We can't outrun it," Tamme said. "We'll have to fight."

She faced the swarm, trying to analyze it for weakness, though she did not know what she was looking for. The thing swirled and pulsed like a giant airborne amoeba, sending out fleeting pseudopods that vanished

34

instead of retracting. Sparks that burned out when flung from the main mass?

"God . . ." Veg said.

"Or the devil," she said, firing one hip-blaster.

The energy streamed through the center of the bright cloud. Points of light glowed all along the path of her shot, but the swarm did not collapse.

"It's a ghost!" Veg said. "You can't burn a ghost!" He was amazed rather than afraid. Fear simply was not natural to him; he had run as one might from a falling tree, preserving himself without terror.

Tamme drew another weapon. A jet of fluid shot out. "Fire extinguisher," she said.

It had no effect, either. Now the swarm was upon them. Pinpoint lights surrounded them, making it seem as though they stood in the center of a starry nebula. Circe jumped up, her mantle spreading broadly, but there was nothing for her to strike at, and it was too late to escape.

Then something strange happened.

# Chapter 4

# SENTIENCE

.
. .
.

First problem: survival in a nonsurvival situation.

Second problem: existence of mobile blight, detectable only by its transitory damping effect on elements.

Each problem seemed insoluble by itself. But together, there was a possibility. The existence of mobile nonpattern entities implied that a nonpattern mode of survival was feasible. Comprehend the mode of the blight, and perhaps survival would develop.

OX's original circuitry had difficulty accepting this supposition, so he modified it. The nagging distress occasioned by these modifications served as warning that he could be pursuing a nonsurvival course. But when all apparent courses were nonsurvival, did it matter?

He put his full attention to the blight problem. First he mapped the complete outline of each blight spot, getting an exact idea of its shape. One was virtually stationary, a central blob with extensions that moved about. Another moved slowly from location to location in two dimensions, retaining its form. The third was most promising because it moved rapidly in three dimensions and changed its shape as it moved.

*This was the way a sentient entity functioned.*

Yet it was blight. A mere pattern of element damping.

Pattern. A pattern of blight was still a pattern, and pattern was the fundamental indication of sentience. Thus, nonsentients were sentient. Another paradox, indicating a flaw in perception or rationale.

Possibility: The blight was not blight but the facsimile of blight. As though a pattern were present but whose presence suppressed the activation of the elements instead of facilitating it. An inverse entity.

Error. Such an entity should leave blanks where those elements were being suppressed: as of the absence of elements. OX perceived no such blanks. When he activated given elements, the presence of an inverse pattern should at least nullify it so that the elements would seem untouched. Instead, they did activate— but not as sharply as was proper. The effect was more like a shield, dimming but not obliterating the flow of energy. A blight, not a pattern.

OX suffered another period of disorientation. It required energy to wrestle with paradox, and he was already short of the reserve required for survival.

In due course he returned to the problem; he had to. It seemed that the ultimate nature of the spots was incomprehensible. But their perceivable attributes could be ascertained and catalogued, perhaps leading to some clarification. It was still his best approach to survival. Where a pseudopattern could survive, so might a genuine pattern.

OX developed a modified spotter circuit that enabled him to perceive the spots as simple patterns rather than as pattern-gaps. The effect was marvelous: Suddenly, seeming randomness became sensible. Instead of ghosts, these now manifested as viable, if peculiar, entities.

The most comprehensible was the outline-changing spot. At times it was stationary, like a pattern at rest. When it moved, it altered its shape—as a pattern entity normally did. But even here there was a mystery: The spot did not change according to the fundamental rules of pattern. It could therefore not be stable. Yet it was; it always returned to a similar configuration.

$\overline{OX}$'s disorientation was developing again. With another effort he modified his rationale-feedback to permit him to consider confusion and paradox without suffering in this fashion. The distress signals accompanying this modification were so strong that he would never have done it had he not faced the inevitable alternative of nonsurvival.

Now he concentrated on the observable phenomena. Possible or not, the spot moved in the manner it moved and was stable.

Another spot moved but did not alter its outline appreciably. It seemed to be circulating so as not to exhaust its elements, which made sense. But it traveled only in those two dimensions.

The third spot did not move. It only shifted its projections randomly. It had occupied the same bank of elements too long—yet had not exhausted them. Another improbability: Elements had to be given slack time to recharge, or they became inoperative.

Of course, a pattern that damped down elements might not exhaust them in the same fashion.

Could $\overline{OX}$ himself achieve that state? If he were able to alternate pattern-activity with pattern damping, he might survive indefinitely.

*Survival!*

Such a prospect was worth the expenditure of his last reserves of energy.

$\overline{OX}$ did not know how such an inversion might be achieved. The spot patterns *did* know, for they *had* achieved it. He would have to learn from them.

It now became a problem of communication. With an entity of his own type $\overline{OX}$ would have sent an exploratory vortex to meet the vortex of the other. But these spot-entities were within his demesnes, not perceivable beyond them.

He tried an internal vortex, creating a subpattern within his own being, in the vicinity of the most mobile spot. There was no response.

He tried a self-damping offshoot—another construction developed as the need manifested. The mobile spot ignored it. Was the spot nonsentient after all—or merely unable to perceive the activation of the elements?

He tried other variants. The mobile spot took no notice.

OX was pragmatic. If one thing did not work, he would try another, and another, until he either found something that did work or exhausted the alternatives. His elements were slowly fading; if he did not discover a solution—nonsurvival.

In the midst of the fifteenth variation of offshoot, OX noted a response. Not by the shape-changing spot at which the display was directed—by the stable-shape mobile spot. It had been moving about, and abruptly it stopped.

Cessation of motion did not constitute awareness necessarily; it could signify demise. But OX repeated the configuration, this time directing it at the second spot.

The spot moved toward the offshoot. Awareness—or coincidence?

OX repeated the figure, somewhat to the side of the first one. The spot moved toward the new offshoot.

OX tried a similar configuration, this time one that moved in an arc before it damped out. The spot followed it and stopped when the figure was gone.

OX began to suffer the disorientation of something very like excitement despite a prior modification to alleviate this disruptive effect in himself. He tried another variant: one that moved in three dimensions. The spot did not follow it.

But a repeat of the two-dimensional one brought another response. This spot always had moved in two dimensions; it seemed to be unable to perceive in three. Yet it acted sentient within that limited framework.

OX tried a two-dimensional shoot that looped in a circle indefinitely. The spot followed it through one full circle, then stopped. Why?

Then the spot moved in a circle of its own beside the shoot. It was no longer following; it was duplicating!

OX damped out the shoot. The spot halted. There was no doubt now: The spot was aware of the shoot.

The spot moved in an oval. OX sent a new shoot to duplicate the figure.

The spot moved in a triangle. $\overline{OX}$ made a similar triangle subpattern.

The spot halted. $\overline{OX}$ tried a square. The spot duplicated it. *So did the shape-changing spot.*

$\overline{OX}$ controlled his threatening disorientation. Communication had been established—not with one spot but with two!

*Survival!*

# Chapter 5

# CITY

• • •
• •
• • •

It was like a city, and like a jungle, and like a factory, all run together for surrealistic effect. Veg shook his head, unable to make any coherent whole of it at first glance.

He stood on a metal ramp beside a vastly spreading mock-oak tree overlooking a channel of water that disappeared into a sieve over a mazelike mass of crisscrossing bars lighted from beneath.

"Another alternate, I presume," Tamme said beside him. "I suspect we'll find the others here. Why not have your mantas look?"

Now Veg saw her standing beside Hex and Circe. "Sure—look," he said vaguely. He still had not quite adjusted to finding himself alive and well.

The mantas moved. Hex sailed up and over the purple dome of a mosquelike building whose interior consisted of revolving mirrors, while Circe angled under some wooden stalactites depending from an inverted giant toadstool whose roots were colored threads.

Veg squatted to investigate a gently flexing flower. It was about three inches across, on a metallic stem, and it swiveled to face him as he moved. He poked a finger at its center.

Sharp yellow petals closed instantly on his finger, cutting the skin. "Hey!" he yelled, yanking free. The skin was scraped where the sharp edges had touched and smarted as though acid had been squirted into the wounds.

He raised his foot high and stamped down hard with his heel. The flower dodged, but he caught the stem and crushed it against the hard ramp. Then he was sorry. "Damn!" he said as he surveyed the wreckage. "I shouldn't have done that; it was only trying to defend itself."

"Better not fool with what we don't understand," Tamme warned a bit late.

"I don't understand *any* of this, but I'm *in* it!" Veg retorted, sucking on his finger.

"I believe that was a radar device—with a self-protective circuit," she said. "This place is functioning."

"Not a flower," he said, relieved. "I don't mind bashing a machine."

There was a humming sound behind him. Veg whirled. "Now *that's* a machine!" he cried.

"Climb!" Tamme directed. She showed the way by scrambling up a trellis of organ pipes to reach a suspended walkway. Veg followed her example with alacrity.

The machine moved swiftly along the original ramp. Its design was different from the one he had battled in the desert. It had wheels instead of treads and an assortment of spider-leg appendages in place of the spinning blade.

It stopped by the damaged flower. There was a writhing flurry of its legs. So quickly that Veg was unable to follow the detail, it had the plant uprooted, adjusted, and replaced—repaired.

Then the machine hummed on down the ramp.

"What do you know!" Veg exclaimed. " A tame machine!"

"I wouldn't count on it. If we do any more damage, we may see a destroyer-machine. And if this is their world, we'll be in trouble."

"Yeah, no sand here." Veg nodded thoughtfully. "If that desert was the hinterland, this is the capital. Same world, maybe."

"No. What we went through felt like a projection— and the atmospherics differ here. That's no certain indication, but I believe it is safer to assume this is another alternate."

"Anyway, we're jungle specimens, picked up and put down, remote control. In case we should bite." He bared his teeth. "And we just *might*."

"Yet it is strange they didn't cage us," Tamme said. "And it was no machine that brought us."

"Well, let's look about—carefully." He walked along the higher path. It extended in a bridgelike arc over a forest of winking lights. These were bulbs, not the scintillating motes that had brought the party here. Which reminded him again: "What *did* bring us?"

Tamme shook her head in the pretty way she had. It bothered him to think that probably all female agents had the same mannerisms, carefully programmed for their effect on gullible males like him. "Some kind of force field, maybe. And I suspect there is no way out of this except the way we came. We're in the power of the machines."

He stopped at a fountain that seemed to start as a rising beam of light but phased into falling water and finally hardened into a moving belt of woven fabric. Very carefully because of his experience with the flower, he touched the belt. It was solid yet resilient, like a rug. "The thing is a loom!"

Tamme looked, startled. "No Earthly technology, that," she said. "Very neat. The light passes through that prism, separates into its component colors, which then become liquid and fall—to be channeled into a pattern of the fabric before they solidify. Some loom!"

"I didn't know light could be liquefied or solidified," Veg remarked. His eyes traced the belt farther down to where it was slowly taken up by a huge roll.

"Neither did I," she admitted. "It appears that we are dealing with a more sophisticated science than our own."

"I sort of like it," he said. "It reminds me of something 'Quilon might paint. In fact, this whole city isn't bad."

But it was evident that Tamme was not so pleased. No doubt she would have a bombshell of a report when she returned to Earth. Would the agents come and burn all this down, as they had the dinosaur valley of Paleo?

Hex returned. "Hey, friend," Veg said. "Did you find them?"

One snap: YES.

"All in one piece?"

Three snaps: confusion. To a manta, fragmentation was the death of prey. The creatures were not sharp on human humor or hyperbole.

But Cal and Aquilon were already on their way. "Veg!" Aquilon called just as though nothing had changed between them. She was absolutely beautiful.

In a moment they all were grouped about the light-fountain-loom. "We've been here an hour," Cal said. "This place is phenomenal!" Then he looked at Tamme, and Veg remembered that Cal had not known about her crossover. "Where are your friends?"

"Two alternates away, I suspect," Tamme said.

"You drew straws, and you lost."

"Exactly."

"She's not bad when you get to know her," Veg said, aware of the tension between the two.

"When you get to know them . . ." Aquilon murmured, and he knew she was thinking of Subble.

"I realize that not all of you are thrilled at my presence," Tamme said. "But I think we have become involved in something that overrides our private differences. We may never see Earth again."

"Do you want to?" Cal inquired. He was not being facetious.

"Is there anything to eat around here?" Veg asked. "We're short on supplies now."

"There are fruiting plants," Aquilon said. "We don't know whether they're safe, though."

"I can probably tell," Tamme said.

"See—lucky she's along!" Veg said.

It fell flat. Neither Cal nor Aquilon responded, and he knew they were still against Tamme. They were not going to give her a chance. And perhaps they were right; the agents had destroyed the dinosaur enclave without a trace of conscience. He felt a certain guilt defending any agent . . . though Subble had indeed seemed different.

It didn't help any that he knew Tamme could read his emotions as they occurred.

"Any hint of the machines' purpose in bringing us here?" Tamme asked.

Cal shrugged. "I question whether any machine was responsible. We seem to be dealing with some more sophisticated entities. Whoever built this city . . ."

"There's some kind of amphitheater," Aquilon said. "With a stage. That might be the place to make contact —if they want to."

"Doesn't make much sense to snatch us up and then forget us!" Veg muttered.

"These entities may not see things quite the way we do," Cal said, smiling.

They examined the fruit plants, and Tamme pronounced them probably safe. Apparently she had finely developed senses and was able to detect poison before it could harm her system.

The amphitheater was beautiful. Translucent colonnades framed the elevated stage, which was suspended above a green fog. The fog seemed to have no substance yet evidently supported the weight of the platform, cushioning it. Veg rolled a fruit into the mist, and the fruit emerged from the other side without hindrance: no substance there!

"Magnetic, perhaps," Cal said. "I admit to being impressed."

"But where are the people who made all this?" Veg demanded.

"Why do you assume *people* made it?"

"It's set up for people. The walks are just right, the seats fit us, the stage is easy to see, and the fruit's good. It wouldn't be like this if it were meant for non-humans."

Cal nodded. "An excellent reply."

"What about the machines?" Aquilon asked. "They move all around, tending it."

"That's just it," Veg said. "They're *tending* it, not *using* it. They're servants, not masters."

"I can't improve on that reasoning," Cal said. That struck Veg as vaguely false; why should Cal try to butter him up? To stop him from siding with Tamme?

"But if human beings built it—" Aquilon started.

"Then where *are* they?" Veg finished. "That's what I wanted to know the first time 'round."

"Several possibilities," Cal said thoughtfully. "This could have been constructed centuries or milennia ago, then deserted. The machines might have been designed to maintain it, and no one ever turned them off."

"Who ever deserted a healthy city?" Veg asked. "I mean, the whole population?"

"It happened at Çatal Huyuk in ancient Anatolia. That was a thriving neolithic city for a thousand years. Then the people left it and started Hacilar, two hundred miles to the west."

"Why?"

"We don't know. It happened almost eight thousand years ago. I suspect they ran out of game because of overhunting, and no doubt the climate had something to do with it."

"I don't like that one," Veg said. "*These* builders didn't have to hunt for a living. If something happened to *them,* it sure could happen to *us.*"

"On the other hand, they could be here now, sleeping —or watching us."

"I don't like that, either," Veg said.

"Or perhaps this is a prison city, made for the confinement of enemies or undesirables until sentence is pronounced."

"You get worse as you go," Veg said, grimacing. "*You* try it, 'Quilon."

Aquilon smiled. That still gave him a nervous thrill, for he remembered when she could not smile back on Planet Nacre. In certain ways things had been better then. "How about a vacation resort for honored guests?"

"Stop there," he said. "I like it."

"At any rate," Cal concluded, "whatever brought us can certainly remove us—and *will* when it so chooses. We would do well to conduct ourselves decorously."

"Segregation of the sexes?" Aquilon asked mischievously.

"He means not to break anything," Veg said—and realized too late that no one had needed any interpretation. Neither girl was stupid; Veg himself was the slow member of the group. It had never bothered him when they were three; now that they were four, it somehow did.

"You understand that, mantas?" Aquilon asked. "We don't want trouble."

The two fungoids agreed with token snaps of their tails. Aquilon had, in her way, taken the sting from his verbal blunder, for the mantas *did* need to have human dialogue clarified on occasion. Still the sweet girl, 'Quilon, and he loved her yet—but not in the same way as before. Oh, if certain things could be unsaid, certain mistakes taken back . . . but what was the use in idle speculation? In time love would diminish into friendship, and that was best.

"For now, let's rest," Tamme said.

Rest! Veg knew Tamme didn't need it half as much as the others did. The agents were tough, awfully tough. And in their fashion, intriguing.

Cal nodded agreement. He would be the most tired. He was much stronger than he had been when Veg met him back in space before Nacre, and now he could eat ordinary foods, but still his physical resources were small. "The mantas will stand guard," Cal said.

Tamme gave no indication, but somehow Veg knew she was annoyed. She must have planned to scout around alone while the others slept; maybe she had some secret way to contact the agents back on Paleo. But she could not conceal it from the mantas!

Then Tamme looked directly at him, and Veg knew she knew what he was thinking. Embarrassed, he curtailed his conjectures. And Tamme smiled faintly. Bitch! he thought, and her smile broadened.

They found places around the chamber. The benches were surprisingly comfortable, as though cushioned, yet the material was hard. Another trick of the city's technology? But there was one awkward problem.

"The john," Aquilon said. "There has to *be* one!"

"Not necessarily," Cal replied, smiling in much the way Tamme had. "Their mores may differ from ours."

"If they ate, they sat," Veg said firmly. "Or squatted.

Sometime, somewhere, somehow. No one else could do it for them."

"They could have designed machines to do it for them."

Veg had a vision of a machine slicing a person open to remove refuse. "Uh-*uh!* I wouldn't tell even a machine to eat—"

"A variant of dialysis," Cal continued. "I have been dialyzed many times. It is simply a matter of piping the blood through a filtration network and returning it to the body. Painless, with modern procedures. It can be done while the subject sleeps."

"I don't want my blood piped through a machine!" Veg protested. "Now I'll be afraid to sleep for fear a vampire machine will sneak up on me, ready to beat the oomph out of me!"

"Dialysis would only account for a portion of it," Aquilon murmured.

"Oh, the colon can be bypassed, too," Cal assured her.

Veg did not enjoy this discussion. "What say we set aside a place, at least until we find a real privy? In fact, I can *make* a real privy."

Cal spread his hands in mock defeat. "By all means, Veg!"

"I will forage for building materials," Tamme offered.

"I'll help," Aquilon said. "Circe?"

"That is kind of you," Tamme said. Veg wondered whether she meant it. Foraging alone, the female agent could have explored the city widely and maybe made her report to Taler. Now she couldn't—and even if she moved out too quickly for Aquilon to follow, the manta would keep her in sight. Smart girl, 'Quilon!

Then he glanced at Tamme to see whether she were reading his reactions again. But she was not watching him this time, to his relief.

His eyes followed as the two women departed. How alike they were, with their blonde hair and shapely bodies—yet how *un*like! Would they talk together? What would they say? Suddenly he was excruciatingly curious. Maybe he could find out from Circe later.

"I think you need no warning," Cal said quietly as

he poked about the suspended stage. "Just remember that girl is an agent, with all that implies."

Veg remembered. Back on Earth the agents had moved in to destroy every vestige of manta penetration. They had burned Veg's northern forest region, gassed the rabbits and chickens of the cellar-farm in Aquilon's apartment complex, and bombed the beaches where Cal had lived. Then they had come to Paleo and brutally exterminated the dinosaurs. That memory was still raw —but years would never completely erase the pain of it. They were agents of what Aquilon called the omnivore: man himself, the most ruthless and wasteful killer of them all. He knew, how well he knew!

Yet—Tamme was a mighty pretty girl.

"Once we had a difference of opinion," Cal said. "I hope that does not occur again."

Veg hoped so, too. He and Aquilon had argued against making any report on the alternate world of Paleo, to protect it from the savage exploitation of man. Cal had believed that their first loyalty had to be to their own world and species. Their difference had seemed irreconcilable, and so they had split: Cal on one side, Veg and Aquilon on the other. And it had been a mistake, for Cal had in the end changed his mind, while the other two had only learned that they were not for each other. Not that way, not as lovers, not against Cal.

This time there was no question: They were all three against the omnivorous government of Earth. The agents were incorruptible representatives of that government, fully committed to their computer-controlled program. In any serious choice, Veg knew his interests lay with Cal and Aquilon, not with Tamme.

Yet it had not worked out with Aquilon, and Tamme was a pretty girl . . .

"It is possible to divorce the physical from the intellectual," Cal said.

God, he was smart—as bad in his way as Tamme was in hers. "I'll work on it," Veg agreed.

They built the privy and also a little human shelter of light-cloth from the fountain-loom. It seemed ridiculous to pitch such a tent inside the doomed auditorium

—but the city was alien, while the shelter seemed human. It served a moral purpose rathen than a physical one.

The mantas found meat somewhere while the humans ate the fruits. Survival was no problem. Veg conjectured that there were either rats or their equivalent in the city: omnivores for the mantas to hunt. Maybe no coincidence.

But as they ranged more widely through the city, they verified that there was no escape. The premises terminated in a yawning gulf whose bottom they could neither see nor plumb. This was, indeed, a prison. Or at least a detention site.

"But we were not brought here for nothing," Cal insisted. "They are studying us, perhaps. As we might study a culture of bacteria."

"So as to isolate the disease," Aquilon added.

"We're not a disease!" Veg said.

Cal shrugged. "That may be a matter of opinion."

Veg thought of the omnivore again, destroying everything from flies to dinosaurs, and wondered. "What happens to the culture—after they know what it is?"

"We'd rather not know," Aquilon said a bit tightly. Veg felt a surge of sympathy for her. She had salvaged nothing from Paleo but the egg—and that was gone.

Tamme didn't comment, but Veg knew her mind was working. She was not about to sit still for the extermination of a used culture.

"That's for sure!" Tamme said, startling him, mocking his own speech mannerism. Once more he had forgotten to watch his thoughts. He knew she was not really a mind reader, but the effect was similar at times.

"It is my suspicion that our captors did not construct this city," Cal said. "Otherwise they would not need to study us in this manner. More likely the city was here, and we were there, so it combined us, trusting that we were compatible."

"That might be the test," Tamme said. "If we are compatible, we have affinities with the city, and so they know something about us. If we had died quickly, they would have known we had no affinities. Other samples, other environments, hit or miss."

"Score one for it," Aquilon said. "I rather like it

here. Or at least I would if only I were certain of the future."

"If my conjecture is correct," Cal continued, "we have two mysteries. The origin of this city—and the nature of the sparkle-cloud. And these mysteries may be mysteries to each other, too, if you see what I mean."

"Yeah, I see," Veg said. "City, sparkle, and us—and none of us really knows the other two.

"With a three-way situation," Aquilon said thoughtfully, "we might have a fighting chance."

"If only we knew how to fight!" Veg said.

Night came again inside the auditorium as well as out. They ate and settled down.

Then Veg saw something. "The sparkle-cloud!" he exclaimed. "It's back!"

It shimmered on the stage, myriad ripples of lights, pattern on pattern. They had seen it in daylight; by night it was altogether different: phenomenal and beautiful.

"A living galaxy!" Aquilon breathed. "Impossible to paint . . ."

"Energy vortex," Cal said, studying it from a different view. "Controlled, complex . . ."

"It's staying on the stage," Veg said. "Not coming after us!"

"*Yet*," Tamme put in succinctly.

"If only we could *talk* to it!" Aquilon said.

"How do you communicate with an alternate-hopping energy vortex?" Tamme inquired. "Even if it had a brain, there's a problem in translation. More likely it is just a field of force generated by some distant machine."

"Even so, communication might be possible," Cal said. "When we use radio or telephone or television, we are actually communicating with each other. What counts is who or what is controlling the machine or the force."

"Translation—that's the key!" Aquilon said, picking up from Tamme's remark. "Circe—send it your signature."

The manta beside her did not move. The eye glowed, facing the vortex.

After a moment Aquilon shrugged, disappointed. "No

connection," she said. "Their energy must be on different bands."

"It is possible that we are seeing the mere periphery of some natural effect," Cal said. "A schism between alternates, a crack in the floor that let us fall through to another level—no intelligence to it."

Suddenly the vortex changed. Whorls of color spun off, while planes of growing points formed within the main mass. Lines of flickering color darted through those planes.

"A picture!" Aquilon exclaimed.

"Must be modern art," Veg snorted.

"So called 'modern art' happens to be centuries old," Cal observed.

"No, there really is a picture," Aquilon said. "You have to look at it the right way. The planes are like sections; the lines show the outlines. Each plane is a different view. Look at them all at once, integrate them . . ."

"I see it!" Tamme cried. "A holograph!"

Then Cal made it out. "A still life!"

Veg shook his head, bewildered. "All I see is sheets and squiggles."

*"Try,"* Aquilon urged him. Oh, she was lovely in her earnestness! He needed no effort to appreciate *that*. "Let your mind go, look at the forms behind the forms. Once you catch it, you'll never lose it."

But Veg couldn't catch it, any more than he had been able to catch *her,* back when he thought she was within his grasp. He strained but only became more frustrated. He saw the flats and curves of it but no comprehensible picture.

"It's all in the way you look," Cal explained. "If you—" He broke off, staring into the vortex. "Amazing!"

Veg looked again, squinting, concentrating, but all he saw was a shifting of incomprehensibly geometric patterns with sparkles flying out like visual fireworks.

"That's Orn!" Aquilon cried. "No, it's a chick—"

"The hatchling," Cal said. "Ornet. Yet how—?"

"And a baby manta!" she continued. "Where *are* they?"

"Back on Paleo, maybe," Veg said, annoyed. "What sort of a game are you folks playing?"

"No game," Tamme assured him. "We *see* them."

" 'Quilon!" Cal cried. "Look! Behind that obscuring sparkle. Can that be—?"

"It *is*," she cried. *"That's a human baby!"* She shook her head, but her eyes remained riveted to the picture. "My God!"

Veg strained anew but could make out nothing. He was getting angry.

"Your God," Cal said. "I remember when you found that expression quaint."

Aquilon drew her eyes momentarily from the stage to look at Cal, and Veg felt the intensity of it, though he was not a part of it. She was moving inexorably to Cal, and that was right; that Veg loved her did not mean he was jealous of his friend. Cal deserved the best.

"I was painting," she said. "That first night on the mountain . . . and you said you loved me, and I cried." Her eyes returned to the stage. "Now I have picked up your mannerisms."

Veg put his own eyes straight at the indecipherable image. The human relations of the trio were just as confused as that supposed picture, only coming clear too late to do any good. He had not known Cal and Aquilon were so close, even back at the beginning of Nacre. He had been an interloper from the start.

Suddenly all three others tensed as though struck by a common vision. Veg knew now this was no joke; they could never have executed such a simultaneous reaction —unless they really had a common stimulus. "What the hell is it?" he demanded.

"A machine!" Aquilon exclaimed, "that whirling blade—"

*"Where?"* Veg cried, looking around nervously. But there was no machine. Aquilon was still staring into the vortex.

"That must be what Veg fought!" Tamme said. "See the treads, the way it moves—no wonder he had such a time with it! The thing's vicious!"

"Sure it was vicious," Veg agreed. "But this is only a picture—or a mass hypnosis. *I* don't see it."

"You know, that's a small machine," Cal said. "A miniature, only a foot high."

"They're *all* babies!" Tamme said. "But the others are

no match for that machine. That's a third-generation killer."

"Throw sand at it!" Veg said. For a moment he thought he saw the little machine buzzing through the depths of sparkle. But the whirling blade spun off into a pin-wheel, and he lost it. He just didn't have the eye for this show.

"They *can't* throw sand," Aquilon said breathlessly. "Ornet and the mantling don't have hands, and the baby can't even sit up yet."

"They would hardly know about that technique of defense yet," Cal added.

"Well, they can run, can't they?" Veg demanded. "Let them take turns leading it away."

"They're trying," Tamme said. "But it isn't—"

Then all three tensed again. "No—!" Cal cried.

Aqualon screamed. It was not a polite noise, such as one makes at a play. It was a full-throated scream of sheer horror.

Veg had had enough. He charged the stage, leaped to the platform, and plunged into the center of the glowing maelstrom, waving his arms and shouting. If nothing else, he could disrupt the hypnotic pictures that had captivated the minds of the others.

He felt a tingling, similar to his experience the last time. Then it faded. He was left gesticulating on the stage, alone. The sparkle-cloud was gone.

# Chapter 6

# FRAMES

Things progressed rapidly. The two blight spots were sentient; they responded to geometric sub-patterns readily and initiated their own. They had individual designations by which they could be identified, and these they made known by their responses. The shape-changing one was Dec, a ten-pointed symbol. The mobile-stable one was Ornet, indicative of a long line of evolving creatures or perhaps, more accurately, a series of shifting aspects of identity. The third was not responsive in the same way, but Ornet identified it as Cub, or the young of another species. Each entity was really quite distinct, once the group was understood.

The blights had a need, as did O̅X̅. He grasped the concept without identifying the specific. Ultimately, the mutual imperative to be SURVIVE. O̅X̅ needed more volume; the spots needed something else.

When the spots were amenable, they made perfect geometric figures. When they were distressed, they made imperfect figures. O̅X̅ did the same. Thus, they played a wide-ranging game of figures: I do *this*—does it please/displease you? Is it nearer or farther from your mode of survival? You do *that*—I am pleased/displeased as it reflects on some aspect of my survival.

Given enough time, they could have worked out an efficient means of communication. But there was no time; OX's elements were fading, and he had to have answers *now*. He had to know what the spots needed, and whether they had what *he* needed.

So he ran a frame-search. Instead of laboriously exchanging symbols, he surveyed the entire range of prospects available to him.

In a few, the spots were more active. They made excellent figures. In others, the elements were stronger, better for him. Guided by this knowledge, OX arranged his responses to direct developments toward the most favorable prospects.

But somehow these prospects faded as he approached them. The spots ceased cooperating.

OX surveyed the framework again, analyzing it in the context of this alteration. Somehow the act of orienting on his needs had made those needs unapproachable.

He tried orienting on the prospects most favorable to the spots—and then his own improved.

Confusion. His survival and that of the spots were linked—but the mechanism was unclear.

By experimentation and circuit modification, he clarified it. The spots needed a specific locale, both physical and frame—that part of the framework where there were certain stationary spots. As they approached that region, they did something that enhanced the strength of his elements.

This was an alternate solution to his problem! He did not need greater volume if his existing elements recharged faster. The proximity of the spots, in some cases, enhanced that recharging. OX directed the responses to further enhance recharging while keeping the needs of the spots in mind.

Suddenly the spots responded. Amazingly, the elements flourished, recharging at such a rate that OX's entire survival problem abated.

In retrospect, comprehension came. The elements were not individual entities; they were the energy termini of larger subpatterns. These systems were physical, like the ground. The spots were physical. The spots catered to

56

the needs of the energy plants and thereby improved $\overline{OX}$'s situation.

Dialogue improved also. $\overline{OX}$ learned that one of the most important needs of spots and element-plants was fluid—a certain kind of liquid matter. In the presence of this fluid, spots of many varieties flourished. Some were mobile spots of semi-sentient or nonsentient nature, distinct from the three he knew. Others were stationary and nonsentient—and these also were of a number of subtypes. Some provided nourishment for the sentient spots, and so these were facilitated by the transfer of liquid and increased access to certain forms of ambient energy. Others, of no direct interest to the sentients, produced nodules of processed energy that projected into adjacent alternate-frames. These were the elements!

The physical sustenance that the spots provided for their own plants also aided the element plants. They became more vigorous, and so the elements were stronger. So, by this seemingly devious chain, when $\overline{OX}$ helped the spots, he helped himself. Not just any spots, for the semi-sentients had no care at all for the plants and would not cater to $\overline{OX}$'s preferences. But the sentient spots, grasping the interaction between them, now cared for the element plants as they cared for their own. It was largely through Ornet, the most sentient spot, that this understanding came about.

Survival seemed assured.

Then the machine came.

$\overline{OX}$ recognized it instantly, though he had never experienced this type of interaction before. Alarm circuits were integral to his makeup, and the presence of the machine activated them. Here was Pattern's deadliest enemy!

In certain respects the machine was like a spot, for aspects of it were physical. But in other respects it was a kind of pattern, or antipattern. It possessed, in limited form, the ability to travel between frames, as $\overline{OX}$ did. Ordinarily, he would have noted only its pattern-aspect, but his necessary study of the spots had provided him with a wider perspective, and now he grasped much more of its nature. Suddenly the spots had enhanced his survival in quite another way, for when he viewed the machine as a double-level entity, he found it both more comprehensible and more formidable.

It could not touch $\overline{OX}$ directly, but it was deadly. It destroyed his elements by shorting out their stores of energy and physically severing the element-plants from their moorings, leaving gaps in the network. Such gaps, encountered unawares, could destroy a pattern entity.

The machine was also a direct physical threat to the spots and hence, in another respect, to $\overline{OX}$'s own survival. He could avoid it, moving his pattern to undamaged elements—but the spots had no such retreat. They could not jump across the frames of probability.

The spots were aware of this. They were furiously mobile, interacting with the machine. Ornet was distracting it by moving erratically, while Dec swooped at it, striking with a sharp extremity. But the machine was invulnerable to such attack. In a moment it discovered less elusive prey. It turned on Cub.

Cub did not take evasive action. He merely lay where he was while the attack-instrument of the machine bore down.

The blades connected. Thinly sliced sections of the physical body flew out as the action continued. The solids and fluids were taken into the machine, and Cub was no more.

After that, the machine departed. It was a small one, and its immediate survival need—its hunger—had been sated by the matter in Cub. The crisis was over.

But Dec and Ornet had a different notion. They suffered negative reaction. They were distressed by the loss of their companion, as though he were related in some way to their own survival. It was a thing they were unable to convey directly to $\overline{OX}$, but he understood their need, if not their rationale. They had expended much attention assisting Cub from the outset, and they required him to be undefunct.

Accordingly, $\overline{OX}$ surveyed the alternates. A number existed in which one of the other spots had been consumed by the machine, but $\overline{OX}$ concluded these were not appropriate. He located those in which all three spots survived intact.

*Knowing* an alternate frame and *entering* it were different things. OX had directed events toward favorable alternates before—but now he had to travel through the fourth dimension of probability, isolate one from many, and take the spots with him—when the options had been greatly reduced by the force of events. He could readily remove the spots to a frame in which they would not suffer immediate attack by the machine; it was much more difficult to do this after that event had actually occurred.

He tried. The consumption of energy was colossal, diminishing his elements at a ruinous rate. Once started, he *had* to succeed, for only in the proper alternate would the elements remain sufficiently charged for the maintenance of his pattern. Failure meant nonsurvival.

The spots could be moved so long as they remained within the boundaries of his animated form. He could not move them physically from place to place, but he could transfer them from one version of reality to another. It was in his fundamental circuits, just as knowledge of machines was in them; he knew what to do—if he could handle himself properly. Moving blight spots was more difficult than merely moving himself.

The framework wrenched. OX fibrillated. The frame changed. OX let go, disoriented by the complex effort. For a time he could not discern whether he had succeeded or failed.

. . . rstanding came about.

Survival seemed assured.

Then the machine came.

OX recognized it instantly, though he had never experienced this type of interaction before. The intrusion of the machine activated his alarm circuits. Here was Pattern's deadliest threat!

OX acted. He formed a decoy shoot designed to preempt the attention of the machine. It resembled ideal prey because it exhibited tokens keyed to the machine's perceptions: the glint of refined, polished metal; the motion of seeming blight; the sparkle of the periphery of a true pattern-entity. The machine was not intelligent enough or experienced enough to penetrate the ruse. It followed the shoot.

The shoot moved out on a simulated evasion course, the machine slicing vigoriously at it. The shoot would fizzle out at a suitable distance from the locale of the spots—by which time the machine would have forgotten them. The threat had been abated, and all the spots were safe.

# Chapter 7

# FOREST

Agents were disciplined; they had firm control over their emotions. Even consciousness-changing drugs could not subvert this, unless their actions overrode the total function of the brain. The subconscious mind of an agent was integrated with the conscious so that there were no suppressed passions, no buried monsters.

But the brutal slaying of a human infant had shaken her. The agent training and surgery could not eliminate the most fundamental drives that made her a woman. To watch, even in replica, a baby being sliced alive like so much bologna and funneled into the maw of a machine . . .

Then Veg had disrupted the image, and it had not returned. Perhaps that was just as well.

Another thing bothered her: the feeling that the image was not a mockup but a transmission. As with a televised picture: a replica of events actually occurring elsewhere. If so, this was no threat to cow the captives; it was the presentation of vital information.

Perhaps the controlling entity expected them to absorb the news like so many sponges. Probably there was more to come. But she was not inclined to wait on alien convenience. It was time to act.

Before she could act, she had to reconnoiter and get back in touch with Taler. That meant giving Cal and the mantas the slip.

But she could not afford to leave the human trio to its own devices. That was why she had come along on this projection! If she left them alone now, they could come up with some inconvenient mischief, just as they had on Paleo.

Answer, straight from the manual: take a hostage.

There was no problem which one. Cal was too smart to control directly—if, indeed, he could be controlled at all. He had given the agents a lesson back at Paleo! Aquilon would be difficult to manage because she was female, and complicated. The mantas were out of the question. So it had to be Veg: male, manageable, and not too smart. And she had primed him already.

Meanwhile, the others were recovering from their shock. No subtlety here; they reacted exactly as human beings should be expected to. Perhaps that was part of the point: The aliens intended to test the party in various ways, cataloguing their responses, much as psychiatrists tested white rats.

"What does it mean?" Aquilon asked, shading her eyes with one hand as though to shut off the glare of the vision.

"It means they can reach us—emotionally as well as physically," Cal said slowly. "Whenever they want to. We could be in for a very ugly series of visions. But what they are trying to tell us—that is unclear."

Tamme turned to the nearest manta. "Did you see it?" she inquired.

"Circe didn't see the vision," Aquilon answered. "Their eyes are different; they can't pick up totalities the way we do. They have no conception of perspective or of art."

Tamme knew that. She had studied the material on the fungoid creatures before passing through the aperture from Earth to Paleo. She knew they were cunning and dangerous; one had escaped captivity and hidden on a spaceship bound for the region of space containing the manta home-world of Nacre. It had never been killed or recaptured despite a strenuous search, and they had had

62

to place a temporary proscription on Planet Nacre to prevent any more mantas from entering space.

The manta's eye was an organic cathode emitting a controlled beam of light and picking up its reflections from surrounding objects. That radar eye was unexcelled for the type of seeing that it did and worked as well in darkness as in light. But it had its limitations, as Aquilon had described. Yet if the mantas had seen the cloud-picture, this would have been highly significant.

Cal understood. "We see with one system, the manta with another. A comparison of the two could have led to significant new insights about the nature of the force that brought us here and showed us this scene." He shook his head. "But we have verified that the mantas see only flares of energy in the cloud, winking on and off extremely rapidly. They can not perceive the source of these flares and are not equipped to see any pictures."

"Let's sleep on it," Veg said gruffly.

"The baby—something about it—" Aquilon said.

"What's a *baby* doing by itself in an alternate world?" Veg demanded. "Whatever you folks thought you saw, it wasn't real."

Tamme differed. "A little manta, a little flightless bird, and a little human being—there's a pattern there, and they looked real. I was able to read the bodily signs on that baby. It was thirsty. I'd say it was real, or at least a projection made from a real model."

"Odd that it should be in a nest," Cal remarked.

"I recognized it somehow," Aquilon said. "I don't know who it was, but it was *somebody*. Maybe one of us, back when . . ."

Cal was surprised beyond what he should have been. Tamme would have liked to question him about that, but this was not the occasion. Why should a conjecture about his infancy make him react? But Aquilon was right: There *was* a certain resemblance to Cal—and to Aquilon herself. Had the alien intelligence drawn somehow from human memories to formulate a composite infant?

They settled down. The trio shared the interior of their tent, unselfconsciously; Tamme, by her own choice and theirs, slept apart. She had not been invited along, and they did not want her, but they accepted her presence as one of the facts of this mission.

Tamme's sleep was never deep, and she did not dream in the manner of normals because of the changed nature of the computer-organized mind. Much of human sleep was a sifting, digesting, and identification tagging of the day's events; without that sorting and filing, the mind would soon degenerate into chaos. But agents were reprogrammed regularly and so required no long-term memory cataloguing. Rather, she sank into a trancelike state while her body relaxed and her mind reviewed and organized developments with a view to their relevancy for her mission. It took about an hour; agents were efficient in this, too.

Now the others were asleep, Cal deeply, Aquilon lightly, Veg rising through a rapid-eye-movement sequence. The two mantas were off exploring; if she were lucky, they would not check on the supposedly quiescent human party for several hours.

She stood and removed her blouse, skirt, and slippers. Her fingers worked nimbly, tearing out friction seams and pressing the material together again in a new configuration. This was one trick male agents didn't have!

When the clothing was ready, she removed her bra, slip, and panties and redesigned them, too. Then she reassembled herself in an artful new format, let down her hair, and relaxed.

Sure enough, Veg's REM proceeded into wakefulness. It was not that he had complex continuing adjustments to make in connection with his rebound from Aquilon —though he did. He had merely forgotten to visit the privy before turning in. Tamme had known he would rouse himself in due course.

Veg emerged from the tent. Tamme sat up as he passed her. He paused, as she had known he would. He could barely see her in the dark, but he was acutely conscious of her locale. "Just goin' to the . . ." he muttered.

"It happens," she said, standing, facing him, close.

Hope, negation, and suspicion ran through him. She picked up the mixed, involuntary signals of his body: quickened respiration and pulse, tightening of muscles, odors of transitory tension. She could see him, of course, for she had artificially acute night vision—but her ears and nostrils would have sufficed. Normals were so easy to read.

Veg walked on, and Tamme walked with him, touching, matching her step to his. There was a faint, suggestive rustle to her clothing now that set off new awareness in him. He did not consciously pick up the cause of this heightening intrigue, but the effect was strong. And in his present emotional state, severed from Aquilon, he was much more vulnerable to Tamme's calculated attack than he would normally have been.

Outside the auditorium there was a light-flower, its neon petals radiating illumination of many wavelengths. Now Veg could see her—and it was a new impact.

"You've changed!"

"You merely behold me in a different light," she murmured, turning slightly within that differing glow.

"Some light!" he exclaimed. She could have traced the process of his eyes by his reactions: warm appreciation for face and hair, half-guilty voyeurism for the thrust of her bosom and newly accented cleavage thereof, wholly guilty desire for the enhanced swell of her hips and posterior.

But his guilt was not straightforward. He ordinarily did not hesitate to appreciate the charms of women. But he had not been exposed to other women for some time. His experience with Aquilon and the knowledge that he was in the company of an agent made him hold back. He felt no guilt about cleavages and posteriors—merely about reacting to them in the present circumstances. This guilt in turn heightened the allure in a kind of reverse feedback. Forbidden fruit!

She turned away, interrupting his view of the fruit, and led the way along the path, accenting her gait only that trifle necessary to attract the eye subtly. Here the way was like a tunnel under swirling mists. Translucent figures loomed within the ambience, never quite coming clear, even to Tamme's gaze. There were so many marvels of this city—if only it were possible to establish contact with Earth so that it all could be studied and exploited!

They had built the privy over the Black Hole: a well of opacity fifteen feet across and of no plumbable depth. Cal had conjectured that it had once been an elevator shaft. Now it served as a sanitary sink.

While Veg was inside, Tamme brought out the miniature components of her projector. It would project a spherical aperture seven feet in diameter that would hold for fifteen seconds. After that, the unit would shut down, conserving its little power cell. The cell recharged itself, but slowly.

One problem was that she could not take the aperture projector with her. She had to step through the sphere while it existed. It would be disastrous to be caught halfway into the field as it closed down! Part of her would be in the other world, the remainder here—and both would be dead. Too bad people did not possess the regenerative powers of earthworms: cut one in half, make two new individuals!

Actually, the apertures were two-way. They were really tunnels between alternates that one could move through in either direction. The trouble was that the device could not be activated from the far side. No doubt in time the technicians would develop a key for that purpose—or perhaps they had already but simply hadn't gotten it into production yet. Alternate-projection was a nascent science.

She expected no difficulty but took no unnecessary chances. She wrote a short message addressed to Calvin Potter and attached it to the generator.

Veg emerged. It had only been a couple of minutes, but the agent had worked extremely rapidly. All was in order.

"What's that?" he asked.

"An aperture generator," she said, rising to approach him.

"You mean you had one of those all along?" he demanded. "We could have gone back anytime?"

"Yes and no," she said. "I could have used it anytime—but it is a calculated risk. Our aperture technology is emergent; we seem to have less than a fifty per cent reliability of destination."

"You're getting too technical for me," Veg said, eying

her displayed torso again. But she knew he understood the essence; he merely liked to assume a posture of country-boy ignorance when anyone used difficult words. This window might or might not take them back where they started from.

"We set our aperture projector on Paleo for Earth," she said. "Instead, it opened onto the machine desert. This one has a complementary setting. It should take us back to where the other one is. But it may not."

"We?" he asked. "You can go where you want to; I'm staying with my friends."

She could knock him out and toss him through. But she wanted his cooperation in case of emergency, and it was always better to keep things positive when possible. "I thought it would be more private this way," she said, using her specific muscular control to twitch her left breast suggestively.

The suggestion scored. But with his flare of desire came immediate suspicion. "What do you want with me?"

Time for a half-truth. "These generators are two-way —but it is better to have an operator. When I'm over *there*"—she indicated the prospective field of the projector— "I can't turn it on again over *here*. And if it doesn't open in the right place, I could be stranded." She shrugged, once more making a signal with her decolletage. "That might please some of you, but . . ."

"Uh-uh," he said, giving her one more correct call. "We're all human beings, up against things we don't understand. We've got to stick together."

"That's right. So—"

"So you want me to cross over first? No thanks! I did that before and almost got gobbled by a machine."

"No, I'll go," she said.

He relaxed, his suspicion warring with his desire to believe her. She knew Cal had warned him not to get involved with an agent. "Then you want me to turn it on in an hour to bring you back?"

"Yes." She took a breath, skillfully accentuating the objects of his gaze in yet another ploy. "Of course . . ."

"Not much privacy," he remarked, "if I'm *here* and you're *there*." Now he was getting angry, as the lure retreated, despite her seeming agreement to his prior objections. Fish on a hook.

"Well, the projector *can* be set to go on automatically after a certain period. A simple clockwork timer. And the limit is not necessarily an hour. It's a combination stress-time parameter with a safety factor. We could slip a load of five hundred pounds through—twice the normal —but then we'd have to wait four hours to return. The time multiplies at the square of the mass, you see. For sustained use, two hundred and fifty pounds per hour is the most efficient."

"I see," Veg said. "So we could both go through. Together we wouldn't weigh more than three fifty—"

"Three sixty."

"Hold on! I'm two hundred, and you can't be more than one thirty—"

"You're two-oh-five; you have prospered in the wilderness, I'm one fifty-five, including my hardware."

"You sure don't look it!"

"Heft me."

He put his big hands under her elbows and lifted her easily. "Maybe so," he said. "Sure no fat on you, though."

"Agents are more solid than they look. Our bones are laced with metal—literally. And the android flesh with which we are rebuilt is more dense than yours. But you're right: no fat in it."

"I know you're tough," he agreed, not altogether pleased. "Still, might be safer if we both went in case there were bad trouble at the other end."

She would be better off alone if there were real trouble. But that was not the point. "Yes. But then there would be a long, uninterrupted wait—and no one could reach us." She breathed again.

Veg was not slow to appreciate the possibilities. Two, perhaps three completely private hours with this seductive woman! "Safety first!" he said. "Let's go take a look."

He had taken the bait, lured by the thrill of exploration as well as her own enticements. And she really had not had to lie. It *was* safer with two, in a routine crossover, and the limitations of the generator were as she had described.

She really had taken more trouble than strictly necessary to bring him along. A knockout or a straight lie would have done the job in seconds. But either of these techniques would have led to complications later. This way, not only would he serve as an effective hostage—he could be of genuine assistance in a variety of circumstances. All she had to do was prepare him.

She could do a lot with a man in three hours.

"All right," she said. "You're armed?" She knew he was; she was merely alerting him.

He nodded. "I keep a knife on me. I lost my other hardware to that machine back in the desert."

"If there's any long-distance threat, I'll cover it."

He glanced once more at her half-exposed breasts. "Yeah—like Taler."

She laughed honestly this time, knowing he knew there was no jealousy between agents. She set the return aperture timer for three hours, leaving a reasonable margin for recharging, then activated the projector.

As the sphere formed, she drew him through the aperture beside her.

There was no passage of time, just the odd transfer wrench. They emerged in a world apart. Where there had been surrealistic buildings, now were trees.

Not the desert world. She had been afraid of this.

"Not Paleo, either—or Earth," Veg said, for once divining her thoughts before she read his.

Tamme looked about warily. "How do you know? This is a forest—and there are forests on both worlds."

"This is the forest primeval," he said, unconsciously borrowing from American literature.

"Evangeline," Tamme said.

"Who?"

"Longfellow's poem from which you quoted. *Evangeline, A Tale of Acadie*, vintage 1847."

"Oh. That's right—you agents do that. Got too much of that dense android muscle in your brains." He grimaced. "What I meant was that this forest has never been touched by man. So it's not Earth—not *our* Earth. And it's a high rainfall district, so it's not the desert world—not this place, not this milennium, anyway. Look at the size of that pine!"

"The aperture does not necessarily lead to the same geographic spot on the alternate," she reminded him. "Each alternate seems to differ in time from the others, so it could differ in space, too, since the globe is moving. For instance, we're in day here instead of night, so we must be elsewhere on the globe. There was vegetation on other parts of what you call the desert world."

"That's what I said. But no trees like this. Those machines ate wood, too. They'd have sawed into this long ago—and they haven't."

He was right. Her perceptions showed a slightly differing chemical composition of this world's atmosphere. Though it would be foolish to judge an entire world by one view of a tiny fraction of it, it *was* a new alternate. The changes were minor but significant.

"I am not surprised," she admitted. "My aperture projector is set for Paleo—but we did not start from the desert world. That sparkle-cloud moved us to an unspecified alternate, so we're out of phase."

"Yeah—like taking the wrong bus."

That was hardly precise, and she was surprised he thought in terms of such an ancient vehicle, but it would do. "It may be a long, hard search for home."

"*Your* home, maybe. I'd settle for Paleo. Or Nacre."

"Nacre is part of the Earth-alternate. So you'd have to—"

"But we can get back to the city-world all right? We're not lost from there?"

"Yes—in just under three hours. We're in phase for that. But we shall have to be standing right on this spot, or we'll miss it."

"Well, let's not waste the time!" he exclaimed. "This is beautiful! Finest softwood forest I ever saw!"

She laughed. "By all means, look at the trees. But how can you be sure this *isn't* Paleo? Plenty of virgin softwood there!" She knew this wasn't Paleo, but was interested in his reasoning.

"Not the same. These are modern pines. See, the needles are different. Trees evolve, you know, same as

70

animals do. This white pine, now—actually, it's different from Earth white pine, in little ways—"

She raised her hands in mock surrender. He was not pretending; at this moment, the forest really did interest him more than she did, and he knew more than she in this area of botany. Agents had an excellent general education, but they could not be experts in every field.

Meanwhile, the social environment had changed as well as the physical one. Just as sex was relatively attractive to this country man when he was confined to the city, this challenging new—rather, *old*—forest was more attractive yet.

Which was not quite what she had anticipated. There were always unexpected wrinkles appearing in normals! Agents, in pleasant contrast, were completely predictable—to other agents. They were designed to be that way.

Pleasant contrast? It actually made for a certain tedium, she realized, when the mission stretched out longer than a few hours or days. In some things, predictability was less than ideal.

*Watch yourself,* she thought then. She was beginning to suffer from an overload of experience, and she had no dream mechanism to restore her mind to its prior equilibrium. It was inevitably shaping her into more of an individual than the computer could readily tolerate. If this went too far, her report would be suspect, even useless. The general rule was that an agent's mission should not continue longer than ten days because of that deterioration of reliability. She had already been nineteen days, and the end was not in sight.

She shuddered. How good it would be to return to computer central to be reset—and how awful to remain out so long she lost her affinity with her series, TA!

Veg was moving among the trees, tapping the trunks, looking at needles. This was his element! He suffered no pangs of dawning identity!

There were, it seemed, plenty of untouched worlds available for man's expansion. Earth's population and resources problem would be solved—just as soon as she got back.

She would have to return, try another setting, and begin a survey of alternate-worlds. It would be too cumbersome to step through every time. She would fashion a spot sensor that used very little power in projection because of its small mass. By bouncing it through and back like a tennis ball, she could check a dozen worlds in an hour, the only delay being the adjustment of the projector settings between uses.

She would not need Veg, after all. Not until she located familiar territory.

Three hours. She could sleep, for she had perfect timing and would wake when the return aperture was due. But first she would make a spot survey of this locale, for it might turn out to be the most suitable one yet discovered for exploitation. Earthlike, modern, no dinosaurs.

She lifted her hands, caught hold of a dead spoke on the huge pine, and hauled herself up. The trunk was a good six feet in diameter at the base, and the top was out of sight. She climbed rapidly, wriggling between the branches as they became smaller and more closely set. She was getting dirty, but that didn't matter. She really should have adjusted the seductive design of her outfit; trees were not much for that sort of thing, and her clothing inhibited progress. A few welts or scratches on the visible surfaces of her breasts would not bother her but could well turn off Veg—and she just might need him.

The trunk thinned alarmingly at the top and swayed in the stiffening wind. At an elevation of two hundred feet she halted, looking about. There were a number of tall trees, some reaching to two hundred and fifty feet. White pine, when allowed to grow, was one of the tallest trees, comparable to the Douglas fir and young redwood. Veg would know all about that! But now these tall trees interfered with her vision, so that all she could see was more forest. She had wasted her time. No doubt Veg could have told her that, too!

She descended, to find him waiting for her, looking up. How like a man! She hardly needed to make an effort to show off her wares; he knew how to find them for himself. Tree-climbing skirt!

"No good climbing," he remarked. "That's boy-scout lore—useless in a real forest. All you see is—"

"More trees," she finished for him.

"I had a better view from the ground."

"Thank you."

"Found something else."

Now she read the signs in him: He was excited, and not merely by his nether-view of her thighs as she came down the tree. He knew that what he had to tell her would affect her profoundly.

Tamme paused, trying to ascertain what it was before he told her. It was not a threat, not a joke. Not a human settlement. What, then?

"Can't tell, can you!" he said, pleased. "Come on, then."

He showed the way to a small forest glade, a clearing made by a fallen giant tree and not yet grown in. The massive trunk, eight feet thick, lay rotting on the ground. And near its sundered stump—

"An aperture projector!" she exclaimed, amazed.

"Thought you'd be surprised. Guess we weren't the first here, after all."

Tamme's mind was racing. There was no way that such a device could be here—except as a relic of human visitation. *Agent* visitation, for this was an agent model, similar to hers. But not identical—not quite.

"Some alternate-world agent has passed this way," she said. "And not long ago. Within five days."

"Because the brush has not grown up around it," Veg said. "That's what I figured. Can't be yours, can it?"

"No." The implications were staggering. If an alternate-world agent had come here, then Earth was not alone. There could be millions of highly developed human societies possessing the secret of aperture travel, competing for unspoiled worlds. What would she do, if she encountered one of those foreign agents, as highly trained as she, as dedicated to *his* world as she was to Earth?

By blind luck she had learned of the other agent first. Before *he* learned of *her*.

This was likely to be the mission of her life—and the fight of Earth's survival.

She had an immediate choice: Return to the surrealist city and commence her survey of alternates, hoping to discover in the process the route home. Or take a more chancy initiative by going after the competing agent and attempting to kill him before he could make his report to his world.

Each alternative was rife with bewildering complexities. She was trained to make quick decisions—but never had the fate of Earth depended on her snap judgment, even potentially. So she sought an advisory opinion. "Veg—if you came across the spoor of a hungry tiger, and you knew it was going to be him or you—what would you do? Follow the trail, or go home for help?"

Veg squinted at her. "Depends how close home is, and how I am armed. But probably I'd go home. I don't like killing."

She had posed the wrong question—another indication of her need for caution. An agent should not make elementary mistakes! Naturally the vegetarian would avoid a quarrel with an animal. "Suppose it was the track of a man as strong and as smart as you—but an enemy who would kill you if you didn't kill him first?"

"Then I'd *sure* go home! I'm not going out *looking* for any death match!"

She ran her tongue over her lips. "Any sensible person would do the same. It's a fairly safe assumption."

"Yeah."

"But the secret of victory is to do the unexpected."

"Yeah."

"All right. The aperture we used will come on again in two hours and eleven minutes. Check your watch; you'll only have fifteen seconds."

"I don't have a watch."

There it was again. She was missing the obvious at a calamitous rate in her preoccupation with larger concerns. She needed computer reorientation—but could not get it. There was no choice but to continue more carefully.

She removed her watch and handed it to him. "All you have to do is stand exactly where we landed. In fact, your best bet is to go there now, camp out on that spot. Then you'll be transported back automatically even if you're asleep. Tell your friends where I went, then wait at the city. Cal will understand."

He was confused. "Where *are* you going? I thought—"

She knelt by the generator. "After the tiger. This will not be pretty, and I may not return. It's not fair to involve you further."

"You're going to fight that other agent?"

"I have to. For our world, Earth."

"You're not taking me along?"

"Veg, I was using you. I'm sorry; I felt it was a necessary safeguard. My purposes are not yours, and this is not your quarrel. Go back to your friends." She was checking over the projector as she talked, making sure it was in working order, memorizing the setting.

"That was the note you left," he said wisely. "Telling Cal and 'Quilon not to try anything if they didn't want anything to happen to me."

She nodded acquiescence. "The projector is vulnerable. If they moved it or changed the setting, even accidentally . . ." Of course she could do the same thing to *this* one and return to the city, but that was no sure way to solve the problem. The other agent might have another projector, so her act would only alert him—and an agent needed no more than a warning! No, she had to go after him and catch him before he was aware, and kill him— if she could.

"Now you're letting me go." His mixture of emotions was too complex for her to analyze at the moment. The projector was more important.

"There was nothing personal, Veg. We do what we must. We're agents, not normal people." All was in order; the projector had not been used in several days, so it was fresh and ready to operate safely. "We will lie, cheat, and kill when we have to—but we don't do these things from preference. I suppose it won't hurt for you to know now: I was extremely sorry to see those dinosaurs destroyed on Paleo. Had I been in charge, we would have left you and them alone. But I follow my orders literally, using my judgment only in the application of my instructions when judgment is required." She glanced up, smiling briefly. "Take it from a trained liar and killer: Honesty and peace are normally the best policies."

"Yeah. I knew you were using me. That's why I lost

interest, once I thought it through. I'm slow, but I do get there in time. Trees don't *use* people."

She took an instant to verify that in him. He was serious; deceptive behavior turned him off even when he didn't recognize it consciously. She had misread him before, and that was bad. She had overrated the impact of her sex appeal; the preoccupation had become more *hers* than *his*. She was slipping.

Veg had loved Aquilon—*still* loved her—in part because of her basic integrity. He had lost interest in Tamme when her agent nature was verified. He was a decent man. Now his interest was increasing again as she played it straight.

"I made you a kind of promise," she said. "Since I may not be seeing you again, it behooves me to keep that promise now." She ran her finger along the seam of her low-fashioned blouse, opening it.

Veg was strongly tempted; she read the signals all over his body. No mistake *this* time! But something in him would not let go. "No—that's paid love. Not the kind I crave."

"Not a difficult payment. Sex is nothing more than a technique to us. And—you are quite a man, Veg."

"Thanks, anyway," he said. "Better get on with your mission." There was a turbulent decision in him, a multi-faceted, pain/pleasure metamorphosis. But he did not intend to betray her. "Time can make a difference— maybe even half an hour."

"I tried to deceive you before," she said. "That discouraged you. Now I am dealing only in truth. I never deceived you in what I was offering, only in my motive, and that's changed now. I would prefer to part with you amicably."

"I appreciate that. It's amicable. But I meant it, about time making a difference. You should go, quickly."

She read him yet again. The complicated knot of motives remained unresolved: He wanted her but would not take her. She did not have time to untangle all the threads of the situation—threads that extended well back into his relation with Aquilon. "Right." She put her blouse back together.

She had not been lying. Veg was a better man than

she had judged, with a certain quality under his superficial simplicity. It would have been no chore to indulge him, merely an inconvenience.

She turned on the projector. The spherical field formed. "By, Veg," she said, kissing him quickly. Then she stepped into the field.

And he stepped into it with her.

# Chapter 8

## ENCLAVE

The episode of the machine attack had brought them together, with new understandings. The spots were interdependent—and $\overline{OX}$ interdependent with them. Dec, the moving shape changer. Ornet, the stable mover. Cub, helpless. $\overline{OX}$, variable and mobile.

The three spots required gaseous, liquid, and solid materials to process for energy. The concepts were fibrillatingly strange despite $\overline{OX}$'s comprehensive new clarification circuits. They needed differing amounts of these aspects of matter in differing forms and combinations. But it was in the end comprehensible, for their ultimate requirement was energy, and OX needed energy, too. They drew it from matter; he drew it from elements. Energy was the common requirement for survival.

Could the spots' method of processing it be adapted to $\overline{OX}$'s need? YES. For when $\overline{OX}$ acted to promote the welfare of the spots, his elements became stronger. He had ascertained that before the machine attacked. When he provided the spots with their needs, they helped the plants, which in turn strengthened their elements. Yet the specific mechanism was not evident.

$\overline{OX}$ concentrated, experimenting with minute shifts in the alternate framework. Gradually, the concepts clarified.

The fundaments of the plants were rooted in certain alternates but flowered their elements in others. The roots required liquids and certain solids; the flowers required pattern-occupation, or they accumulated too much energy and become unstable. Their energy would begin spilling, making chaos. The reduction of that energy by the patterns kept the plants controlled, so that they prospered. The plants had both material and energy needs, and the spots served the first, the patterns the second.

The spots served another purpose. One of them, Ornet, had knowledge—a fund of alien information that compelled $\overline{OX}$'s attention, once he established adequate circuitry to hold detailed dialogue with this particular spot. For this information offered hints relating to survival.

Ornet had a memory circuit quite unlike that of $\overline{OX}$. Yet $\overline{OX}$ had become wary of ignoring difficult concepts; survival kept him broadening. Ornet's memory said that his kind had evolved a very long time ago, gradually changing, aspects of itself continually degenerating and renewing like a chain of self-damping shoots. That much was comprehensible.

But Ornet's memory also said that there were many other creatures, unlike Ornet or the two other spots or the machine, and that they, too, expanded, divided, and degenerated. This was significant: *a host of other spots.* Yet only the three were here. What had happened to the others?

Ornet did not know. There were a few in the enclave, mobile nonsentients, but those were only a tiny fraction of those described. $\overline{OX}$ was not satisfied that all were gone. They seemed to have existed in another framework and might exist there still. Where was that framework?

Further, Ornet's perception said that the machines had evolved in somewhat similar fashion. He knew this from his observation of the one that attacked. And he also said that $\overline{OX}$ himself had evolved somehow from some different pattern.

Alien nonsense! But $\overline{OX}$ modified his circuits, creating the supposition that all of this could be true, and followed the logic to certain strange conclusions.

Yet something was missing. OX realized, in the moment this special circuit functioned, that he could not have evolved here as the first pattern; he had come into existence only recently, whereas the plants had been here for a long time. And what about the spots? All were of recent origin, too, like OX. Even his special circuits could not accept this as the only reality.

Because the spots enhanced the elements, OX's immediate problem of survival had been abated. He could afford to consider longer-range survival. In fact, he *had* to—for survival was not complete until all aspects were secure. Control of his immediate scene was not enough. Was there some threat or potential threat beyond?

OX explored as far as he was able. His region was bounded on all sides by the near absence of elements; he could not cross out. There were only diminishing threads of elements that tapered down to thicknesses of only a few elements in diameter. It was impossible for OX to maintain his being on those; he had to have a certain minimum for his pattern to function.

He sent his shoots across these threads regularly; this was part of the way he functioned. Most were self-damping processes resulting from more complex circuits; some were simple self-sustaining radiations. A few were so constituted that they would have returned had they encountered a dead end. None did return, which showed OX that the threads continue on into some larger reservoir beyond his perception.

Radiations were inherent in the pattern scheme. Had another pattern-entity existed within OX's limited frame, OX would have been made aware of its presence by its own radiations. It was essential that patterns not merge; that was inevitable chaos and loss of identity for both. Because of the natural radiations of shoots, patterns were able to judge each other's whereabouts and maintain functional distances. This OX knew because it was inherent in his system; it would be nonsurvival for it to be otherwise. Once he had reacted to the seeming presence of another pattern because he had intercepted alien shoots, both self-sustaining and damping . . . but upon investigation it had turned out to be merely the reflection of his own projections, distorted by the irregular edge of his confine.

He knew there were other patterns . . . somewhere. There had to be. He had not come equipped with shoot-interpretation circuits by coincidence!

Perhaps beyond the barrier-threads? OX could not trace them—but the spots *could*. OX held dialogue with the communicative spot, Ornet. He made known his need to explore beyond the confines of this region.

Ornet in turn communicated with Dec, the most mobile spot. Dec moved rapidly out of OX's perception. When he returned, his optic generator signaled his news: This frame, one of the limited myriads of alternates that comprised the fabric of OX's reality, did indeed have other structures of elements. Dec had located them by following the element-threads that OX could not. Dec perceived these elements only with difficulty but had improved with practice. At varying physical distances, he reported, a number of them re-expanded into viable reservoirs. And in one of these Dec had spied a pattern.

The news threw OX into a swirl of disorientation. Hastily he modified his circuits; he had now confirmed, by observation of his own nature and indirect observation of the external environment, that he was not the only entity of his kind.

The other patterns had to know of him. His radiations, traveling the length of the element-threads, had to notify them of his presence. Yet never had a return-impulse come. That had to mean the others were damping out their external signs. Their only reason would be to abate a threat, as of a shoot-detecting machine or a pattern-consuming nonsentient pattern, or to conceal their presence for more devious internal reasons. On occasion, OX damped out his own radiation when he did not wish to be disturbed; his circuits did this automatically, and analysis of them showed this to be the reason. Actually, such damping was pointless here, there were no intrusive patterns, and the spots were not affected: additional evidence that OX was equipped by nature to exist in a society of patterns, not alone.

Why would other patterns, aware of him, deliberately conceal themselves from him? In what way was he a threat to them? He was a fully functioning pattern; it was not his nature to intrude upon another of his kind. The other patterns surely knew this; it was inherent, it was survival.

Something very like anger suffused $\overline{OX}$. Since his nature responded only to survival-nonsurvival choices, it was not emotion as a living creature would know it. But it was an acute, if subtle, crisis of survival.

A compatible pattern would not have acted in the fashion these outside patterns did. Therefore, their presence was a strong potential threat to his survival.

$\overline{OX}$ sent Dec out to observe again more thoroughly, and he sent Ornet out to the same physical spot in an adjacent frame. The two observers could not perceive each other, for they could not cross over alternates, and $\overline{OX}$ could observe neither since they were beyond his element-pool. But this difficult cooperative maneuver was critical.

Their report confirmed what $\overline{OX}$ had suspected.

Dec had observed a pattern fade, leaving the points unoccupied. Then it, or another like it, had returned. But Ornet's location had remained vacant.

$\overline{OX}$ understood this, though the spots did not. The pattern was traveling through the frames. Because of the configuration of the pool as $\overline{OX}$ had mapped it, he knew that the foreign pattern had to move either toward Ornet or away from him. It had moved away. And that meant that the other pool of elements extended beyond $OX$'s own pool, for his did not go farther in that direction.

The other pools, in fact, were probably *not* pools. They were aspects of the larger framework. The other patterns were not restricted as $\overline{OX}$ was.

They were keeping him isolated, restricted, confined to an enclave, while they roamed free. This, by the inherent definition of his circuitry, was inimical behavior.

$\overline{OX}$ sank into a long and violent disorientation. Only by strenuous internal measures was he able to restore equilibrium. Then it was only by making a major decision that forced a complete revamping of his nature.

He was in peril of nonsurvival through the action of others of his own kind. He had either to allow himself to be disrupted at their convenience or to prepare himself to disrupt the other patterns at *his* convenience. He chose the latter.

$\overline{OX}$ was ready to fight.

## Chapter 9

# LIFE

The two mantas, Hex and Circe, showed them the place, then disappeared again on their own pursuits. They seemed to like the city and to enjoy exploring it.

Cal and Aquilon stood on either side of the projector, not touching it. "So she had a way back all the time—and she took Veg with her," Aquilon said bitterly. "While we slept, blissfully ignorant." She crumpled the note and threw it away in disgust.

"I knew she had some such device," Cal replied. "I told the mantas to let them go."

She was aghast. "Why?"

"We could not stop the agent from doing as she wished —but Veg will keep an eye on her and perhaps ameliorate her omnivoristic tendencies. Meanwhile, it is pointless to remain idle here. I suspect we shall be able to make contact with the pattern-entities better on our own. They may or may not attempt to contact us again on the stage. If they do, I would prefer that Veg not break it up and that Tamme not receive their information. If they don't, it will be up to us to make a move."

"You really have it figured out," she said, shaking her head. Then: *"Pattern* entities? What—?"

"I have been doing some thinking. I believe I understand the nature of our abductor, and how we can communicate with it."

She lifted her hands, palms up. "Just like that!"

"Oh, it was simple enough, once I had the key," he said modestly. "Pattern."

"That's what you said before. I still don't follow it."

"First we have to capture a suitable machine."

"Capture a machine!" she exclaimed.

"If we can immobilize it long enough for me to get at its control unit, I should be able to turn it to our purpose."

She looked at him in perplexity. "Lure it under an ambush and knock it on the head with a sledgehammer?"

Cal smiled. "No, that would destroy the delicate mechanism we need. We shall have to be more subtle."

"Those machines aren't much for subtlety," she cautioned him. "If there are any of the whirling-blade variety around—"

"The menials will do," he said. "Preferably one with an optic-signal receiver."

Aquilon shook her head. "Well, you know best. Tell me what to do."

"Locate a flower or other device that will attract the right type of machine."

"Something optical, you mean?"

"Something that requires optical repair, yes." He faced away. "Hex! Circe!"

Aquilon shrugged and went looking. Cal knew what she was thinking: He was far more the mystery man than he had been on Nacre or Paleo. Those had been comparatively simple, physical worlds; this was a complex intellectual-challenge situation. His area of strength! But he would soon explain himself.

The two mantas arrived, sailing down to land beside him. "You have observed the tame machines?" he inquired.

They did not need to snap their tails. His rapport with them had progressed beyond that stage. He could tell their answer by the attitude of their bodies, just as he had divined their disapproval of his directive regarding Tamme and her projector. YES. As he had already known.

"Can you broadcast on their optical circuits?"

Now they were dubious. There followed a difficult, somewhat technical dialogue involving wavelengths and intensities. Conclusion: They *might* be able to do what he wanted. They would try.

Aquilon returned. "The light-loom seems best," she reported. "If something interfered with the original light-beam, the entire fabric would be spoiled. Seems a shame . . ."

"We shall not damage it," Cal assured her. "We want only to attract the relevant machine." He glanced again at the little projector. "This we shall leave untouched, as I believe it has been set to bring them back at a particular moment. They have no chance to reach Earth; I hope they find equivalent satisfaction."

Aquilon's eyes narrowed. "Are you implying—"

"As the agents experience more of reality away from their computer, they become more individual, more human. We stand in need of another human female if we are to maintain any human continuity away from Earth."

Her lip curled. "Why not wish for a cobra to turn human while you're at it?"

They went to the fountain. "Distort that light," Cal told the mantas. "Play your beams through it if you can keep it up without hurting your eyes."

They dutifully concentrated on the rising light.

"This may take a while," Cal said, "because it is subtle."

"Too subtle for me," she murmured.

"I will explain it." He dusted off the clear plastic panel covering the tapestry storage chamber. This was unnecessary, for there was no dust. He brought out a small marking pencil.

"Where did you get that?" she asked.

"The marker? I've had it all the time."

She smiled ruefully. "He travels through Paleocene jungles, he battles dinosaurs, he tackles self-willed machines, he carries a cheap pencil."

Cal put his hand on her arm, squeezing. "Life does go on."

She turned her lovely blue eyes upon him. "Did you mean it, on Nacre?"

Nacre, fungus planet: There was no mistaking her allusion. Now he regretted that he had made reference to it in front of Veg; that was not kind. He looked into the depths of those eyes and remembered it with absolute clarity.

They had been climbing, forging up a narrow, tortuous trail between ballooning funguses and the encompassing mist. Aquilon, instead of resting, had painted—not despite the fatigue, as she explained, but *because* of it. And though her subject had been ugly, the painting itself had been beautiful.

"You match your painting," Cal had told her, sincerely.

She had turned from him, overcome by an emotion neither of them understood, and he had apologized. "I did not mean to hurt you. You and your work are elegant. No man could look upon either and not respond."

She had put away her painting and stared out into the mist. "Do you love me?" Perhaps a naïve question since they had only known each other three months, and that aboard a busy spaceship; they really had had little to do with each other until getting stranded on the pearl-mist planet.

And he had answered: "I'm afraid I do." He had never before said that to a woman and never would again except to her.

Then she had told him of her past: a childhood illness that destroyed her smile.

Now she had her wish: She could smile again. That was the gift of the manta. But it had not brought her satisfaction.

"Yes, I meant it," he said. And did not add: *But Veg loved you, too.* That had formed the triangle, and she had seemed better suited to healthy Veg, especially on Paleo. Unfortunately the two had proved not wholly compatible and were in the process of disengaging. Cal hoped he had done the right thing in exposing Veg to Tamme. He had tried to warn Veg first, but the whole thing had a jealous smell to it as though he were throwing a rival to the wolves. Wolf, cobra—by any metaphor, an agent was trouble. Unless, as with Subble, there was some redeeming human quality that transcended the mercilessly efficient and ruthless program. A long, long shot—but what else was there?

"Look—the pattern is changing! Aquilon exclaimed, looking through the plastic at the slowly moving material.

"Excellent—the mantas have mastered the trick. Now we'll see how long it takes for a repair-machine to come."

"You were about to explain what you're doing."

"So I was! I am becoming absent-minded."

"*Becoming?*"

Such a superficial, obvious gesture, this bit of teasing. Yet how it stirred him! To Cal, love was absolute; he had always been ready to die for her. Somehow he had not been ready to banter with her. It was a thing he would gladly learn. At the moment, he did not know the appropriate response and would not have felt free to make it, anyway. So he drew three dots on the surface: $\therefore$ "What do you see?"

"A triangle."

"How about three corners of a square?"

"That, too. It would help if you completed the square, if that's really what you want to indicate."

"By all means." He drew in the fourth dot: $\because$ And waited.

She looked at it, then up at him. "That's all?"

"That's the essence."

"Cal, I'm just a little slower than you. I don't quite see how this relates to comprehension of the so-called 'pattern entities' and travel between alternate worlds."

He raised an eyebrow. "You don't?"

"You're teasing me!" she complained, making a moue.

So he was learning already! "There's pleasure in it."

"You've changed. You used to be so serious."

"I am stronger—thanks to you." On Nacre he had been almost too weak to stand, contemplating death intellectually and emotionally. He still had a morbid respect for death—but Veg and Aquilon had helped him in more than the physical sense.

"Let's take your square another step," she suggested. "I know there's more. There always is with you."

He looked at the square. "We have merely to formulate the rule. Three dots are incomplete; they must generate the fourth. Three adjacent dots do it—no more, no less. Otherwise the resultant figure is not a—"

"All right. Three dots make a fourth." She took his marker and made a line of three: • • • "What about this?"

"Double feature. There are two locations covered by three adjacent dots. So—" He added two dots above and below the line: • • •

"So now we have a cross of a sort." She shook her head. "I remain unenlightened."

"Another rule, since any society must have rules if it is to be stable. Any dot with three neighbor-dots is stable. Or even with two neighbors. But anything else—more than three or less than two—is unstable. So our figure is not a cross."

"No. The center dot has four neighbors. What happens to it?"

"Were this the starting figure, it would disappear. Cruel but necessary. However, the five-dot figure does not form from the three-dot figure because the ends of the original one are unstable. Each end-dot has only a single neighbor." He drew a new set: • • • Then he erased the ends, leaving one: •

"But what of the new dots we already formed?"

"Creation and destruction are simultaneous. Thus our figure flexes so." He numbered the stages: 1 • • • 2 • • •

3 • • • 4 • "We call this the 'blinker.' "

She looked at him suspiciously. "You mean this has been done before?"

"This is a once-popular game invented by a mathematician, John Conway, back in 1970. He called it 'Life.' I have often whiled away dull hours working out atypical configurations."

"I haven't seen you."

He patted her hand. "In my head, my dear."

"That would sound so much better without the 'my.' "

" 'In head?' "

She waggled a forefinger at him. " 'Dear.' "

"You are becoming positively flirtatious." Perhaps she was rebounding from Veg.

"Was Taler right on the ship?"

The ship. Again he looked into her eyes, remembering. The Earth government had not waited for the trio's report; it had sent four agents to Paleo to wrap it up, which agents had duly taken the normals prisoner and destroyed the dinosaur enclave. "Interesting," Taler had remarked while Tamme watched, amused. "Dr. Potter is even more enamored of Miss Hunt than is Mr. Smith. But Dr. Potter refuses to be influenced thereby."

"I suppose he was," Cal said.

She sighed as though she had anticipated more of an answer. "There must be more to life than this."

He glanced at her again, uncertain which way she meant it. He elected to interpret it innocuously. "There is indeed. There are any number of game figures, each with its own history. Some patterns die out; others become stable like the square. Still others do tricks."

Now she was intrigued. "Let me try one!"

"By all means. Try this one." He made a tetromino, four dots: .·.

Aquilon pounced on it. "There's an imaginary grid, right? The dots are really filling in squares and don't mesh the same on the bias?"

"That's right." She was quick, now that she had the idea; he liked that.

"If this is position one, then for position two we have to add one, two, three spots, and take away—none." She made the new figure: ·.·

"Correct. How far can you follow it?"

She concentrated, tongue between her lips. At length, she had the full series. "It evolves into four blinkers. Here's the series." She marked off the numbers of the steps in elegant brackets so as the avoid the use of con-

fusing periods. [1] .·.   [2] ·.·   [3] :.:   [4] ·.·

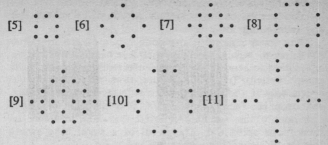

[5]     [6]     [7]     [8]

[9]     [10]     [11]

"Very good. That's 'Traffic Lights.'"

"Fascinating! They really work, too! But still, I don't see the relevance to—"

"Try this one," he suggested, setting down a new pattern: ⠂⠂ "That's the 'R Pentomino.'"

"That's similar to the one I just did. You've just tilted it sideways, which makes no topological difference, and added one dot."

"Try it," he repeated.

She tried it, humoring him. But soon it was obvious that the solution was not a simple one. Her numbered patterns grew and changed, taking up more and more of the working area. The problem ceased to be merely intriguing; it became compulsive. Cal well understood this; he had been through it himself. She was oblivious to him now, her hair falling across her face in attractive disarray, teeth biting lips. "What a difference a dot makes!" she muttered.

Cal heard something. It was the hum of a traveling machine. The bait had finally been taken!

He moved quietly away from Aquilon, who did not miss him. He took his position near the light fountain. The next step was up to the mantas.

The machine hove into sight. It was exactly what Cal had hoped for: a multilensed optical specialist—the kind fitted out to analyze a marginally defective light-pattern. One of the screens on it resembled an oscilloscope, and there seemed to be a television camera.

Excellent! This one must have been summoned from

moth-balling, as light-surgery was no doubt necessary less frequently than mechanical repairs. This was an efficient city, which did not waste power and equipment.

The two mantas turned to concentrate on the machine. Cal knew they were directing their eye-beams at its lenses, attempting to send it intelligible information and usurp its control system. If anything could do it, the mantas could—but only if the machine were sufficiently sophisticated.

It stopped, facing the mantas. Was the plan working?

Suddenly the machine whirled, breaking contact. Its intake lens spied Cal. The snout of a small tube swung about with dismaying authority.

Cal felt sudden apprehension. He had not expected physical danger to himself or Aquilon, and he was not prepared. His skin tightened; his eyes darted to the side to assess his best escape route or locate a suitable weapon. There was a nervous tremor in his legs.

He had played hide-and-seek with Tyrannosaurus, the largest predator dinosaur of them all. Was he now to lose his nerve before a mere repair robot?

Cal leaped aside as the beam of a laser scorched a pinhole in the plastic wall behind the place he had just stood. He had seen the warm-up glow just in time. But now it was warmed up and would fire too fast for his reflexes. He scurried on as the laser projector reoriented.

His plan had malfunctioned—and now the machine was on the attack. They were in for it!

The mantas tried to distract it, but the thing remained intent on Cal. Wherever he fled, it followed.

Aquilon, jolted out of her concentration, stepped forward directly into the range of the laser, raising her hand. Her chin was elevated, her hair flung back, her body taut yet beautiful in its arrested dynamism. For an instant she was a peremptory queen. "Stop!" she said to the machine.

It stopped.

Startled, Cal turned back. Had the machine really responded to a human voice—or was it merely orienting on a new object? Aquilon's life depended on that distinction!

Aquilon herself was amazed. "I reacted automatically, foolishly," she said. "But now—I wonder." She spoke to the machine again. "Follow me," she said, and began to walk down the path.

The machine stayed where it was, unmoving. Not even the laser tube wavered, though now it covered nothing.

"Wait," Cal murmured to her. "It begins to come clear. You gave that machine a pre-emptive directive."

"I told it to stop," she agreed. "I was alarmed. But if it understood and obeyed me then, why not now?"

"You changed the language," he said.

"I what?"

"The first time you addressed it, you used body language. Everything about you contributed to the message. You faced it without apparent fear, you raised your hand, you gave a brief, peremptory command."

"But I spoke English!"

"Irrelevant. No one could have mistaken your meaning." He put his hand under her arm, pulling her gently toward him. "Body language—the way we move, touch, look—the tension of our muscles, the rate of our pulse, our respiration—the autonomic processes. The agents virtually read our minds through those involuntary signals."

"Yes," she said, seeing it. "Your hand on me—that's speaking, too, more than your words."

He let go quickly. "Sorry. I just wanted you to understand—"

"I did," she said, smiling. "Why does that embarrass you?"

"This city is, despite its weirdities, essentially human. It was made to serve human beings, perhaps women like you—"

"A matriarchy?"

"Possibly. Now those people are gone, but the city remains, producing breathable air, growing edible fruit, supporting at least some omnivorous wildlife as though in anticipation of the needs of the mantas, manufacturing things for human use. Surely the machines remember their erstwhile masters!"

"Then why did it attack you?"

"I was acting in an unfriendly manner, associating with aliens who were interfering with the business of the city. I was giving the signals of an enemy or a vandal—as indeed I regarded myself. The machine reacted accordingly."

Aquilon nodded. "So we know the builders, though not their language."

"We *are* the builders—on another variant. Perhaps this city is an artifact of a human alternate many thousands of years in our future. With the alternate framework, it stands to reason that many worlds are ahead of us as well as many behind."

"Dinosaurs on one—super science on another," she agreed.

"But I do not think the sparkle-cloud is part of this human scheme—as I was explaining."

"You *were*?"

"The Life game."

She grimaced. "I haven't gotten through your R Pentomino yet."

"I wouldn't worry about it," he said. "It only achieves a 'steady state' after eleven hundred moves."

"Eleven hundred moves!" she exclaimed indignantly. "And you set me innocently to work with a pencil—"

"The point is, the entire game is determined by the opening configuration. But that hardly means that all openings are similar, or that a five-point figure does not have impressive complexities in its resolution. Most simple patterns quickly fade or become stable. A few are open-ended, especially when they interact with other figures. So larger opening patterns might conceivably—"

"Cal!" she cried. "Are you saying that this little dot-game—the sparkle-pattern—"

He nodded. " 'Life' is a simple two-dimensional process that nevertheless has certain resemblances to the molecular biology of our living life. Suppose this game were extended to three physical dimensions and given an indefinitely large grid?"

She shook her head so that her hair flew out enticingly. Had she picked up that gesture from Tamme? "It would still be predetermined."

"As *we* are predetermined, according to certain philosophies. But it becomes extremely difficult to chart that course before the fact. Suppose a number of forms were present on that grid, interacting?"

"If their patterns got too large, they'd mess each other up. There's no telling what would happen then." She paused, his words sinking in. "It would still be predetermined by the initial figures and their relation to each other on the grid—but too complicated to predict without a computer. Maybe there's no computer that could handle the job if the grid were big enough and the figures too involved. Anything could happen."

"And if it existed in four or five dimensions?"

She spread her hands. "I'm no mathematician. But I should think the possibilities would approach those of organic processes. After all, as you pointed out, enzymes in one sense are like little keys on the molecular level, yet they are indispensable to the life processes. Why not dot-pattern enzymes, building into—" She paused again. "Into animate sparkle-clouds!"

"So we could have what amounts to independent, free-willed entities," he finished. "Their courses may be predetermined by their initial configurations and framework —but so are ours. We had better think of them as potentially sentient and deal with them accordingly."

"Which means establishing communication with them," she said. "It was a giant mental step, but at last I am with you." She looked down at the complex mess of her R Pentomino and blew out her cheeks.

"That's good," he said. "Because we need that machine —and you seem to be able to control it. Bring it to the auditorium."

Aquilon struck a dramatic pose before the machine. "Come!" she commanded, gesturing imperatively. And it did.

"You know, I rather enjoy this," she confided as they walked.

# Chapter 10

# PHASE

$$\begin{matrix} \bullet & \bullet & \bullet \\ \bullet & & \bullet \\ \bullet & & \bullet \\ \bullet & \bullet & \bullet \end{matrix}$$

$\overline{OX}$ was ready to fight. He now knew he was under observation by pattern-entities resembling himself who declined to communicate with him. Had they merely been there, unaware of him, they would not have cut off their normal radiation shoots—and since he had not cut off his, they had to know of him. So he was certain of his diagnosis.

His combat circuitry, laboriously developed in the process of restoring equilibrium, informed him that it would be nonsurvival to permit the outside patterns to learn of his change of condition. He therefore fashioned a pseudoplacid circuit whose purpose was to maintain normal radiation despite the internal changes. The observing patterns would thus receive no evidence of $\overline{OX}$'s real intent.

It was also probable that the outside patterns did not comprehend the significance of the spots. That was thus an asset, for the spots had already proved themselves as both element-stimulators and sources of exterior information. In fact, the spots represented $\overline{OX}$'s major potential weapon. He had ascertained that they, like he, were of recent origin; they, like he, possessed the powers of growth and increased facility. According to the Ornet-Spot memory, the stationary stable Cub was a member of a type that had greater potential than many others. But this needed a great deal of time and concentration to develop. OX decided to exploit this potential.

Each alternate was separated from its neighbors by its phase of duration. OX had verified this by study of the elements he activated: They gradually matured as the plants charged them, and this maturation represented a constant within the individual frame. Even an element that had been activated and recharged many times still reflected its ancestry and age. But the equivalent elements of adjacent alternates differed, one frame always being newer than the other.

Since OX was a pattern having no physical continuity, this differential of alternates did not affect him except as it affected the elements. Generally the older, more established elements were more comfortable; fresh ones were apt to release their energy unevenly, giving him vague notions of nonsurvival.

That differential could, however, affect the spots, who were almost wholly physical. OX could move them from one frame to another as they were, allowing them to change in relation to their environment because of the shift in that environment—as when he had moved them to a more favorable habitat. He could also, he discovered, modify the transfer so that the alternates remained fixed —and the spots changed. He had done that when Cub perished before the blade of the machine. It was merely an aspect of crossover: A physical difference between creature and alternate always had to be manifest.

What it amounted to was a method for aging the spots. When OX moved them this way, they were forced to assume the duration they would have had, had they always existed there. Then he shifted them back, this time letting them be fixed while the frame seemed to change. It was an artificial process that cut the spots off from the untampered frames beyond the enclave—but he was barred from that, anyway.

In this manner he brought the spots from infancy to maturity in a tiny fraction of the time they would normally have required. Of course to *them* it seemed as though their full span had passed in normal fashion; only OX knew better. But he explained this to them and offered certain proofs for their observation, such as the apparent cessation of the growth of the fixed life around them, the immobile plants. Only those plants within the radius of the frame-travel advanced at the same rate. They discussed this with increasing awareness and finally believed.

The little machine, always hovering near, was also caught up in the progress. OX tried to leave it behind, but with inanimate cunning it moved in whenever it sensed his development of the complex necessary circuits, staying in phase. Originally it had been impervious to the spots' attacks; had they advanced without it, they would have been free of it one way or another, either by getting completely out of phase with it or by becoming large and strong enough to overcome it. Thus, they always had to be on guard against its viciousness.

OX also arranged education shoots that facilitated the expansion of awareness in the spots. Though this almost wholly occupied OX's available circuitry, it did not have a large effect on either Dec or Ornet. They seemed programmed to develop in their own fashions regardless of his influence. But for Cub it was most productive. Ornet's conjecture had been accurate: Cub had enormous potential, in certain respects rivaling OX's own. How this could be in a physical being OX could not quite grasp; he had to assume that Cub had a nonphysical component that actually made rationality feasible. At any rate, Cub's intellect was malleable, and OX's effort was well rewarded.

OX watched and guided according to his combat nature as Dec became large and swift, able to disable a semi-sentient animal with a few deadly snaps of his tail-appendage, able to receive and project complex information efficiently. He was the fastest-moving spot physically, useful for purely physical observations and communications.

Ornet served to protect and assist Cub—but Ornet's memory clarified as he grew and offered many extraordinary insights into the nature of spots and frames that influenced OX's own development. Ornet, limited as he was physically, nevertheless had vested within him more sheer experience than any of the others, including OX himself. That was a tremendous asset, like a stabilizing circuit, guiding him through potential pitfalls of nonsurvival. OX always consulted with Ornet before he made any significant decision.

But Cub was his best investment. He grew from a non-mobile lump to a slowly mobile entity, then to a creature approaching Ornet in physical capability. His intellect became larger and larger. Soon he was grasping concepts that baffled both Dec and Ornet. Then, as he approached maturity, his reasoning ability interacted with OX's on something other than a teacher-pupil level. He began to pose questions that OX could not resolve—and that in turn forced OX to ever-greater capacities.

What about the killer machine? Cub inquired once after they had driven it off. Do you think it gets lonely as we do? Doesn't it have needs and feelings, too?

The very notion was preposterous! Yet OX had to make a new circuit and concede that yes, in machine-terms, it would have needs and feelings, too, and perhaps was lonely for its own kind.

Or maybe for sapience of any kind—including ours? Cub persisted. Could it be that when it tries to consume us, it is really seeking intellectual dialogue, not aware that we do not integrate physically as it does?

OX had to allow that possibility, also. Still, he pointed out, it remains a deadly enemy to us all because we *don't* integrate as mechanical components. We can never afford to let down our guard.

But long after that dialogue, his circuits fibrillated with the intemporate concept. A machine, seeking intellectual dialogue. A *machine*!

# Chapter 11

# HEXAFLEXAGON

.
.
.

... ...

.
.
.

They emerged into a blinding blizzard. Snow blasted Veg's face, and the chill quickly began its penetration of his body. He was not adequately dressed.

Tamme turned to him, showing mild irritation. "Why did you come?" she demanded.

He tried to shrug, but it was lost in his fierce shivering. He did not really understand his own motive, but it had something to do with her last-minute display of decency. And with her beauty and his need to disengage irrevocably from Aquilon.

Tamme removed her skirt, did something to it, and put it about his shoulders. He was too cold to protest. "This is thermal," she said. "Squat down, hunch up tight. It will trap a mass of warm air, Eskimo-style. Face away from the wind. Duck your head down; I'll cover it." And she removed her halter, formerly her blouse, adjusted it, and fashioned it into a protective hood.

He obeyed but did finally get out a word. "You—"

"I'm equipped for extremes," she said. "You aren't. I can survive for an hour or more naked in this environment—longer with my undergarments. So can you—if you just sit tight under that cloak. After that, we'll both exercise vigorously. We have to stretch it out three hours, until the projector brings us back. We'll make it—though for once I wish I'd set it for the minimum safe-return time."

He nodded miserably. "Sorry. I didn't know—"

"That you would only be in the way? *I* knew—but I also knew your motive, confused as it might be, was good. You have courage and ethics, not because you've been programmed for them, but because you are naturally that way. Perhaps agents should be more like that." She paused, peering around. Snowflakes were hung up on her eyebrows, making little visors. "I'll make a shelter. Maybe we won't *have* to go back."

He watched her move about, seemingly at ease in the tempest . . . in her bra and slip. He was chagrined to be so suddenly, so completely dependent on a woman, especially in what he had thought of as a man's natural element: wilderness. But she was quite a woman!

Tamme made the shelter. She cleared the loose snow away, baring a nether layer of packed snow and ice, a crust from some prior melting and refreezing. She used one of her weapons, a small flame thrower, to cut blocks of this out. Soon she had a sturdy ice wall.

"Here," she directed.

He obeyed, moving jerkily into the shelter of the hole behind the wall. The wind cut off. Suddenly he felt much better. The cloak *was* warm; once the wind stopped wrestling with it, stealing the heated air from the edges, he was almost comfortable. He held it close about his neck, trapping that pocket of heat. But his feet were turning numb.

Tamme built the wall around him, curving it inward until she formed a dome. It was an igloo!

"I think you'll manage now," she said. "Let me have my clothing; I want to look about."

She crawled into the igloo beside him while he fumbled with cloak and hood. And she stripped off her underclothing.

Veg stared. She was an excellent specimen of womanhood, of course; not lush but perfectly proportioned, with no fat where it didn't belong. Every part of her was lithe and firm and feminine. But that was not what amazed him.

Strapped to her body was an assortment of paraphernalia. Veg recognized the holster for the flame thrower she had just used: It attached to her hip where a bikini would have tied—a place always covered without seeming to be, filling a hollow to round out the hip slightly. There was another holster, perhaps for the laser, on the other hip. An ordinary woman would have padded that region with a little extra avoirdupois; Tamme's leanness only served to delineate her muscular structure without at all detracting from her allure. There was similar structures near her waist, which was in fact more slender than it had seemed. And at the undercurves of her breasts.

How artfully she had hidden her weaponry while seeming to reveal all! Her thighs had seemed completely innocent under her skirt as she came down the pine tree. And who would have thought that the cleavage of her bosom had been fashioned by the push of steel weapons so close below! Had she been ready to make love to him that way, armed to the . . . ?

"No, I'd have set aside the weapons," she said. "Can't ever tell where a man's hands may go."

She tore the bra, slip, and panties apart, then put them back together a different way. Evidently she could instantly remake all her clothing for any purpose—functional, seductive, or other. He had no doubt it could be fashioned into a rope to bind a captive or to scale a cliff. And of course her blouse had become first a revealing halter, then a hood for his head.

The female agent was every bit as impressive as the male agent! It was an excellent design.

"Thanks," Tamme said.

She donned her revised underthings, once more covering the artillery. Veg now understood about her weight: She probably weighed a hundred and fifteen stripped but carried forty pounds of hardware.

She held out her hand unself-consciously. Hastily he passed the cloak and hood across and watched her convert them back into skirt and blouse. But not the same design as before; the skirt was now longer for protection against the storm, and the blouse closed in about her neck, showing no breast. Quite a trick!

She scrambled out the igloo door and disappeared into the blizzard. While she was gone, Veg chafed his limbs and torso to warm them and marveled at the situation in which he found himself. He had gone from Earth to Paleo, the first alternate; then to Desertworld, the second alternate. And on to Cityworld, Forestworld, and now to Blizzard—the third, fourth, and fifth, respectively. Now he was huddled here, shivering, dependent on a woman—while all alternity beckoned beyond!

How had they come here, really? Who had left the aperture projector so conveniently? It smelled of a trap. As did the blizzard. But for Tamme's strength and resourcefulness, it could have been a death trap.

Yet death would have been more certain if the aperture had opened over the brink of a cliff or before the mouth of an automatically triggering cannon.

No—that would have been too obvious. The best murder was the one that seemed accidental. And of course their immediate peril might well *be* accidental. Surely this storm was not eternal; this world must have a summer as well as a winter and be calm between altercations of weather. Tamme had said the projector could have been left five days ago. This storm was fresh. So maybe another agent had passed this way, leaving his projector behind as Tamme had left hers at Cityworld.

That meant the other agent was still around here somewhere. And that could be trouble. Suppose the agent overcame Tamme and stranded Vag here alone? She was tough and smart—and mighty pretty!—but another agent would have the same powers.

Unless—

Veg straightened up, banging his head against the curving roof wall. Suddenly a complex new possibility had opened to his imagination—but it was so fantastic he hardly trusted it. He didn't want to embarrass himself by mentioning it to Tamme. But he could not ignore it. He would have to check it out himself.

He wriggled out of the igloo. The wind struck him afresh, chilling him again, but he ducked his head, hunched his shoulders, and proceeded. This would not take long.

He counted paces as he slogged through the snow. At a distance of twenty steps—roughly fifty feet since he could not take a full stride in two-foot-deep snow—he halted. This was a tissue of guesswork, anyway, and here in the storm it seemed far-fetched indeed.

He tramped in a circle, backward into the wind where he had to, eyes alert despite being screwed up against the wind. His face grew stiff and cold, and his feet felt hot: a bad sign. But he kept on. Somewhere within this radius there might be—

There wasn't. He retreated to the igloo, half disappointed, half relieved. He didn't regret making the search.

Tamme returned. "What have you been doing?" she demanded. "Your tracks are all over the place!"

"I had a crazy notion," he confessed. "Didn't pan out."

"*What* crazy notion?"

"That there might be another projector here, part of a pattern."

She sighed. "I was hoping you wouldn't think of that."

"You mean that's what *you* were looking for?" he asked, chagrined.

She nodded. "I suspect we are involved in an alternate chain. We started from the city alternate—but others may have started from other alternates, leaving their projectors behind them, as I did. One started from the forest. Another may have started from here. In which case there will be a projector in the area."

"That's what I figured—only I didn't really believe it. Projectors scattered all through alternity."

"Alternity! Beautiful."

"Well, it's as good a name for it as any," he said defensively. "Anyway, if it's all happening like that—what do you care? No one's trying to torpedo Earth."

"How do you know?" she asked.

"Well, I can't *prove* anything, but what about the Golden Rule? We're not trying to do anything to *them*, so—"

"Aren't we?"

He faltered. "You mean, we *are?*" He had thought she was just going after one agent, not the whole universe.

"Our government is paranoid about Earth-defense. We're out to destroy any possible competition before it destroys us. Remember Paleo?"

"Yeah . . ." he agreed, wishing she hadn't reminded him of that. She, like all agents, was a ruthless killer.

"So it behooves us to catch them before *they* catch *us*."

"But *we're* not paranoid! We don't have to—"

"*You* aren't. As an agent of our government, I *am*."

He didn't like that, but he understood it. "You have to serve your master, I guess. But if you ran the government—"

"Things would change. I don't like paranoia; it's inefficient. I don't like killing to maintain a defective system. But that is academic. Right now I have to trace this chain —if that's what it is—to its end. And deal with what I find there."

"Yeah . . ."

"You assumed the projector would be within fifty feet because the last one was. That does not necessarily follow."

"Hell of a better chance to find it than looking three miles out."

"Yes. I ranged three miles. The snow covers all traces."

"Maybe it's under cover—in a hollow tree or under a rock or something. Because of its being winter."

"Good idea. I'll check for that." She moved out again.

She found it. The mound gave it away. Another aperture projector, very similar to the others.

"You can still go back," she told Veg.

"I'm getting curious," he said, "Let's go. It's cold here."

She shrugged and activated the device. They stepped through.

Veg braced himself for any extreme of climate or locale—hot, cold, lush, barren, metropolis, wilderness. And stood amazed, caught unbraced for the reality.

It was an alien orchestra.

The instruments were conventional, even archaic: strings, woodwinds, percussion. The technique was flawless to his untrained ear. The melody was passionate, stirring mind, heart, and entrails. It was only the players who were alien.

Tamme looked about warily, as bemused as he. Veg knew she was searching for the next projector.

There was no sign of it.

Meanwhile, the alien orchestra played on, oblivious of the intrusion. The players on the violins had at least twelve appendages, each terminating in a single finger or point. These fingers moved over the strings, pressing to change the pitch; half a dozen fingers bunched to control the bow. The creatures on the flutes were bird-like, with nozzle-like mouths with gill-like apertures around the neck that took in air alternately so that there was always pressure. Those on the drums had arms terminating in hard balls on flexible tendons; they did not need to hold any drumsticks.

Veg wondered whether the creatures had been designed for the instruments or the instruments for the creatures. If the latter, as seemed more reasonable, what did this signify about music on Earth? Human beings adapting to instruments that were designed for aliens? That would mean strong crossover between alternates . . .

He tried to speak, but the music was loud, coming at them from every side, and he could not hear his own voice. Not surprising since the two of them had apparently landed right in the orchestra pit, huge as it was. They had to get out of it before they could communicate.

He looked for the edge of it—and only saw more musicians. They were really devoted to their art to ignore creatures as strange as he and Tamme must seem to them. He started to walk between the players, but a hand on his arm restrained him. It was Tamme, shaking her head "No."

He realized why: There was no distinguishing feature about this spot, and they could readily lose it. For that matter, they could lose each other if they stayed apart. There seemed to be no end to this orchestra!

Tamme pointed to a spot on the floor. "Stay!" she mouthed several times until he read her lips and understood. He would be the place marker, she the explorer. Ordinarily he would have insisted on reversing the roles, but he knew she was more capable. He squatted where she had indicated.

Tamme moved through the formations of musicians.

They were not exactly in lines or groups, but they were not random. There was a certain alien order to it—a larger pattern like that of the leaves on a tree or the stars in the sky.

Somewhere, here, was another projector—maybe.

Where? It was not visible. Could the aliens—actually they were not aliens but natives, as this was their alternate—could they have moved it? Somehow he doubted it. The creatures had taken absolutely no notice of the human intrusion; why should they bother with a mechanical device that did not play music? Maybe it was inside one of their instruments. No—when they left, it would be lost, and that was no decent alternative!

He contemplated the musicians. Where *did* they go during their breaks? Or were they anchored here forever? He had seen none move. Strange!

But back to the projector: Could it be in one of the boxlike seats? There seemed to be room. Which one? There were fifty or a hundred of them in sight. And how could he get *at* it?

Tamme was moving in widening spirals. He caught intermittent glimpses of her between the musicians. After a couple more circuits she would be invisible; the massed musicians blocked every line-of-sight pathway beyond a certain distance.

Well, that was one problem he would let Tamme handle. She didn't want him interfering, and maybe she was right. Still, it took some getting used to—but Tamme was different from Aquilon.

Veg shook his head. He wasn't sure which type of girl he preferred. Of course it was over between him and Aquilon, and pointless with Tamme, even for the one-night stand she had offered; she was not his type. Still, no harm in speculating. . . .

This shifting randomly through alternates—or *was* it random? It reminded him of something. A children's game . . . puzzle . . . fold-a-game, flex-a-gone . . .

"Hexaflexagon!" he exclaimed. "Alternity hexaflexagon!"

Tamme was there so fast he jumped, startled. "What's the matter?" He could hear her now; the music had subsided to a delicate passage.

"Nothing," he said sheepishly. "I was just thinking."

She did not waste effort on the matter. "I have located the projector."

"Great!" he said, relieved. Now that they were on this rollercoaster, he preferred to continue forward. He had not relished the notion of staying here or of returning to the blizzard world. "How'd you figure which box?"

"Sound. The boxes are hollow; the projector changed the acoustics."

"Oh. So you used the music. Smart." Music and hexaflexagons, he thought. He followed her to the place.

It was the stool of a bass-strings player. The octopus-like creature almost enveloped the box, four of its tentacles reaching up to depress the ends of the four strings, four more manipulating the bow. The sounds it made were low and sweet: It really had the musical touch!

"You're pretty good," Veg told it. But the volume had swelled again, drowning him out. The creature made no acknowledgment.

Tamme squatted, touched the box, and lifted out a panel. Inside was one of the little aperture projectors. She didn't ask whether he was ready to go; she knew it. She reached in, her arm almost brushing the overlapping bulk of the octopus, and turned the machine on.

And they were on a steeply inclined plane. "Yo!" Veg cried, rolling helplessly.

Tamme caught his wrist and brought him up short. He had known she was strong, but this disconcerted him. Seemingly without effort, she supported the better part of his weight.

Veg's flailing free hand found purchase, and he righted himself. They were perched on a steeply tilted sheet of plastic. It was orange but transparent; through it he could see the jumbled edges of other sheets. He had caught hold of the slanting upper edge. Tamme had done the same farther up.

Below them were more sheets, some edge-on, some angeled, some broadside. Above them were others. And more to the sides. All sizes and colors. What held them in place was a mystery; they seemed firm, as if embedded in clear glass, yet there was no support.

Veg peered down, searching for the ground. All he could see was an irregular network of planes. The jungle, like the orchestra they had just vacated, was everywhere, endless.

Tamme let go, slid down, and landed gracefully on a purple horizontal plane to the side. She signaled Veg to stay put.

"It figures," he muttered, hoisting himself up to perch on the thin edge. The worlds were fascinating in their variety, but he certainly wasn't being much of a help so far.

Soon she was partially hidden behind the translucency of angled planes; he could detect her motion, not her image. She was looking for the next projector, of course.

Suppose she didn't find it? There was no guarantee that a given world had a projector or that it would be within a thousand miles. There had to be an end to the line somewhere.

A chill of apprehension crawled over him. No guarantee the next world would have air to breathe, either! They were playing one hell of a roulette game!

Maybe they would go on and on forever, meeting such a bewildering array of alternates that eventually they would forget which one they had started from, forget Earth itself.

Well, he had volunteered for the course!

Tamme was now invisible. Veg looked about, becoming bored with the local configurations. He wanted to explore some on his own, but he knew he had to remain as a reference point. This alternate was pretty in its fashion, but what was there to *do?*

He noticed that the plastic plane he perched on was not in ideal repair. Strips of it were flaking off. Maybe it was molting, shedding its skin as it grew. Ha-ha.

Idly, he peeled off a length of it, moved by the same mild compulsion that caused people to peel the plastic from new glossy book restorations. The stuff was almost colorless in this depth, flexible and a bit crackly. He folded it over, and it made a neat, straight crease without breaking.

That gave him a notion. He began folding off triangular sections. He was making a hexaflexagon!

"Let's go," Tamme said.

Veg looked up. "You found it, huh?" He tucked his creation into a pocket and followed her, leaping from plane to plane, stretching his legs at last.

It was hidden in the convergence of three planes, nestled securely. "Kilroy was here, all right," he murmured.

Tamme glanced at him sharply. "Who?"

"You don't know Kilroy? He's from way back."

"Oh—a figure of speech." She bent over the projector.

So that was a gap in the agent education: They didn't know about Kilroy. He probably wasn't considered important enough to be included in their programming. Their loss!

The projector came on,



                                   and they were back in the blizzard.

"A circuit!" Tamme cried in his ear, exasperated. "Well, I know where the projector is." She bundled him into her clothes and plunged forward.

"Maybe it's not the same one!" Veg cried.

"It is the same. There's our igloo." Sure enough, they were passing it. But Veg noted that they had landed in a slightly different place this time, for the igloo had been built at their prior landing site. This time they had arrived about fifty feet to the side. Was that significant? He was too cold to think it out properly.

In minutes they found it. "There's been time to recharge it—just," she said. Then: "That's funny."

"What?" he asked, shivering in the gale.

"This is a left-handed projector, more or less."

"Same one we used before," he said. "Let's get *on* with it."

"I must be slipping," she said. "I should have noticed that before."

"In this blizzard? Just finding it was enough!"

She shrugged and activated it.

They were now in the alien orchestra.

Veg shook the snow off his cloak and hood and looked about. This time they seemed to have landed in exactly the same place as before; he saw the stain of their prior water-shedding as the snow melted.

"We're stuck in a loop of alternates," Tamme said. "I don't like this."

"There's got to be a way out. There was a way *in*."

"That doesn't necessarily follow." She glanced about. "In any event, we ought to rest while the local projector is recharging."

"Sure," he agreed. "Want me to stand watch?"

"Yes," she said, surprising him. And she lay down on the floor and went to sleep.

Just like that! Veg's eyes ran over her body, for she was still in bra and panties. The hardware didn't show, and in repose Tamme looked very feminine. And why shouldn't she? he asked himself fiercely. Every woman in the world did not have to be stamped in the mold of Aquilon!

Of course Tamme wasn't a woman at all but an agent. She really *was* stamped from a mold—the TA-distaff-series mold. All over the world there were more just like her, each every bit as pretty, competent, and self-reliant.

He shied away from that concept. Instead, he looked around the orchestra at the now-familiar creatures. They looked the same: octopi, gillbirds, drumstick drummers. But something had changed somehow. What was it?

He concentrated, and it came to him: *This* alternate was the same, but the blizzard-alternate had been different. The igloo, as he passed it . . . no, he couldn't quite pin it down. Different, yet the same, indefinably.

Veg blew out his breath, removed Tamme's cloak, and discovered his plastic hexaflexagon. This was proof he had been to the plane world, at least! He completed the folds, bit on the ends to fasten them properly, and flexed the device idly.

This was a hexa-hexaflexagon. It was hexagonal in outline, and when flexed, it turned up a new face from the interior, concealing one of the prior ones. But not in regular order. Some faces were harder to open than others.

He fished in his pocket and brought out a stubby pencil. He marked the faces as he came to them: 1 for the top, 2 for the bottom. He flexed it, turning a new blank face to the top, and marked it 3. He flexed it again, and 2 came up.

"Closed loop," he muttered. "But I know how to fix that!" He shifted his grip to another diagonal and flexed from it. This time a new face appeared, and he marked this 4.

The next flex brought up 3 again. Then 2. And 1.

"Back to where we started," he said. And changed diagonals. A blank face appeared, which he marked 5. Then on through 2, 1, 3, and finally to the last blank one, 6.

"Those loops are only closed if you let them," he said with satisfaction. "I'd forgotten how much fun these hexes were! You can tell where you are because the faces change orientation."

Then the realization hit him.

"Hey, Tam!" he breathed.

He had spoken no louder than before, and the volume of the ambient music had not abated, but she opened her eyes immediately. "Yes?"

"Maybe this is a bum lead—but I think I know why we're repeating worlds. And maybe how to snap out of the loop in controlled fashion."

She sat effortlessly, the muscles in her stomach tightening. "Speak."

He showed her his plastic construct, opaque because of its many layers. "You know what this is?"

"A doodle from plane-frame material."

"A hexa-hexaflexagon. See, I flex it like this and turn up new faces."

She took it and flexed it. "Clever. But to what point?"

"Well, they don't come up in order—not exactly. Look at the face numbers as you go—and at the composition of the repeats."

"One," she called off. She flexed. "Three . . . Two . . . One . . . Five . . . Two, inverted." She looked up. "It's a double triad. Intriguing, not remarkable."

"Suppose we numbered the worlds we've been going

through—and found a repeat that was backwards? I mean, the same, but like a mirror image?"

For the first time, he saw an agent do a double take. "The second blizzard was backwards!" she exclaimed. "Or rather, twisted sixty degrees. The igloo—the irregularities in it and pattern of our prior tracks, what was left of them, the projector—all rotated by a third!"

"Yeah. That's what I figured. Didn't make sense at first."

"Flexing alternates! Could be." Rapidly she flexed through the entire sequence, fixing the pattern in her mind. "It fits. We could be in a six-face scheme on this framework. In that case our next world will be—the forest."

She certainly caught on rapidly! "But we can't go home from there."

"No. The face will be twisted, part of a subtriad. But we would know our route."

"Yeah," he agreed, pleased.

She pondered momentarily. "There's no reason the alternates should match the hex faces. But there *is* a clear parallelism, and it may be a useful intellectual tool, in much the way mathematics is a tool for comprehending physical relations. Our problem is to determine the validity of our interpretation without subjecting ourselves to undue risk."

"You sound like Cal now!"

"No shame in that," she muttered. "Your friend has a freakishly advanced intellect. We could travel the loop again just to make sure—but that would mean a delay of several hours, waiting for the projectors to recharge. In that time our competition could gain the advantage."

"So we just go ahead fast," Veg finished. "We can follow the flex route and see if it works. If it does, we've got our map of alternity."

"In your bumbling male-normal fashion, you may have helped me," Tamme said. "Come here."

Veg knelt down beside her.

She put both hands to his head, pulled him to her, and kissed him. It was like the moment in free fall when a spaceship halted acceleration in order to change orientation. His whole body seemed to float, while his own pulse pounded in his ears.

She let him go. It took him a moment to regain composure. "That isn't the way you kissed me before."

"That was demonstration. This was feeling."

"You do feel? I thought—"

"We do feel. But our emotions are seldom aroused by normals other than amusement or distaste."

Veg realized that he had been paid an extraordinary compliment. But that was all it was. He had helped her, and she was appreciative. She had repaid him with a professionally executed gesture. Case dismissed.

"We should have a choice here," she said. "Repeat the triad indefinitely—or break out of it. Only way to break out is to project elsewhere than to the plane world. But how can we do that—without interfering with the settings on the projector?"

Veg appreciated the problem. Touch those settings, and they could be thrown right out of this hex framework and be totally lost—or dead. That would accomplish nothing worthwhile. They wanted to follow the existing paths wherever they led, and catch up to—whom?

"These settings are built into the hexaflexagon," he said. "All you have to do is find them."

"Yes. Too bad alternity isn't made of folded plastic."

They remained in silence for a time, while the music swelled around them. And Veg had a second revelation. "The music!"

Again she caught on almost as fast as he thought of it and quickly outdistanced his own reasoning. "In phase with the music! Of course. Catch it during one type of passage, go on to Plane. Catch it during another—"

"Now's the time!" Veg cried.

They ran to the projector. Tamme had it on instantly.

And they were in the forest.

"Victory!" Veg exclaimed happily. Then he looked about uncertainly. "But is it—?"

"Yes, it is rotated," Tamme said. "So it is part of a different triad. There'll be another odd-handed projector here."

They located it, and it was. "Hypothesis confirmed," she said. "Now if our interpretation is correct, we won't have to worry about being sent back to Blizzard because this inverted version is part of a different loop. The next one should be new. Brace yourself." She reached for the switch.

"Sure thing," Veg said. "I'm braced for one

new world."

It was new, all right. Veg's first impression was of mist. They stood in a tangibly thick fog. He coughed as the stuff clogged his lungs. It wasn't foul, just too solid to breathe.

"Get down," Tamme said.

He dropped to the ground. There was a thin layer of clear atmosphere there, below the fog bank, like air trapped beneath river ice. He put his pursed lips to it and sucked it in.

"Crawl," she said, her voice muffled by the fog.

They crawled, shoving aside the fog with their shoulders. Suddenly the ground dipped—but the bottom of the fog remained constant. It was too stiff to match the exact contour of the land. Now there was squatting clearance beneath, then standing room.

"That's some cloud!" Veg remarked, peering up. The stuff loomed impenetrably, a pall that blacked out all the sky. Wan light diffused through it. "Stuff's damn near solid!"

"You liked it better under the pine tree?" Tamme inquired. She was already looking for the next projector.

"Sure did!" He had the nagging feeling the fog bank could fall at any moment, crushingly.

A valley opened out before them. Tamme stared.

Veg followed her gaze. "A fog house?" he asked, amazed.

It was. Blocks of solidified fog had been assembled into something very like a cabin, complete with slanting, overlapping fog tiles on the roof. Beyond it was a fog wall or fence.

"This we have to look into," Tamme said. She moved toward the house.

A curtain of fog parted, showing a doorway and a figure in it. "Inhabited yet," Tamme murmured. Her hands did not move to her weapons, but Veg knew she was ready to use them instantly.

"Let's go ask directions," he suggested facetiously.

"Yes." And she moved forward.

"Hey, I didn't mean—" But he knew that she had known what he meant since she could read his emotions. Awkwardly, he followed her.

Up close, there was another shock. The inhabitant of the house was a human female of middle age but well preserved—with a prehensile nose.

Veg tried not to stare. The woman was so utterly typical of what he thought of as a frontier housewife—except for that proboscis. It twined before her face like a baby elephant trunk. It made her more utterly alien than a battery of other nonhuman features might have—because it occupied the very center of attention. It was repulsively fascinating.

Tamme seemed not to notice. "Do you understand my speech? she inquired sociably.

The woman's nose curled up in a living question mark.

Tamme tried a number of other languages, amazing Veg by her proficiency. Then she went into signs. Now the woman responded. "Hhungh!" she snorted, her nose pointing straight out for a moment.

"Projector," Tamme said. "Alternates." She shaped the projector with her hands.

The woman's nose scratched her forehead meditatively. "Hwemph?"

"Flex," Veg put in, holding out the hexaflexagon.

The woman's eyes lighted with comprehension. "Hflehx!" she repeated. And her nose pointed to the fog bank from which they had emerged, a little to the side.

"Hthankhs," Veg said, smiling.

The woman smiled back. "Hshugh."

Veg and Tamme turned back toward the fog. "Nice people," Veg remarked, not sure himself how he intended it.

"There have been others before us," Tamme said. "The woman had been instructed to play dumb, volunteering nothing. But we impressed her more favorably than did our predecessors, so she exceeded her authority and answered, after all."

"How do you know all that?" But as he spoke, he

remembered. "You can read aliens, too! Because they have emotions, same as us."

"Yes. I was about to initiate hostile-witness procedures, but you obviated the need."

"Me and my flexagon!"

"You and your direct, naïve, country-boy manner, lucking out again." She shook her head. "I must admit: Simplicity has its place. You are proving to be a surprising asset."

"Shucks, 'taint nothin'," Veg said with an exaggerated drawl.

"Of course, our predecessors were the same: Tamme and Veg. That's why they obtained her cooperation."

"I noticed she wasn't surprised to see us. I guess our noses look amputated."

"Truncated. Yes."

He laughed. "Now she's punning. Truncated trunks!"

They were at the fog bank. "Stand here. I need another orientation point. The projector will be within a radius of twenty meters, or about sixty feet."

"You sure can read a lot from one nose-point!"

She plunged into the bank. The stuff was so thick that her passage left a jagged hole, as if she had gone through a wall of foam. It bled into the air from the edges, gradually filling in behind her. "Talk," Tamme said from the interior. "The sound will help me orient on it, by the echo."

It figured. She didn't ask him to talk because of any interest in what he might have to say! "This place reminds me of Nacre in a way. That was all fog, too. But that was thinner, and it was everywhere, made by falling particles. The real plant life was high in the sky, the only place the sun shone; down below was nothing but fungus, and even the animals were really fungus, like the mantas. So it wasn't the same."

There was no response from the bank, so he continued. "You know, I read a story about a fog like this once. It was in an old science-fiction book, the kind they had in midcentury; I saw a replica printed on paper pages and everything. This thick fog came in wherever the sun didn't shine—they spelled it 'phog'—and inside it was some kind of predator you never saw that ate people. It never left the fog—but nobody dared go *in* the fog, either. All they heard was the scream when it caught somebody—"

"YAAAGH!"

Veg's mouth gaped. "Oh, no!" He plunged into the fog, knife in hand.

A hand caught his wrist and hauled him back out. "Next time don't try to tease an agent," Tamme said, setting him down. "I found the projector."

"Sure thing," he said, chagrined. Still, it was the first clear evidence of humor he had seen in her.

"Crawl under," Tamme said.

They crawled under the fog, snatching lungfuls of clear air from the thin layer on the ground. The projector was there.

"Not far from where we landed," Tamme said. "But the pattern is not consistent enough to be of much aid. We still have to search out the projector on each new world and figure out the mechanism for breaking out of loops. I don't like that."

Veg shrugged noncommittally. Except for Blizzard, he hadn't minded the searches. But of course if there were danger, they would not be able to afford much delay. "With the hexaflexagon, you can run through every face just by flexing the same diagonal as long as it will go. When it balks, you switch to the next. So maybe if we just keep going straight ahead, we'll get there, anyway."

Tamme sat up. She did not seem to be bothered by fog in her lungs. "We'll play it that way. If we get caught in a repeating loop, we'll look for something to change. Meanwhile, I want a concurring opinion."

"Another man-versus-tiger choice?"

She brought out a slip of paper. "Call off the order of your hexaflexagon faces."

Veg, hunched nose down to the ground to avoid the fog, was surprised at this request. Tamme knew the order that the faces appeared; she had flexed through them, and agents had eidetic recall. He could only confirm the obvious! But he brought out his toy and went through the whole pattern, calling off the numbers. "One. Five. Two. One. Three. Six. One. Three. Two. Four. Three. Two. One."

Tamme made a diagram of lines and numbers and little directional arrows. "This is triangular," she said. "A three-faced hexaflexagon would simply go around the central triangle. Your six-faced one adds on to the angles. Would you agree to the accuracy of this diagram?"

She showed him what she had drawn.

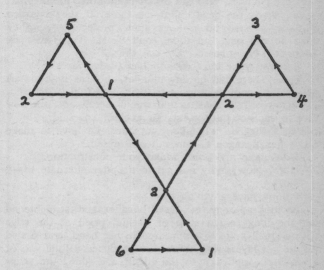

Veg traced around it, starting from the northwest face 1. "One, five, two, one, three—yeah, that's the order. Makes sense of it finally!"

Tamme nodded. He could barely make out her gesture since her head was almost concealed by the fog. "As I make it, we actually started on Five, the City. That would make Two the Forest, One the Blizzard, Three the Orchestra, Six the Planes, and back to our first repeat, One/Blizzard. Then repeat Three/Orchestra. And repeat Two/Forest. And now face Four/Fog."

"I guess so," Veg said, having trouble keeping up. "We're here now."

"Our next stop should be repeat Three/Orchestra—this time twisted because it is on a separate loop. Then

119

on to Two/Forest, One/Blizzard, and home to Five/City."

"It figures," he said. "We've used up all the faces."

"In which case we'll be back where we started—closed loop, and nobody but ourselves."

"I guess so, right now. The others must have gotten off. Is that bad?"

"I can't buy it. Who set up all these other projectors?"

Veg shook his head. "Got me there! If they'd gotten off, they'd have taken back their projectors—so they must be still on. And there can't be six Veges and six Tammes." He sobered. "Or *can* there?"

"Suppose your hexaflexagon had twelve faces?"

"Sure. There can be any number of faces if you start with a long enough strip of triangles and fold it right."

"A twelve-face construction would merely add one new face to each of the six exterior angles," she said.

Veg shrugged. "I'll take your word. I'd have to make a live hexaflexagon to check it out myself."

"*Don't* take my word. Make your construction."

"Here? Now? Why not get to a better alternate to—"

"No."

"I don't have anything to—"

She took apart the six-faced hexaflexagon, straightened out the long folded strip of plastic, pried at the edge with a small knife that appeared in her hand, and peeled it into two layers lengthwise. She produced a little vial of clear fluid, applied it to the edges, and glued the strips together endwise. The result was a double-length strip.

Veg sighed. He took it and folded it carefully. He made a flat spiral so that the double length became the size of the original but with two layers instead of one. Then he fashioned a normal hexaflexagon.

"Run through it and number your faces," Tamme said.

"Okay." This was a more complicated process, involving thirty flexes, but in due course he had it. Meanwhile, Tamme had been making a new diagram.

"Now start at face One and flex," she said. "I will call off your numbers in advance. Five."

He flexed. "Five it is."

"Seven."

He flexed again. "Right."

"One."

"Right again. Hey, let me see that diagram!"

She showed it to him. It was an elaborated version of the prior one, with new triangles projecting from each of the six outer points. One angle of each of the outermost triangles carried the number of a new face, bringing the total to twelve.

They flexed through the rest of the construct. It matched the diagram.

"As I make it," Tamme said, "We could be on this one instead of the six-faced one. In that case our starting point would be Seven, followed by One, Five, Two, Eight, Five, Two, One, and now Three. If so, both our next two stops may be new worlds, Six and Nine."

"Instead of repeats!" Veg said. "That's the proof right there. All we need to do is try it. If we don't like the new ones, we just skip on to Three, there in the loop— that's here. Our map is still good."

"Unless this is actually a mere subsection of an infinitely large configuration," she cautioned. "In that case, it is only a hint of a route through it. But we could probably find our way back, though there is no longer any way to travel back the way we came." She paused, peering at him through the mist. "If something should happen to me, you use this diagram to return to your friends in the City."

"Not without you," he said.

"Touching sentiment. Forget it. Your philosophy is not mine. I will leave you instantly if the need arises."

"Maybe so," Veg said uncomfortably. "So far there hasn't been any real trouble. Maybe there won't be."

"I rate the odds at four to one there *will* be," she said. "*Someone* set up these projectors, and in at least one case it was another agent just like me. Of course I'm used to dealing with agents just like me—but they have been Tara, Tania, and Taphe, not alternate Tamme's. I mean to find that other agent and kill her. That will be difficult."

"Yeah. Different philosophies," Veg said. He knew she read the disapproval in him. Maybe it would be better to leave her if it came to that.

"Precisely," Tamme said. And activated the projector.

They were in a curving hall. Checkerboard tiles were on the floor and a similar but finer pattern on the flat ceiling. The walls were off-white. Light shone down from regularly spaced squares in the ceiling pattern. It was comfortably warm, and the air was breathable.

"So you were right," Veg said. "A new alternate, a larger pattern. No telling *how* many agents in the woodwork."

"It is also possible that these are all settings on the same world," Tamme said. "That would account for the constancy of gravity, climate, and atmosphere."

"That blizzard wasn't constant!"

"Still within the normal temperature range."

"If they're all variations of Earth, that explains the gravity and climate. You said yourself they were different alternates. Trace distinctions in the air, or something."

"Yes. But perhaps I was premature. It could be as easy to regulate the air of a particular locale as to arrange for travel between alternates. Matter transmission from one point on the globe to another would cover it. I merely say that I am not *sure* we are actually—" She stopped. "Oh-oh."

Veg looked where she was looking but didn't see anything special. "What's up?"

"The walls are moving. Closing in."

He didn't see any difference but trusted her perception. He was not claustrophobic, but the notion made him nervous. "A mousetrap?"

"Maybe. We'd better locate that projector."

"There's only two ways to go. Why don't I go down here, and you go there? One of us is bound to find it."

"Yes," she said. There was a slight edge to her voice, as if she were nervous. That was odd because agents had excellent control. They were seldom if ever nervous, and if they *were,* they didn't show it.

"Okay." He walked one way, and she went the other. But it nagged him: What was bothering her so much that even he could notice it?"

"Nothing," he muttered to himself. "If I pick it up, it's because she wants me to." But what was she trying to tell him?

He turned about to look back toward her. And stood transfixed.

The walls were moving—not slowly now but rapidly. They bowed out from either side between him and Tamme, compressing the hall alarmingly. "Hey!" he yelled, starting back.

Tamme had been facing away. Now she turned like an unwinding spring and ran toward him, so fast he was astonished. Her hair flew out in a straight line behind her. She approached at a good thirty miles an hour: faster than he had thought it possible for a human being on foot.

The walls accelerated. Tamme dived, angling through just as the gap closed. She landed on her hands, did a forward roll, and flipped to her feet. She came up to him, not even out of breath. "Thanks."

"That mousetrap!" he said, shaken. "It almost got you!" Then: "Thanks for what?"

"For reacting in normal human fashion. The trap was obviously geared to your capacities, not mine. That was what I needed to ascertain."

"But what was the point?"

"The object is to separate us, then deal with us at leisure. No doubt it feeds on animal flesh that it traps in this manner."

"A carnivorous world?" Veg felt an ugly gut alarm.

"Perhaps, or merely a prison, like the City. We see very little of the alternates we are visiting."

"I'm with you. Let's find the projector and get out!"

"It will have to be in a secure place—one that the walls can not impinge on."

"Yeah. Let's stay together, huh?"

"I never intended to separate," she said. "But I wasn't sure who might be listening."

Hence the edgy tone. He'd have to be more alert next time! "You figure it's intelligent?"

"No. Mindless, perhaps purely mechanical. But dangerous—in the fashion of a genuine mousetrap."

"Yeah—if you happen to be the mouse."

They moved on, together. The walls were animate now, shifting like the torso of a living python. They pushed in—but the air in the passage compressed, preventing complete closure. There was always an exit for the air, and Veg and Tamme were able to follow it on out.

"But watch out when you see any air vent or duct," Tamme warned. "There the walls could close in all the way quite suddenly because there would be an escape for the air."

Veg became extremely interested in air vents.

Sometimes they encountered a fork in the way and had to judge quickly which branch would lead to a broader hall. But now that they understood this region's nature, they were able to stay out of trouble.

"Hey—there it is!" he exclaimed ."The projector."

The walls were rolling back ahead of them, while closing in behind, as though herding them forward. A projector had now been revealed. It was on wheels, and a metallic ring surrounded it.

"Clever," Tamme said. "Wheels and a circular guard so that it always moves ahead of the wall and can't be trapped or crushed. So long as the walls do not close precisely parallel—and that does not seem to be their nature—it will squirt out. See the bearings on the ringguard." She moved toward it.

Veg put out his hand to stop her. "Cheese," he said.

She paused. "You have a certain native cunning. I compliment you."

"Another kiss will do."

"No. I am beginning to respect you."

Veg suffered a flush of confused emotion. She did not kiss those she respected? Because a kiss decreased it—or increased it? Or because her kisses were calculated sexual attractants, not to be used on friends? Was she becoming emotionally involved? This was more the way Aquilon reacted. The notion was exciting.

"The notion is dangerous," Tamme said, reading his sentiment. "You and I are not for each other on any but the purely physical level, strictly temporary. My memory of you will be erased when I am reassigned, but yours of me will remain. When emotion enters the picture, it currupts us both. Love would destroy us."

"I'd risk it."

"You're a normal," she said with a hint of contempt. She turned to the projector. "Let's spring the mousetrap."

124

She brought a thread from somewhere in her uniform, then made a lasso. She dropped this over the switch, jerked it snug, then walked away. The thread stretched behind her, five paces, ten, fifteen.

"Hide your eyes," she said.

Veg put his arms up to cover both ears and eyes. He felt the movement as she tugged at the thread, turning on the projector.

Then he was on the floor. Tamme was picking him up. "Sorry," she said. "I miscalculated. That was an agent's trap."

"What?" He stared back down the hall, his memory coming back. There had been a terrific explosion, knocking him down—

"Directional charge. We were at the fringe of its effect. You bashed your head against the walls."

"Yeah." He felt the bump now. "Good thing that wall has some give. You people play rough."

"Yes. Unfortunately, I have been overlong on this mission. My orientation is suffering. I am making errors. A fresh agent would have anticipated both the trap and its precise application. I regret that my degredation imperiled your well-being."

"Mistakes are only human," he said, rubbing his head.

"Precisely." She set him on his feet. "I believe the blast stunned the walls temporarily. You should be safe here while I make a quick search."

"I like you better, human."

"Misery loves company. Stay."

"Okay." He felt dizzy and somewhat nauseous. He sat down and let his head hang.

"I'm back." He had hardly been aware of her absence!

She took him to a "constant" spot she had located: six metal rods imbedded in floor and ceiling, preventing encroachment. On a pedestal within that enclosure was another projector.

"This one is safe," Tamme said.

Veg didn't ask her how she knew. Probably it was possible to booby trap a projector to explode some time after use so that a real one could be dangerous, but that would be risky if the alternate-pattern brought the same person back again. Best not to mess with the real projectors at all! Like the way the desert Arabs never poisoned the water no matter how vicious the local politics got. Never could be sure who would need to drink next.

"I hope the next world is nicer," he said.

"Bound to be." She activated the device.

Chapter 12

# CUB

· · ·

Cub finished his meal of fruit, roots, and flesh. He had gorged himself in case it were long before he ate again. Beside him Ornet preened himself, similarly ready.

Dec sailed in from his last survey. By minute adjustments of his mantle he made the indication: All is well.

Cub raised his wing-limb, flexing the five featherless digits in the signal to O̅X̅: We are ready.

O̅X̅ expanded. His sparkling presence surrounded them as it had so many times before. But this time it was special. The field intensified, lifted—and they were moving. Not through space; through time.

At first there was little change. They could see the green vegetation of the oasis and the hutch they had built there for shelter and comfort. Farther out there were the trenches and barriers they had made to foil the predator machine.

The machine. Mach, they called it. The thing had grown right along with them because it was part of the enclave O̅X̅ had aged. It was a constant menace—yet Cub respected it, too, as a resourceful and determined opponent. Had it been in his power to destroy it, he would not have done so because without it the group would be less alert, less fit, and bored.

Do we *need* adversity to prosper? he asked himself, linking his fingers so that he would not inadvertently sig-

127

nal his thoughts to the others. Apparently so. That ever-present threat to survival had forced them all to advance much faster and better than they would have otherwise. Perhaps, ironically, it was the machine more than anything else that was responsible for their success as a group. This was a concept he knew the others would not understand, and perhaps it was nonsensical. But intriguing. He valued intrigue.

Then the hutch vanished. The trees changed. They expanded, aged, and disappeared. New ones grew up, matured, passed. Then only shifting brush remained, and finally the region was a barren depression.

Cub moved his digits, twisting them in the language that Ornet, Dec, and $\overline{OX}$ understood. Our oasis has died, he signaled. The water sank, the soil dried, the plants died. We knew this would happen if we were not there to cultivate the plants and conserve the water they need. But in other frames water remains, for $\overline{OX}$'s elements remain.

A shoot formed within $\overline{OX}$'s field. This is temporal, it said, using its blinker language that they all understood. All alternates extend forward and back from any point. All are distinct, yet from any point they seem to show past and future because of the separation in duration between frames.

Obvious, Cub snapped with an impolite twitch of his fingers.

Ornet made a muffled squawk to show partial comprehension. He was a potent historian but not much for original conjecture. His language, also, was universally understood: Cub could hear it, Dec could see it, and $\overline{OX}$ could field the slight variations it caused in his network of elements.

Dec twitched his tail in negation: The matter was not of substantial interest to him.

I would include a geographic drift, $\overline{OX}$'s shoot flashed. But I am unable, owing to the limit of the enclave.

Nonsense, Cub responded. We're all advanced twenty years. In terms of real framework, we exist only theoretically—or perhaps it is the other way around—so we can travel on theoretical elements.

Theoretical elements? the shoot inquired.

Your elements were cleared out by the external patterns, Cub signaled. Once they were there, and once they will be there, instead of mere threads. They still exist, in alternate phases of reality, serving as a gateway to all the universe. Use them.

Theoretical elements? The shoot repeated.

Cub had little patience with the slowness of his pattern-friend. Make a circuit, he signaled, much as he would have told Ornet to scratch for arths if he were hungry. Analyze it. Accept this as hypothesis: We can theoretically travel on theoretical elements. There has to be an aspect of alternity where this is possible, for somewhere in alternity all things are possible. To us, geography may be fixed, for we are restricted to the enclave. Theoretically, that geography can change elsewhere in relation to ours just as time does. We have merely to invoke the frames where this is so.

Uncomprehending, OX made the circuit. Then he was able to accept it. Such travel was possible. And—it was.

The geography changed as they slid across the aging world. They saw other oases growing and flexing.

Cub was surprised. He had been teasing OX, at least in part. He had not really believed such motions would work; the enclave isolation had prevented any real breakout before. But when OX made a circuit, OX became that circuit, and his nature and ability were changed.

Perhaps OX had at last transcended the abilities of the outside patterns. If so, a genuine breakout was now feasible. But Cub decided not to mention that yet, lest the outside patterns act to remedy that potential breach. It was not wise to give away your abilities to the enemy.

That was how they had given Mach the slip. Always before, OX had made certain preparatory circuits, which the machine had sensed. This time Cub had had OX make spurious shoot-circuits, deceiving Mach. Thus, when they were ready to move, the machine had thought it was another bluff and had not appeared.

But soon Cub became bored with flexing oases. Let's cut across the alternates, he signaled. See some really different variations. We can go anywhere now . . .

Another test—but OX obliged. The oasis is sight stopped growing and started changing. The green leaves on the trees turned brown; the brown bark turned red. The bases thickened, became bulbous. Creatures appeared, rather developed from the semisentients already present. Like Ornet but with different beaks: tubular, pointed, which they plunged into the spongy trunks of the trees, drawing out liquid.

This was more like it! Cub watched, fascinated by sights he had never seen before and hardly imagined. A feast of experience!

The trees flowered, and so did the creatures. The flowers expanded until there were neither trees nor creatures, only flowers. The oasis itself expanded until there was no desert at all, only large and small flowers.

A streak appeared. Cub couldn't tell whether it was a wall or a solid bank of fog. It cut off some of the flowers. They did not wither; they metamorphosed into colored stones. The fog-wall increased until it concealed everything. Then it faded, and in its wake were planes, multi-colored, translucent, and set at differing angles. Machines rolled up and down them, chipping away here, depositing there, steadily altering the details of the configuration without changing its general nature. Cub hardly bothered to question why; he knew that there would be too many whys in all alternity to answer without squeezing out more important concerns.

The planes dissolved into bands of colored light, and these in turn became clouds, swirling in very pretty patterns, developing into storms. Rain came down, then snow—Cub recognized it, for snow fell on the enclave seasonally, forcing him to fashion protective clothing. But this was not only white; it was red and green and blue, shifting as the alternates shifted.

In due course it solidified into walls of stone: They were passing through a cavern, a huge hollow in the ground. Cub recognized this also, for last season he had fashioned digging and chipping tools and dug deep, deep into the ground, trying to ascertain whether there was any escape from the enclave in that direction. He had, in fact, made a small cavern. But it was useless, and he had given up and closed it over. Now they used it for winter storage and occasionally for shelter from storms.

A tremendous room opened out on one side, far larger

than the cave Cub had made. Then the stone closed in again as though the very walls were moving.

Wait! Cub signaled. I saw something. Go back.

The shoot gave a controlled fadeout equivalent to the drooping of Ornet's tail feathers or Cub's own shrug of the shoulders. The moving walls reversed, opening into the cavern.

There! Cub indicated. Geographically—move over.

Now the others spotted it. In the center of the cavern a creature was doing something. It was working on some sort of machine . . . no, the thing was too simple to be a machine, merely a mechanical device, perhaps the ancestor of a machine. Sound emerged, pleasant, harmonious. The thing was playing music, similar to that Cub himself could make with voice and the beat of his hands on a log, but smoother, prettier. The creature's tentacles touched the device here and there, and the melodious sound issued.

Follow that frame, Cub directed, as though the other members of his party had no preferences. But they were content to follow his lead in this. In physical motion, Dec was supreme; in memory, it was Ornet. In imagination, it was Cub, and they all knew it.

OX oriented—and the single alien musician became two, then eight, and then a myriad of players. The music swelled resoundingly. Then the creatures changed, becoming humanoid, and finally human.

Your kind! Ornet squawked.

Startled, Cub examined them more carefully. My kind!

They changed to tall green plants, playing the instruments with leaves and roots. Wait! Cub signaled, too late.

But OX was already backing up. The Cub-type players re-formed, went alien, returned, went naked, elaborately clothed, and finally focused on a compromise.

My kind! Cub repeated, half dazed. But what are those others? He gestured toward some individuals that differed slightly. They resembled him, but their torsos varied, and their faces were bare as though they were not yet grown.

Female of your species, Ornet squawked. Show the natural version, OX.

OX obliged, shifting to the unclothed players.

Mam females lack the urinary appendage, Ornet explained, gesturing with his beak. But they possess structures for the nursing of infants. My ancestors have not observed your particular species, but these are merely modifications of the type.

Cub stared at the nursing structures, appalled yet fascinated. I would like to put my hands on those, he signaled.

This can not be done, the shoot replied. We can not interact.

I know it! Cub gestured irritably, though for a moment he was tempted to challenge $\overline{OX}$ to make a circuit for the attempt. Let's go on.

They went on—but after that Cub's attention was on his memory of his kind, on the bare-fleshed females. If only there were some way to get across the barrier physically!

Suddenly Mach appeared, rising up out of the storage cave. All of them were caught off guard. Once more the machine had been too cunning for them and had arranged to come on their special frame-trip, after all!

The thing came whirling its blade and spinning its treads, forcing the physical beings out of its way, and its pattern-disruptive emanations were so strong that $\overline{OX}$ had to move explosively to avoid nonsurvival effects. Cub could see the sparkles flying out like a stellar display on a chill night.

Then the group mobilized, as it had so many times before. Ornet served as decoy, flapping his wings and squawking just outside the range of the blade. Dec swooped by, flicking his tail at the perceptor bulbs. Cub stood back and threw stones into the blade. And $\overline{OX}$ formed shoots that spun across the elements in the machine's vicinity, distracting its alternate-frame perspective.

They could hardly damage Mach, let alone distroy it; it was invulnerable to their attack. But their combined harassment made it uncomfortable and always drove it back.

This time it persisted for an extraordinary time. It was undeniably strong. But finally the stones and sand that Cub shoveled at its blade and into its hopper discouraged it. Sand did not hurt it, but it was unable to disgorge it while under attack. And so it retreated—just far enough to abate their defensive action.

Through the years they had come to a kind of understanding with Mach. Once the machine retreated, they would let it alone—and it would not attack again that day. Truce, while both sides recuperated. Neither side had ever broken that tacit agreement; that temporary security was too important. Mach actually seemed to be honest; perhaps the mechanical circuits prevented dishonesty in any form. This was one of the things about the machine that Cub respected. Sometimes he and Dec and Ornet sought out Mach and attacked it merely to invoke the truce so that they could be assured *it* would not attack *them* while something important was going on.

Cub threw himself down, panting, as the machine became quiescent. It remained within the area of $\overline{OX}$'s influence—but Cub had no desire to drive it outside. They had brought it along on this trip, and they would have to return it to the normal enclave. It would not be right to leave it stranded.

Once he had wished for some way to rid the enclave of this constant menace. Now he had the chance—and would not take it. Not merely because of his interpretation of their truce; because he was even more certain that Mach was a sentient entity, too, and deserved a certain measure of respect.

But then he remembered what he had seen beyond the enclave, in the cave of the musicians, and forgot the machine.

# Chapter 13

# DREAMS

. . .
. .
.

Aquilon wiped her eyes with her fists. "This R Pentomino is a menace!" she complained. "I'm getting a headache! It just goes on and on."

Cal pulled his head out of the innards of the machine. "I told you it was an impressive dead end after eleven hundred and three moves."

"I know. I wanted to see for myself."

"Try the glider," he suggested.

"The what?"

"You have been dealing with stationary forms. There are others. Here." He extricated himself and came over. "This is the glider." He made the pattern of dots on her canvas-sheet:

"That's another pentomino!" she said indignantly.

He shrugged and returned to his work. "I hope to convert this machine to a specialized oscilloscope, or facsimile thereof, so that we can translate our signals into pattern-language. I have the feeling that the pattern-entities are as eager to talk with us as we are to talk with them. Think how confusing we must be to them!"

"But we are solid and visible!" she said, working on the new figure. It had gone from [1] to [2] to [3] . . In fact, it was now a mirror image of its original form, turned endwise. Funny.

"Precisely. An entity whose system is based on patterns of points would find our mode of operation virtually incomprehensible."

She made the next figure, jumping straight from one to the next without such laborious additions and erasures.

[4]  • •  "Do you think Veg is all right?"

"I doubt I ever get used to the caprices of female thought," he remarked. "Veg is with Tamme."

"That's what I meant."

"Jealousy—at your age?"

She looked at the next figure: [5]   •  "Hey—this thing repeats itself on new squares! It's like a blinker—only it moves!"

"Precisely. Patterns can travel. The glider moves diagonally at a quarter the speed of light."

"Speed of light?"

"An advance of one square per move is the maximum possible velocity in this game, so we call it the speed of light. The glider takes four moves to repeat itself, one square across and one down, so that is one quarter light-speed."

She looked at it, nodding. "Beautiful!"

Veg would have said, "So are you." Not Cal. He said: "A variant of that formation is called the Spaceship. Spaceships of various sizes can move at half the speed of light. As they go, they fire off sparks that vanish, like propulsion."

"The sparkle cloud did that!" she cried.

"Yes. We also know of a 'glider gun' that fires off gliders regularly. And another figure that consumes gliders. In fact, it is possible to fire several gliders to form new figures at the point of convergence—even another glider gun that shoots back at its parent guns, destroying them."

"If I were a pattern, I'd be very careful where I fired my gliders!" Aquilon said. "That game plays a rough game!"

"It does. As does all nature. I should think assorted defensive mechanisms would appear by natural selection, or the game would be unstable—assuming it were self-willed. The possibilities are obvious."

135

"Especially when you get into three dimensions!"

"Yes. It is a three-dimensional computerized grid I am working on now. I wish I were a more experienced technician!"

"I think you're a genius," she said sincerely. And she felt a flare of emotion.

"You can help me now if you will. I'll need some figures for my three-dimensional grid."

"What's wrong with the ones we have? The R Pentomino, the glider—"

"They won't be the same. A line of three points would manufacture four new ones, not two—because of the added dimension. That would form a short cross, which would in turn form a kind of hollow cube. I believe that's an infinitely expanding figure—and that is not suitable for our purpose. We need figures that are approximately in balance—that neither fade out too rapidly nor expand to fill the whole framework."

"Hm, I see," she murmured, trying to trace the three-dimensional permutations of the figure on her two-dimensional canvas. She compromised by using color to represent the third dimension. "Your line becomes an indefinitely expanding three-dimensional figure, as you said. Looks like two parallel caterpillar treads with eight cleats in each, if I haven't fouled it up. But almost any figure expands; there are just too many interactions."

"Agreed. So we must modify the rules to do for three dimensions what 'Life' does for two. Perhaps we must require four points to generate a fifth and let a point be stable with three or four neighbors. Perhaps some other combination. If you can suggest viable rules and figures, it will save me time, once I have this equipment modified."

"I'll try!" she said, and bent to it.

They both had difficult, intricate jobs, and from time to time they had to break off. They also chatted intermittently during the work.

"Say—did you ever find the missing earthquake?" Aquilon asked suddenly.

Cal paused momentarily at his labor. She knew he was finding his mental place, as she had just made another momentous leap of topic. To her surprise, he placed her reference accurately. "We were separated three days on Paleo, during which time there were two tremors, a minor and a strong one. I remember them clearly."

"For a genius, you have a poor memory," she said, smiling over her complex dot-pattern. "We were separated four days, and there were quakes on the first three. You must really have been absorbed with that dinosaur not to notice."

"Odd that we should differ on something so easy to verify," he said. "Shall we compare notes in detail?" It was as though he were inviting her to a duel, certain that she would lose.

Aquilon was intrigued. "Let's."

"You and Veg went to the island—"

"Not *that* much detail," she said, embarrassed. Then she reconsidered. "No—let's put it out in the open. You wanted to make a report on Paleo that would surely lay it open to exploitation and destruction—"

"I changed my mind."

"Let me finish. I wanted to help Orn and Ornette survive because they were unique, intelligent birds and I liked them. Veg went with me." She took a breath and forced herself to continue. "Veg and I made love that night. Next morning he went to see you at the raft—and the first tremor came."

"Yes. After he left the raft, I set sail. I was aware of the tremor; it made the water dance. About fifteen seconds, mild."

"Even a mild earthquake is horrible," she said, giving her head a little reminiscent shake. "That was the first day, the first quake. So we agree."

"So far." She could tell from his tone that he was still sure she was wrong about the tremors. She was also a bit uneasy about the seemingly bland response to her confession concerning Veg. "The second day Circe came and told us a predator dinosaur was after you, but you wouldn't let the mantas help you. I thought we should leave well enough alone. Veg hit me and headed off."

"He should not have done that." Again, too mild a response.

"Cal, I didn't want you to die—but I thought it was

more important that you be allowed to do what you felt you had to do, your own way."

"Precisely. Veg blundered."

So it was all right. Cal understood. She should have known he would. "Later that day the second quake came. It shattered the eggs—all but one. It was violent, awful."

"I was on the mountainside. The tremor knocked Tyrannosaurus off his feet and rolled him down the mountain. I was afraid he was too badly hurt to continue the chase. Fortunately, he suffered minimal damage."

Aquilon grimaced, knowing he was not being facetious. Cal had wanted to conquer the dinosaur himself, without the help of an act of God. "So we agree on the second day, the second quake."

"We agree. I continued on up the mountain and slept in a volcanic cave. Next day the agents came—Taler, Taner, and Tamme."

"No," she said firmly. "Next day there was a third quake. It tore the island apart. A plesiosaurus got Ornette, so Orn and I had to ferry the egg to the mainland the day following—the morning of the fourth day, the day the agents came. I'll never forget that awful journey through the water, protecting the egg! I had to use Orn for support—"

Cal nodded thoughtfully. "So you really did experience an extra day and tremor!"

"You lost a day, Cal. What happened to it?"

He sighed. "This suggests something too fantastic to believe. In fact, I *don't* believe it."

So there *was* something! "This sounds fascinating! You have a secret?"

"In a manner of speaking. I didn't think it was anything significant. You would have been the first to know had there been anything to it. All men have fantasies—and all women, too, I'm sure. But now—I wonder. Alternates *do* exist, and in some of them are virtual duplicates of ourselves. The woman you met, the naked Aquilon—"

"Don't tell me you dream of naked Aquilons!" she said, pleased. But at the same time, the memory of the lost egg upset. her. She had so wanted to save the Orn species . . .

"More than that, I'm afraid. After all, I have seen you naked in life."

She remembered the time she had run nude on Paleo before they found the dinosaurs. She had not realized that he had paid attention. "You always loved me. You said so back on Planet Nacre. And I love you. But there's never been much of a—a physical component, has there?"

"The major component," he said seriously.

"Oh? I thought all things were intellectual to you."

He peered at her over the machine. "You are leading me on."

"That's what I mean. You are too smart for me, and we both know it. I couldn't deceive you with feminine wiles if I tried. You intellectualize everything to the point where you feel no physical passion." She felt a little shiver as she said it, wanting him to deny it. She had taken the initiative with Veg, and that had been wrong; he had resented it and repaid her with a blow. Not a conscious motivation, perhaps—but she was sure that it had been one of his unconscious ones.

"Intelligence is irrelevant. You have shown me my error in the counting of tremors, for example."

"That's right. What *did* you do with that day and that quake? Chase naked Aquilons?"

"Yes."

She looked at him sharply, for he sounded serious. "You *did?*"

"Bear with me if I affront your sensitivities. I think this is something you should know."

"I'm not affronted," she said, keeping her eyes on her diagrams. "Intrigued, though . . ." She certainly was; the three-dimensional life-game analysis was now no more than a pretense.

He buried his head in the machine so that only his voice reached her. She returned to her work with an effort and listened, visualizing what he described.

"I escaped Tyrannosaurus by hiding in a volcanic cave, the night of the day we had the second tremor. It was warm in there, for the water of the stream was hot. I was extraordinarily tired, yet keyed up: It had been the greatest adventure of my life. I had, in my fashion, conquered the dinosaur!

"I found myself a comfortable ledge, sprawled out, and fell into a perspiring stupor. I thought of dinosaurs and conjectured that one of the duck-bills like *Parasaurolophus,* with the enormous nasal crest, might have been able to survive the heat of that cave. Its breath through the inside of that crest would have cooled its tissues, as the breath of a dog cools its tongue and thus its body. But if the creature stayed too long or strayed into the cave and got lost, it might have died and been washed out through the river-canyons of the far side of the mountain range. Idle speculation of the type that entertains me."

"I know," she agreed softly. Who else but Cal would care whether the body of a duck-billed dinosaur washed out one side of the mountain or the other?

"I must have slept off and on. It was not really comfortable in that heat. Toward morning that conjecture about the duck-bill roused me. *Could* it get out of the dinosaur enclave through the mountain? Could *I?* Driven by curiosity, I began to explore the cavern, going far back into the mountain. The heat was terrible; when it reached about one hundred forty degrees Fahrenheit I turned back. I was naked; I was sweating so profusely that clothing would have been useless.

"Then I saw something. It was nestled in a recess, invisible from the mouth of the cave. I would have missed it but for my acute night vision, sharpened by my night in the cave. It was a little machine. Its presence amazed me, for it suggested that man had been there before. I fiddled with it, trying to ascertain its condition and purpose. I lifted a kind of key from it.

"A cone of pale light projected from the device and bathed me. I felt a strange wrenching. For an instant I feared I had been victimized by some type of booby trap, though why anything of that nature should be placed there I could not guess. Then the machine was gone, and I stood in the cave, the key in my hand.

"Astonished, I set it down on a convenient ledge and looked about. Far down at the mouth of the cave I saw a glow; dawn was coming.

"I went back to that entrance to check on Tyrann, my reptile nemesis. He was still there, sleeping, his great nose almost touching the cave. In fact, his bulk blocked the flow of water, making it form into a puddle. Beyond him was the snow of the mountain, covering the canyon rim where the heat of the river did not reach. An odd sight: dinosaur in snow!

" 'Cal!' someone cried. 'I thought you were dead!'

"I turned, startled. You were there, 'Quilon, nude and lovely. Your yellow hair floated down your back like the glorious mane of a thoroughbred horse, and your blue eyes were bright. I doubt you can appreciate how lovely you were to me in that instant. I had come very near death, and you were an angel.

" 'I escaped, thanks to this convenient cave,' I said, as though it were of no moment. I do not remember my exact words, of course, but it was something equivalently inane.

" 'So did I,' " you said. 'Cal, I could have sworn I saw Tyrann get you! It was awful. Then he came after me, and I just made it here—'

" 'I told the mantas not to interfere. Why did you come?'

" 'I love you,' you said.

"You were not speaking intellectually or theoretically or platonically. Your voice trembled with the devotion of a woman for her lover. You were wild and forward, and I—I was powerfully moved by it. *You meant it.*

"Your vision of seeming death had charged you, first with grief, then with enormous passion. We were naked, and in love, and it seemed wholly natural that we resort to the natural culmination. All the suppressed urges I had entertained toward you were released in the bursting of that dam; it seemed I could never get my fill of your body. And you were eager for me; you were a creature of lust. It was as though we were two animals, copulating interminably, driven by an insatiable erotic imperative.

"All day we remained in that cave. Once there was a terrible tremor. It bounced Tyrann half awake; it dislodged stalactites from the back of the cave. We were afraid the mountain would collapse in on us—so we made love again, and slept, and woke, and did it yet again.

"At night I woke, disgusted with myself for using you like that. Yet even as I looked at you in your divine sleep, the passion rose in me again, and I knew that I had to get out of the sight of you if I were not to succumb again. So I retreated to the back of the cave.

"I remembered the key and searched for it in the dark. My hand found it on the ledge. I picked it up and shook it—and suddenly there was a illumination about me, and I experienced that dizzy feeling—and there was the machine in front of me again.

"Alarmed, I returned to where you slept—but you were gone. You could not have left by the cave mouth, for Tyrann was there, and there were no fresh tracks in the powdering of snow near him. I was sure you had not left by the rear passage, for I had been there. Yet there was absolutely no evidence of your presence; even the lichen on the ledge where we had made love was undisturbed, as though no one had ever been there.

"Forgive me: My first thought was intense regret that I had not awakened you for one more act of love before you disappeared. Then I cursed my sordid nature, for I would love you as strongly were I a eunuch. I lay down and tried to piece it out, and finally I slept again. In the morning I knew it had been a dream—an extravagant, far-fetched, ridiculous, wonderful, masculine wish fulfillment. And so I put it out of my mind, ashamed of the carnal nature underlying my love for you, and I have maintained a proper perspective since."

Aquilon sat leaning over her diagrams, stunned. The episode Cal had so vividly described had never happened, and it was shocking to hear him speak so graphically, so uncharacteristically. Yet it mirrored the secret passion she had longed to express if only there were some way around her inhibitions and his. And it touched upon something hideous, something she herself had buried until this moment.

"Cal—" she faltered but had to force herself to go on, lest he think it was revulsion for the sexual description that balked her. Yet she could not say what she had intended, and something almost irrelevant came out instead. "Cal, the key—what happened to it?"

"What happens to any dream artifact when the sleeper wakes?" he asked in return, as though glad for the change of subject.

"No—did you keep it, or put it back? Did you check for that machine again? It should have—"

"I must have replaced the key automatically," he said. "I never returned to the rear of the cave. It was part of my disgust, and I refused to humor the passions of the dream by checking."

"Oh!" It was a faint exclamation of emotional pain. He had never even checked! But that pang freed her inhibition somehow, and now she was able to approach her own hidden concern. "Cal, you said I thought you had died in your dream. What did I say?"

He did not answer, and she knew he was suffering from acute embarrassment, realizing how frankly he had spoken.

"Please, Cal—this is important to me."

His voice came back from the machine. "Not very much. We did talk about it some, but it was not a pleasant subject, and there obviously had been some error."

Aquilon concentrated. "Tyrann galloped after you, those awful double-edged teeth snapping inches short of your frail body, the feet coming down on you like twin avalanches. Snap! and your rag-doll form was flung high in the air, striped grisly red, reflected in the malignant eyes of the carnosaur. Tyrann's giant claw-toes crushed your body into the ground; the jaws closed, ripping off an arm. Your head lolled from a broken neck, and your dead eyes stared at me not with accusation but with understanding, and I screamed."

Now Cal's head jerked out of the machine. "Yes!" he exclaimed. "That's what you said in essence. How could you know?" Then he did a double take. *"Unless you actually were there in that cave—"*

"No," she said quickly. "No, Cal, I wasn't there. I was stranded on an earthquake-torn island with Orn's egg. I swear it."

Still he looked at her. "You desired my death?"

"No!" she cried. "I dreamed it—a nightmare. I told

that dream to the birds, Orn and Ornette, that third day, before the last quake. That I had seen you die."

"You dreamed it—the same time I dreamed my—"

"Cal," she said, another shock of realization running through her. "In some alternate—*could it have happened?*"

He came to her. "No. How could I have made love to you if I were already dead?"

She caught his hand, shaken, desperate. "Cal, Cal—your dream was so much better than mine. Make it come true!"

He shook his head. " 'Quilon, I did not mean to hurt you. It was only that if there were an unaccounted day for me, I would be compelled to believe that somehow—but the whole thing is insane. I do love you—that much has never been in doubt—but I slept around the clock in that cave, recovering from the ravages of that chase, and it is hardly surprising that exaggerated fancies emerged, an ugly expression of—"

"I don't care!" she cried. "Your dream was *not* ugly; *mine* was. Yours was more accurate than your belief. I *am* like that—or could be, would be, if I thought I'd lost you. You like to think I'm cold and chaste, but I'm not. I never was! I seduced Veg—it's no platonic triangle. I made a mistake, but *this* is no mistake. I want to love you every way I can!"

He studied her uncertainly. "You *want* the dream—and all that it implies?"

"Your dream, not mine. Then you'll know me as I am. Yes, I want it—now!"

He shook his head, and she was suddenly, intensely embarrassed, afraid she had repulsed him by her eagerness. Did he only love the ethereal image, not the reality?"

"I take you at your word," he said. Relief and surprise flooded her, made her weak. "After we complete this project."

"Communication with the pattern-entities? But that may take days!"

"Or weeks or years. There will be time."

"But the dreams, the cave—"

"We are not in the cave."

144

She saw he was not going to re-enact the dream-orgy of lovemaking he had described. Had she really thought he would? This was Cal, civilized, controlled. The chaste, celestial personification—it was not of her but of *him*.

Yet he had acceded. Why?

Because he wanted to give her time to reconsider. The impulse of the moment was too likely to lead to regret, as with her and Veg, or with Cal and his dream-girl in the cave. He would not grasp what he was not assured of holding.

It was better this way.

He kissed her. Then she was sure of it.

So it was not the dream. It was love, shifted from the suppressed to the expressed—gentle, controlled, and quiet. It was more meaningful than any wild erotic dream could have been, this simple affirmation of commitment.

Glowing inside, she completed her charts while he worked on the machine, as though there had been no interruption. It was as though they had walked through a desert and suddenly been admitted to an exotic garden filled with intriguing oddities and fragrances that could be explored at leisure together. Yes—there would be time!

"I worked out 'ideal' rules for one, two and three dimensions," she said brightly. "One dimension would be a line. It takes one dot to make another, and any dot with two neighbors or no neighbors vanishes. It doesn't work very well because one dot makes a figure that expands at the speed of light indefinitely, and you can't even start a figure with less than one. For two dimensions, same as now: Three dots make a fourth, and a dot is unstable with less than two or more than three neighbors. Since up to eight neighbors are possible, it has far more variety than the one-dimensional game."

"Of course," Cal agreed.

"For three dimensions there are twenty-seven potential interactions, or up to twenty-six neighbors. We should require seven neighbors to make a new dot, and the figure is stable with six or seven. Less than six or more than seven will eliminate a given dot. So a cube of eight dots would be stable, each dot with seven neighbors— like the four-dot square in the two-dimensional version."

Cal nodded. "I believe it will do. Let's try some forms on our cubic grid, applying those rules."

*I believe it will do.* And Aquilon was as pleased with that implied praise for her work as with anything that had happened.

## Chapter 14

# FORMS

. .
. .
. .

Cub had become minimally communicative during the tour, and $\overline{OX}$ did not understand this. Had he been injured during the battle with Mach?

It is the mating urge, Ornet explained, delving again into his memory-experience of mams. Sight or smell of the mature female stimulates the male to interact with her.

Why? $\overline{OX}$ inquired, finding the concept obscure.

It is the way they reproduce their kind. My kind performs similarly; Dec's has a separate mechanism. The machines are distinct from us all.

Why should any kind of being require reproduction?

We originate, we age, we die, Ornet squawked. It is the way of physical species. If we do not reproduce ourselves, there will be nothing.

Still $\overline{OX}$ could not grasp it. I do not reproduce myself. I exist as long as my elements are charged and numerous.

You surely do reproduce yourself, Ornet squawked. I have not seen enough of your type to fathom the mechanism, but my memory indicates that it must be—for all entities. In some way you were conceived by your forebears, and in some way you will transmit your heritage to your successors. Perhaps if you encountered a female of *your* species—

There are no pattern-females, OX replied. I read that in my circuits. I have the potential to become anything that any pattern can be.

Ornet drooped his tail feathers. He never engaged in speculation; the past was his primary interest.

OX sent a shoot to question Dec. Why should spots die or reproduce themselves? it flashed.

The two are synonymous, Dec replied. To die is to reproduce.

This did not satisfy OX, either. A pattern needed neither to die nor to reproduce. Why should a spot?

Dec was emitting a complex array of signals. OX adjusted his circuitry to pick up the full spectrum. Dec was capable of far greater communication than either of the others, for he used light, the fastest of radiations. OX could perceive it by the effect of his elements: minute but definite. He had long since intensified his perceptions of such variations so that observations that had once been beyond his means were now routine. Now he activated a really intricate perception network, more comprehensive and sensitive and responsive than ever before.

Then Dec's whole mind was coming across on the transmission, as clearly as if it were a barrage of pattern-radiation shoots:

[DEATH]        [SPORES]        [MERGING] [REPRODUCTION]
   *              *                *          *
[cessation ]   [carriers of ]   [two sources] [growth of cells]
[animation]    [genetic code]   [crossover  ]
   *             *                            [chain of habitats]
[philosophical] [♀♂]
[ramifications ]


OX assimilated it and fed back his questions on the aspects of the concept. The dialogue was complex, with loops of subdefinitions and commentary opening out from the corners af the major topics, with both obvious and subtle feedbacks and interactions between concepts. It required maintenance of a circuit larger than the rest of his volume. OX stayed with it, devoting whatever attention was necessary. He refined his circuits, added to them, revised . . .

And found himself within the mind of Dec.

Now he felt the force of gravity, a vital component of Dec's motion; the pressure of atmosphere, another essential; the impact of physical light on his eye. He felt the musculature of the single-foot, opposing the constant pull and unbalance.

These things had been mere concepts to him before, described but not really understood. It was one thing to know that a physical body had weight that held it to the ground; it was quite another to experience that ubiquitous force on every cell of the body. A factor that was of no importance to OX in his natural state was a matter of life and death to this physical being; a fall could actually terminate Dec's existence! Thus, gravity equated with survival. Yet gravity was only one of an entire complex of physical forces. No wonder the spots were different in their reactions from OX; their survival depended on it!

And he understood the synonymity of death and reproduction, how the primed body dissolved into its component cells that became floating spores that met and merged with the spores of another deceased fungus entity and then grew into new entities. Without death there was no replication, and without replication there would be no more entities of this type. Yet this process was necessary to the evolution of the species, and without evolution it would also pass. Death equated with survival—death of the individual, survival of the species —because the demands of the physical environment were always shifting. OX now understood the essential nature of these things, and the rightness of them. Multiple physical imperatives set fantastic demands, requiring complex devices of survival unknown to pattern-entities.

Then he was out of the physical, back in his own nature, fibrillating. He had never before experienced sensation and thinking of this type; there was a phenomenal amount of data to assimilate and circuits to modify. The physical was a whole separate existence, with its unique imperatives!

OX had learned more in this one encounter than in any prior one. He now realized all the way through his being that the intellectual systems of the spots were as complex and meaningful as his own. The spots were, indeed, complete entities.

He modified his circuits to incorporate a perpetual awareness and appreciation of this fact. Just as alternity was infinitely variable, so was intellect! His comprehension of existence would not be complete until he had experienced the inner nature of each spot—and of a machine.

He formed a shoot to approach Ornet. By motions and flashes that coincided with the creature's mode of communication, OX made known his mission: to exchange minds for a moment. Ornet was receptive; he had long been curious, in a paleontological way, about the inner nature of patterns, since they had so little place in his memory.

The mechanism of exchange differed from the one that had been effective with Dec, for there was no mass-level tool of light. Instead, OX had to create a shoot-circuit that duplicated the bird's every observable contour and function, correcting it as Ornet directed. OX made himself into another Ornet, with feet and claws and wings and beak, subject to gravity and all the other manifestations of the physical aspect. Then this form moved to coincide with the presence of Ornet, and the shoot's points picked up the signals of the body's nervous functioning, the living animation of its cells.

Slowly, the mapping progressed, merging the element pattern with the physical pattern. And as the overlap became sufficient, OX began to receive Ornet's sensations and thoughts directly.

Ornet was old. His species was normally adult in the third year after hatching and faded after twenty. Ornet was twenty now. His powers were receding, his feathers losing their gloss, his beak its sharp edge. He felt a kind of vacuum in his life, but he had not been able to define it until OX had questioned him about Cub. Then his memory had been evoked, making it clear—but far too late. He had never had contact with a female of his kind, never been aroused—and so had lived without really missing it. He was not given to speculative thought or to emotional recations; he accepted what was and worked only to enhance survival and comfort.

This personality, in a manner quite different from Dec's, was compatible with $\overline{OX}$'s own mode. But because Ornet's reproductive aspect was quiescent, $\overline{OX}$ still had no direct comprehension of it. And so long as his understanding was incomplete, he lacked a potential tool for survival.

It was evident that Ornet did not have to die in order to reproduce his kind. But if the death/reproduction connection were not valid, what *was?*

$\overline{OX}$ phased out, moving the shoot away from coincidence with the body of the bird. Deprived of their guidance by the minute electrical stimuli of the physical nervous system, the subcircuits collapsed. It was a nonsurvival jolt—but only for the shoot. In a moment $\overline{OX}$ reorganized in a more stable format, recovering equilibrium.

He had absorbed another vast segment of reality and comprehended to some extent the process of aging and its relation to death. But it was not enough.

Now he came to Cub. Cub, by the reckoning of Ornet's memory, was now in the young prime of his life. And he had, as $\overline{OX}$ himself knew, a marvelously powerful and versatile reasoning mechanism. He was the source of $\overline{OX}$'s confusion; now perhaps he would be the resolution of it.

$\overline{OX}$ made another phase-in shoot, this one in the form of Cub. Small and tight as it was, this lone shoot was nevertheless far more complex than $\overline{OX}$'s entire being had been at the time of his first emergence into awareness. I wish to join you, to understand you completely, the shoot signaled.

Do as you like, Cub responded indifferently.

$\overline{OX}$ attuned his subcircuits to the nervous impulses of living matter, as he had so recently mastered with Ornet. He slid the shoot over to merge.

There was a period of adjustment, for though the principle of functioning was similar, between Ornet and Cub, the detail differed. Then awareness focused.

It was a maelstrom. Rational misgivings warred with

unattainable urges. The picture of a naked-Cub-species female formed, her arms and legs outstretched . . . dissipated in an aura of revulsion . . . re-formed.

OX watched, felt, experienced. Now he, too, felt those amazing urges. The attraction/repulsion of the reproduction/death complex; the need to overtake, to grasp, to envelop, to penetrate—countered by inability, confusion, and guilt. Desire without opportunity, force without mechanism. Compulsion so great it threatened to nullify survival itself. Emotion.

OX twisted out of phase with such an effort that he carried the entire enclave into another frame. His system was in terrible disarray; his circuits warred with each other.

But now he understood the spots' need to reproduce their kinds. He knew what emotion was. Having discovered that, he was unable to eliminate it from his system; the profound new circuits were part of his pattern.

But OX realized that his survey was still incomplete. He had learned marvelous and dismaying new things—but that only increased the need to learn the rest. Perhaps little of significance remained, and there were nonsurvival aspects to the continuation of this search—but he had to do it. Survival and emotion drove him.

He searched out Mach, the wild machine.

OX anticipated resistance, but Mach was quiescent. Perhaps it was waiting to ascertain the nature of this new attack. OX formed a shoot-image of it, then cautiously phased in.

This was dangerous because the machine, unlike the living spots, had certain pattern-aspects. It was aware of the elements, though its existence did not depend on them, and it could use them to make those special patterns that extended across frames. This ability was very limited, but this was one reason why OX had such trouble nullifying Mach's attacks. Mach could almost match OX's maneuverability across frames, provided that travel was restricted to adjacent or nearly adjacent ones. And the machine could drain the elements of so much energy that they would not serve a pattern-entity for some time.

OX found the nerve circuits on the physical level of

the machine, adapting to them as he had for Ornet and Cub. And slowly he became Mach.

The machine intellect was distinct from those of the living spots. Its impulses ran along metal conduits with appalling force and dealt with motors and transformers and switches and harsh chemical reactions rather than the subtle interactions of life or pattern. Yet it was sentient.

This was Mach—and now $\overline{OX}$ understood. The machine had needs fully as compelling as those of the other entities. Its prime motive was similar to theirs: SURVIVE. But it required energy transformed from matter by more brutal processes. Most of the physical substances it could obtain from its environment, but a few were in critical shortage here in the enclave.

It was the lack of these substances that made Mach desperate and dangerous. The machine required them in order to develop its potential to reproduce its kind— and some of them could be filtered from the bodies of the living spots. There was no inherent personal animus; Mach attacked because it was driven by a need that could not be denied, in much the fashion of Cub's need. Gradually, as it realized that the spots were in fact sentient, it came to equate destruction of them as long-range nonsurvival and tried to resist the urge to take what beckoned. But it could not.

Supply those substances, and Mach would no longer be an enemy. The machine might even cooperate with the other members of the enclave. Its strength on the physical level was such that it could be of substantial assistance to them—especially in the effort to break out of the enclave.

$\overline{OX}$ had developed combat circuits to oppose the inimical behavior of the external patterns. Now he comprehended that patterns were ill equipped to indulge in such activities. Their intellectual comprehension translated only poorly into action. This was one reason the external patterns had done nothing but observe after arranging the enclave.

Machines, in contrast, were entities of action. Mach's mind contained pragmatic instructions for accomplishing many tasks, provided the tools existed. $\overline{OX}$ now saw that he, as a pattern, had tools that the machine did not.

Now $\overline{OX}$ understood enough, and he had a new sense of motivation. He made ready to act.

# Chapter 15

# ALTERNITY

They stood on a metal highway, and a tank was bearing down on them. It was a monster, with treads as high as a man and a nose needling forward like that of an atmosphere-penetrating rocket.

Veg's dizziness left him. He charged to the side. Tamme was right beside him, guiding his elbow in case he stumbled.

The tank careened on by, not swerving.

"Was that another trap?" Veg asked breathlessly.

"Coincidence, more likely. Do you recognize this alternate?"

He looked about. All around them were ramps and platforms, and on these structures vehicles of every size and shape sped by. Some were quite small, and some were tiny—the size of mice, or even flies. But all were obviously machines.

"A bit like downtown Earth," he muttered. "But not—" He paused. "The machine world! This is where they breed!"

"I doubt they breed," she said. "Nevertheless, this is a significant discovery."

"Significant! Those machines are half the problem! I had to fight one of them halfway across the desert to protect our supplies!"

"Only to fall prey to the sparkle-cloud," she reminded him.

"Yeah . . ."

A dog-sized machine headed for them. It had perceptor-antennae extending from the top, and it emitted a shrill beeping.

"We're discovered," Tamme said. "I think we'd better move on."

But it was already too late. The seemingly aimless paths of the machines suddenly became purposeful. From every side they converged.

"I think we'd better not resist," Tamme said. "Until we locate the projector, we're at a disadvantage."

They certainly were! They were now ringed by machines, several of which were truck-sized, and there was a dismaying assortment of rotating blades, pincers, and drills. But she had already noted a containment pattern to their activity rather than an attack pattern.

A container-machine moved up, and two buzz saws herded them into its cage. The mesh folded closed, and they were prisoners.

"You figure this is the end of the line?" Veg asked. "I mean, maybe the hexaflexagon goes on, but if the machines catch every visitor . . ."

"Uncertain," Tamme said. "Some may avoid capture, some may escape, some may be freed."

"How many agents do you figure are traveling around here?"

"It could be an infinite progression."

Veg was silent, chewing over that. She could read his concern: an endless chain of human beings parading through the worlds, right into the maw of the machine? That would explain how the machines knew so well how to handle them! And why the nose-woman on the fog world had not been surprised or afraid. The alternates would be like tourist stops . . .

They cruised up to a metal structure. "A machine-hive," Veg muttered, staring out through the mesh, and his description was apt. It rose hugely, bulging out over the landscape, and from every direction machines of all sizes approached, while others sped outward. The hum of their engines was constant and loud, like that of

156

hornets. A number were flying machines, and these ranged from jet-plane to gnat size. They zoomed in and out of appropriately diametered holes.

Their own vehicle headed for one of the truck-sized apertures. The machine-hive loomed tremendously as they approached; it was a thousand feet high and as big around.

"Any way out, once we're *in?*" Veg asked apprehensively.

"I could short the gate mechanism and get us out of this vehicle," Tamme said. "But I don't think that would be expedient."

Veg looked out of the rushing landscape. They were now on a narrow, elevated railroad-trestle like abutment fifty feet above the metal ground. Small buzz-saw machines flanked them on trestles to either side, and a pincer-tank followed immediately behind. There was no clearance for pedestrians.

"We must be doing a hundred miles per hour," he remarked.

"More than that. The lack of proximate and stationary objects deceives the eye."

"Well, if the machines wanted to kill us, they'd have done it by now," he said. But he hardly bothered to conceal his nervousness.

So they stayed put. In moments their truck plunged into the tunnel—and almost immediately stopped. Tamme, anticipating this, caught Veg about the waist before he was flung into the wall. "Well, aren't we cozy," she murmured as she let him go.

"I wish you wouldn't do that," he muttered. He meant that she could have warned him instead of demonstrating her superior strength again—and he also knew that she was aware of his reactions to contact with her body. She nodded to herself; she was in fact teasing him, probably trying to build up her own self-image in the face of her deterioration of set, of agent-orientation. This was a weak human device, and she would stop.

The gate opened. They stepped out. The gate closed, and the truck departed. But other bars were already in place, preventing them from following the vehicle out.

"Now we can make our break," Veg said. He put his hands on the bars and shook them. "Yow!"

Tamme knew what had happened. The metal was electrified. "They have had prior experience with our form of animation," she said. "Possibly the first agent escaped, but we shall not. We'll have to wait and see what they have in mind for us."

"Yeah," he agreed dubiously.

Tamme was already exploring their prison. It was brightly lit by glowing strips along the corners, the light reflecting back and forth across the polished metal walls. One wall had a series of knobs and bulbs. They were obviously set up for human hands and perceptions. The machines would have no use for such things!

There was a pattern to the bank of knobs. It resembled the controls to a computer. The knobs would be to activate it, the lights to show what was happening.

"Very well," she murmured. She turned the end knob quickly, removing her hand as it clicked over.

There was no shock. The light above that knob brightened. Sound came from hidden speakers: raucous, jarring.

Tamme reversed the knob. The sound died.

"Alien juke box," Veg muttered.

"Close enough," Tamme agreed. She turned the next knob.

Sound rose again: a series of double-noted twitterings, penetrating.

She turned that off and tried the third. This was like the roar of ocean surf, with a half-melodious variable foghorn in the background.

There was over a hundred knobs. She tried them all— and got a hundred varieties of noise. Then she started over. On the second round the sounds were different; there were no repeats.

"This may be fun to you, but it's my turn to sleep," Veg said. He lay down on a raised platform that seemed made for the purpose.

Just as well. She could work more efficiently if he were safely out of mischief. She could have zeroed in on the sounds she was looking for much faster but preferred to wait until Veg got bored, for a reason she did not care to tell him. Now she got down to serious business.

Still it took time. For two hours she tried new sounds until she got one vaguely resembling human speech. She turned this off, then on again—and it was a different, yet similar patter. She tried again on the same knob, but though the human-sounding voice continued, it was no closer to anything she understood.

"Have to find the key," she murmured inaudibly. "Not getting it yet."

She left the knob on and turned to the next. The voice modified, becoming less human. So she went to the knob on the other side, and now the voice became more familiar.

In this manner, slowly, she centered on a language approximating contemporary English. She knew she could narrow it down to her exact dialect but refrained.

Veg woke with a start. "Hey—that's making sense!"

Tamme warned him into silence with a fierce gesture. Now that the language was close, the machine could probably identify their precise alternate—which was the point of all this. She wanted communication without complete identification, lest her world be in peril.

But the machine—actually it was an input to the main hive intellect—had heard. "Curminicate, yez," it said.

"Yez," she agreed, while Veg looked bewildered.

"Ujest noob; abdain edenddy."

*That's what you think!* she thought. *I'll unjest your noobs but not to abdain edenddy. I want an approximation, not identity.*

She adjusted knobs, bringing it closer. She pretended to be trying to obtain identity while actually adapting herself to the new pattern so that the machine would be satisfied the language was her own. This was a clever trap: letting the captives pinpoint their own alternates so that their worlds could be nailed.

Meanwhile, she hoped Veg had sense enough to keep his mouth shut. A few words from him now could tip off the machine.

"Now—gestons," she said.

"Esk."

"Furst geston: wheer or we?"

"Machina Prime, sender of ralofance."

Mentally she translated: Machine Prime, center of relevance. No modesty about this alternate!

"Wat wont with os?" Already the artificial speech pattern was becoming set so that she could think in it and use it automatically. So while Veg's brow furrowed in confusion, to her it was like an ordinary conversation: What do you want with us?

"Merely to identify you and to establish amicable relations between our frames."

Tamme was glad Veg could not follow the machine's dialect readily, for he would have laughed aloud. Amicable relations between the home-alternate of the killer machines and Earth? Unlikely!

Fortunately, she was an expert liar. "This is what we want, too. We shall be happy to cooperate."

"Excellent. We shall send an emissary to your frame and establish an enclave there."

Which enclave would be blasted out of existence—if it came anywhere close to true-Earth. But it wouldn't. "We shall make a favorable report on our return," she said. "But at present we must continue on through our pattern of frames."

"By all means. We are conversant with your pattern. In fact, we have entertained many of your life-forms before. But we must advise you: There is danger."

Friendly advice from the machine? Beware! "Please explain."

"Your form of sentience is protoplasmic; ours mechanical. Yet we have many similarities, for we both require physical housings and must consume matter in order to produce functioning energy. The enemy is not physical, consumes no matter, and is inimical to rational existence. No physical being is secure on any frame, for the enemy is far more skilled in frame-shifting than either machine or life. But your pattern takes you through an enemy home-frame, and there the danger is magnified."

Oho! So the machines sought liaison against a common antagonist. This just might be worthwhile. "We do not understand the nature of this enemy.

"Its nature is not comprehensible by material beings.

160

It resembles a cloud of energy-points, sustained on a framework of nodes."

The sparkle-pattern! This was an insight indeed! "We have encountered such entities but did not appreciate what they were. They moved us from one frame to another involuntarily. From that frame we escaped and are now attempting to find our way home."

"They do this to our units, also. We are able to resist to a certain extent, but they are sronger than we in this respect."

"Stronger than we, too," Tamme said. "We are very clumsy about frame travel." All too true—which was one of the things that rang false about this proposition. If the machines had true alternate-travel, as this one implied, they had little need of human liaison. If they *didn't*, there was not much help Tamme's world could offer.

"Two frames are stronger than one."

"We agree. What next?"

"Will your world accede to a contract?"

Contract? What was this? Now she wished she could interpret the physical mannerisms of the computer the way she did with men! "That depends on its content."

"Agreement to interact for mutual benefit. Establishment of interaction enclaves. Transfer of beneficial resources."

Now she was catching on. "I believe my world would be interested. But once our government has ratified the contract—"

"Government?"

"That select group of individuals that formulate the mechanisms and restrictions of our society so that there will not be chaos."

"Individuals?"

Oh-oh. "Your machines are not separate entities?"

"They are separate physically but part of the larger entity. Separated from the society, our units become wild, subsapient, without proper control. Only in unity is there civilization. This is why we are unable to travel far between frames; our units become separated from the hive and degenerate into free-willed agents."

"That is a difference between us. We ar distinct subentities; we retain our sentience and civilization when isolated from our hive." But privately she wondered: did human beings really prosper in isolation. Agents certainly did not! For normals it might take a generation, but individuals cut off from their societies did degenerate. Apparently the effect was more intense with the machines. That would explain why this hive-computer was rational, while the machine Veg had met was vicious. Without its civilized control, it had reverted to primitive savagery.

"That is now apparent. It explains what had been a mystery about your kind—though you behave more rationally than your predecessors."

So some had tried to fight "Perhaps you have made it easier for us to *be* rational by providing an avenue for communication. It would also help if you made available those substances we require for our energy conversions —organic materials, water, clean air."

"This we shall do on your advice."

Very accommodating; she almost wished she could afford to trust the machine. Aspects of its society were fascinating. "How should we reach you again? Our meeting here is random; we would not be able to locate your frame again." Maybe she could turn the tables, identifying the machine-alternate without giving away Earth.

"We shall provide you with a frame-homer. This is a nonsentient unit that will broadcast a signal across the framework. We shall be able to locate it by that signal, once it is activated."

"Excellent. We shall activate it when the contract is ready."

A slot opened below the knobs. Inside a little drawer was a lentil-sized button. "No need. This will activate itself when the occasion is proper."

So they weren't gambling overmuch on the good faith of the other party, either! Tamme took it and filed it away in a pocket. "Good. Now we must proceed."

"We shall provide you with your material needs if you will explain them."

She hesitated, then decided to gamble. Why should the machine poison them when it already had them in its power? More likely it would do them every possible little service in the hope of getting them and its unit

162

safely to Earth, thus making firm contact. So she described the type of vitamins, proteins, and minerals that life required.

After some experimentation, the machine produced edible, if unappetizing, food synthesized from its resources. Tamme and Veg were hungry, so they ate and enjoyed. She kept Veg silent while she gave advice for future cuisine. Though she did not regard any human beings that might follow as her friends, the common enemies were a greater threat; let the humans settle their differences in private. Also, let some *other* Earth be taken over if that was the way of it.

"You understand," she said at the conclusion of the meal, "we can not guarantee when we will reach our home-world, or *if* we will. Alternity is complex."

"We understand. We shall conduct you to your projector."

"Thank you."

A truck appeared. The bars lifted. Tamme gestured Veg inside, at the same time touching her finger to her lips. She did not want him blabbing anything while they remained within the hearing of any machine, which she now knew to be no more than a unit of the hive.

They rode out of the giant complex, and she felt a very human relief. Shortly they were deposited at a platform. Set on a pedestal was a projector.

Tamme wasted no time. She activated it. And they

were
standing in mist again.

"Okay—now can I talk?" Veg demanded.

"Should be safe," she said. She had considered whether the lentil-signal could overhear them but decided not. If it were sentient, it would lose its orientation away from the hive-frame, and if it were not, it would probably be inactive until activated. Why should Machine Prime care about their dialogue when their world of Earth was so near its grasp? Calculated risk; she was not ready to throw it away yet but did not want to keep Veg silent forever.

She forged through the mist toward the next projector. Veg followed her with difficulty. He had to crawl on hands and knees, taking deep breaths from air pockets near the ground. "That pidgin English you were jabbering—sounded as though you made some kind of deal—"

"The machine culture wants permission to exploit Earth," she said. "Apparently they have very limited alternate-transfer capacity, hardly ahead of ours, and unless the whole hive goes, the machines become wild. So they want to place an identifying beacon on our alternate—they call it a 'frame'—so that they can zero in with a full self-sustaining enclave. That means a hive-brain. They say they need a contract between alternates, but I don't believe that. Who would enforce such a document?"

"Yeah, who?" he echoed.

She found the projector and activated it.

They stood within the closing walls.

"I don't think it's smart, showing them where Earth is," Veg said.

"Don't worry. If there's one thing I'm not going to do, it's take their button to Earth. I'll find a good place for it—somewhere else in alternity."

"Yeah." He was right behind her as she moved toward the next projector, avoiding capture by the walls. "But what was this about a common enemy?"

"The sparkle-cloud. They can't handle it, either. It is the ultimate alternity traveler. But the fact that we have a mutual enemy does not necessarily make us allies. I played along with the hive-brain only to get us out of there. Which it probably knew."

"Then why did it—?"

"That beacon-button is probably indestructible short of atomic fusion. We're traveling through alternate frames. It's bound to key the machine boss in somewhere even if we throw it away—and it could pay off big if we actually get it to an exploitable world."

"Like Paleo?" They skirted the burned-out decoy projector, mute evidence that this was the same frame they had visited before.

"Like our *Earth*. From what I observed, those machines with their physical power and hive-unity could probably devastate Earth. Our population would become an organic source of nutrition, and our terrain would represent expansion room for their excess units."

Veg scratched his head. "Are we sure they would do that? Maybe they really are trying to be—"

"It is what we would do to *them*."

He nodded. "I guess so. The old omnivore syndrome. Do unto others before they do it unto you. You know you agents wanted to save the alternates for Earth to exploit. Now that we're running into tough civilizations, or whatever—"

"Right. It may be better to close off the alternate frontier entirely. I shall make a complete report on my return. It may be that your dinosaur worlds will be saved after all."

"That's great!" he exclaimed, giving her arm a squeeze with his big hand. He was so strong that she felt discomfort, though no ordinary man could harm her. "Even though it's too late for the *real* Paleo."

"There will be countless alternate Paleos—and it is not certain that we eliminated all the dinosaurs from that one. It was the manta spores we were after, you know."

He was silent. She knew the memory of the destruction of the Cretaceous enclave of Paleo still tormented him, and she had been one of the agents responsible.

They reached the projector. This one was charged, though it would not have been had they not spent that time interviewing the hive-computer. Sooner or later they would return to a frame too quickly and be unable to project out despite pressing need to do so. She would have to prepare for that, if possible. What would be the best way to survive for two hours under pressure? Educate Veg?

Meanwhile, they both needed some rest, and they could not be assured of getting it on an untried world. Veg had slept in the hive, but he was still tired, and she was not in top form.

She activated the projector.

They stood in the forest again, as she had anticipated.

165

"I believe this location is secure," she said. "We'll rest for six hours before continuing."

"Good enough!" Veg agreed. But he hesitated.

"You will not be able to relax here while I'm in sight," she told him. "Short of obliging you or knocking you out—"

"Uh-uh! I'll take a snooze down beside the other projector. That way we can guard both spots."

She nodded acquiescence. His discipline in the face of his powerful passion for her body was remarkable, if somewhat pointless. He had indulged himself with the woman Aquilon and had been unsatisfied, so now he was doubly careful. He wanted more than the physical and was content to gamble against the odds in the hope of achieving it. Unfortunately for him, the odds were long—perhaps a thousand to one, against. She was human, at the root, so theoretically could fall in love. But agents were thoroughly conditioned against irrelevant emotion, and they had virtually no subconscious with its attendant ghosts and passions.

It would be better for him to accept the reality and indulge the passing urge he felt for her, knowing that there was no deeper commitment. That would abate his tension and make this alternate tour easier. Yet she had learned just enough respect for him to let him do it his own way. His human capriciousness and curiosity had already opened several profitable avenues, such as the hexaflexagon parallel, and might do it again. They were a good team: disciplined agent, variable normal.

If his indecision became a threat to her mission, she would have to act to abate it. That could mean seducing him directly or stranding him on some safe alternate. Neither action would leave him satisfied, and that was unfortunate.

Perhaps she would have to deceive him, pretending to love him. She could do it if she really tried. But she did not care to. "Maybe I'm getting too choosy, like him," she muttered. "The real thing, or nothing . . ."

Now she needed rest. She slept.

They stepped from the forest into a forest. Flexible green plants stood on a gently sloping bank of black dirt. As trees they were small, but as vegetables, large. In either case, strange.

"No problem here," Veg said cheerfully. "Just vegetables, like me."

"Trouble enough," Tamme murmured.

"I know. You wish I'd lay you or forget you. Or both. And I guess it makes sense your way. But I don't have that kind of sense."

Good. He was coming to terms with the situation. "These plants are strange."

He walked to the nearest and squatted beside it. "I've seen strange plants before. They all—oh-oh!"

She had seen it, too. "It moved."

"It's got thick leaves and tentacles. And what look like muscles."

Tamme surveyed the assemblage. "We had better find the projector rapidly. The plants are uprooting themselves."

They were. All about the two intruders, the plants were writhing and drawing their stems from the earth.

"I'm with you!" Veg cried. "Next thing, they'll be playing violins . . . over our bones."

Together they ran up the slope, casting about for the projector. This brought them out of the region where the plants were walking and into one where the foliage had not yet been alerted. But the new plants reacted to the alien presence the same way.

"They can't move rapidly, but there are many of them," Tamme said. "You'd better arm yourself with a stick or club if you can find it."

"Yeah." Veg ran over to a stem lying on the ground. He put his hands on it. "Yow!"

It was no dead stalk but a living root. The thing twisted like a snake in his hands, throwing him off.

Meanwhile, the other plants were accelerating. Now they were converging with creditable alacrity, their thick, round roots curling over the ground, digging in for holds.

"Here's a weapon," Tamme said, drawing a yard-long metal rod from her clothing.

Veg paused to stare. "Where'd you hide *that?* I've *worn* that outfit of yours! No club in it."

"It telescopes," she explained. "Be careful—it's also a sword. It weighs only ounces, but it has a good point and edge. Don't cut yourself."

"Edge? Where?" He looked at the blunt-seeming side.

"There's an invisibly thin wire along the leading face, here. It will cut almost anything with almost no pressure. Trust me; *don't* rub your thumb on it."

Veg took the blade and held it awkwardly in front of him. He had obviously never used such a weapon before, but she had no time to train him now. "Just do what comes naturally. Stab and hack. You'll get the feel of it."

He stepped out and chopped at a branch of the nearest plant. The sword sliced through easily, the broad part wedging open the cut made by the wire. "Hey—it works!"

Tamme let him hold off the plants while she searched for the projector. She hoped there *was* one; they always ran the risk of a dead end, a frame in which the original projector had been destroyed or was inaccessible.

The walking plants did not seem to feel much pain, but after Veg had lopped off quite a few branches and stems, they got the message and withdrew. Veg was able to clear a path wherever Tamme wanted to go. He was enjoying this, she knew; though he would not kill animal life to eat, he would kill attacking vegetables.

Then something else appeared. Not a plant; it was vaguely humanoid, yet quite alien. It had limbs that terminated in disks and a head that resembled a Rorschach blob. It emitted a thin keening.

"Is that a machine, plant, or fungus?" Veg asked.

"Mixture," she replied tersely. "Inimical."

"I'll hold it off," Veg said. "You find the projector."

"No, the thing is dangerous. I'll tackle it."

"Thanks," Veg said sourly. But he moved off, allowing her to make a stand while he searched.

Aliens were hard to read, but the malevolence seemed to radiate out of this thing. Obviously it recognized her general type and intended to exterminate it. Had a human agent done something on a prior visit to arouse justified antipathy, or was the creature a hater of all aliens? Or could it be the farmer growing these plants they were mutilating? In that case, its attitude was more that of

168

a man with bug spray. It hardly mattered now; she had to deal with it.

The creature came close and suddenly charged her, its hand wheels leading. They were spinning like little buzz saws—which they surely were. She leaped aside, not wishing to reveal her technology by using a power weapon. The longer she fenced with it, the more she would learn about it. Was it intelligent, civilized—or was it more like a vicious guard dog? The evidences were inconclusive so far.

The saw-wheels came at her again. This time she stepped in, blocking the two arms with her own, forcing the wheels out while she studied the musculature and perceptive organs of the torso. The thing's skin was cold and hairy, like that of a spider.

In the moment her face was close, an aperture opened and spewed out a fine mist. Caught off guard, she did not pull her face away in time. It was an acid, and it burned her skin and eyes, blinding her.

She touched her hip. Her blaster fired through her skirt, bathing the creature in fire. It's body crackled as it was incinerated. The keening stopped.

"Yo!" she heard Veg call.

She ran to him, orienting on the sound. She had been trained to handle herself regardless of injuries. She used the echoes from her own footsteps to identify obstructions, such as the tall moving plants.

"Here—in a pile of rocks," Veg said as she came up.

"Is it charged?"

"Think so. I've never been quite sure how you could tell."

"Time to learn." While she talked, she focused on her autonomic system, blocking out the pain. "There's a little dial in the base with red-green markings. Read it."

He stooped. "It's on green."

"Right," she said, though she could not see anything. The flaming in her face retreated as her pain-block took effect, but that was only part of the problem. The damage was still being done, but she could not yet wash the acid off. "Now let's see if you can activate it."

"That I know. You shove this thing, this little lever—"

She heard the echoes of his voice and knew that the changing walls were there. They had made the shift.

"Now let's see if you know the way to the next projector."

"Hey—how come all this practice *now?*" He paused. "Hey—your face—it's bright red! What happened?"

"That animal-mineral-vegetable was also a skunk."

"Acid!" he cried, alarmed. "Acid in the face! We've got to wash that off!"

"No water here. Let's move on."

"Your eyes! Did it get your—?"

"Yes. I am blind."

She did not need the visual input to pick up his shock and hurt anger. "God, Tamme—"

"I can function. But it will help if you find that projector."

"Come on!" He took her hand.

"You run ahead. I am well aware of your location."

"Okay." He let go. They moved down the flexing passage.

He did know the way. They reached the projector. "Lefthanded—and it's not ready," he announced.

And the next frame should be the forest—safe, pleasant, with plenty of fresh cold water in a nearby stream. Out of reach.

"Someone must have used it since we did," he said. "Been almost eight hours since we were here last." Then he caught himself. "No—I'm thinking of the time we slept. We *left* here only about an hour ago. Hey—I never gave you back your watch. You don't need it right now, though, I guess."

It was a pitifully naïve attempt to distract her from the insoluble problem. "I doubt anyone has been here since we were," she said. "But we have no notion how many are traveling this pattern. This is an inversion, possibly part of another hexaflexagon, with its own personnel."

"Can't we push it?" he asked plaintively. "The dial is getting toward the green . . ."

"Dangerous. An incomplete transfer might deliver dead bodies. We don't know."

"We've got to clean out those eyes. Make them

170

tear." Another hesitation. "Or do agents ever cry—even for that?"

"My eyes teared. The damage was done in the first seconds, and after that it was probably too late for water, anyway." Had she not been preoccupied with their escape, she would have thought of this before. It was another mark of the pressure she was under and her loss of capacity as an agent, quite apart from her vision.

"Permanent or temporary?"

"Temporary, I think. It is a superficial burn, clouding the retinas."

"Then we're okay. We'll rest until you heal."

"We may not have time."

"Stop being so damned tough and act sensibly! Going off handicapped is stupid—you know that."

She nodded. "It was stupid letting myself fall into the acid trap. I've been making too damn many human errors."

"Now you even *sound* human." He sounded pleased.

"We'll give it a few hours. Agents recover quickly."

"Any other girl'd be crying and dependent," he grumbled.

Tamme smiled. "Even Miss Hunt?"

"Who?"

"Deborah Hunt. I believe you were close to her at one time."

"You mean 'Quilon!" he exclaimed. "We never use her original name, any more than we use yours." He paused. "What *was* yours?"

"I have no other name."

"I mean before you were an agent, you were a girl. Who were you? Why did you change?"

"I do not know. I have no memories of my civilian status—or of my prior missions as a TA-series agent, female. The debriefing erases all that. All agents of a given series must start their missions with virtually identical physical and intellectual banks."

"Don't you miss it sometimes?"

"Miss what?"

"Being a woman."

"Like Aquilon Hunt? Hardly."

"Listen, don't cut at her!" he snapped.

"I admit to a certain curiosity about the nature of this emotion that grips you," she said. "Passion, pleasure, pain, hunger, I can understand. But why do you maintain an involvement with a woman you know must go to your best friend and avoid one with me that would carry no further entanglements?" The question was rhetorical: She knew the answer. Normals lacked fit control over their emotions and so became unreasonable.

"You *want* my involvement with you?" he asked incredulously.

"It is a matter of indifference to me except as it affects my mission." Not wholly true; she had no real emotional interest in him but would have appreciated some entertainment during her incapacity. This conversation was another form of that entertainment.

"That's why," he said. "You are indifferent."

"It would be useful to know what she has that I do not."

"Any other woman, that would be jealousy. But you only want to know so you can be a more effective agent."

"Yes." Another half truth. The continuing strain of too long a mission made her desire some kind of buttressing. The temporary love of a man offered that. But it would not be wise to tell him that; he would misinterpret it.

"Well, I'll answer it. 'Quilon is beautiful—but so are you. She's smart, but you're smarter. As a sex object, you have it all over her, I'm sure; she has the body, but she doesn't know how to—well, never mind. What it is, is, she needs a man, and she *cares*."

"Agreed. You have not answered my question."

Veg choked. "You *don't* care. You could drop me in a volcano if it helped your mission. You don't need anyone—even when you're blind."

"True. I have never denied this. I have no such liabilities. But what positive asset does she have that—"

"I guess I can't get through to you. Her *liabilities* are her assets—that's how Cal would put it. Me, I just say I love her, Cal loves her, and she loves *us*. I'd let the universe go hang if that would help her. It has nothing much to do with sex or strength or whatever."

Tamme shook her head, intrigued. "This is far-fetched and irrational. It should be informative to put it to the test."

"Shut up!"

"That, too, is intriguing."

Veg got up and stomped away. But he did not go far, for the walls were waiting.

Tamme threw her mind into a healing state, concentrating on the tissues of her face and eyes. She, like all agents, had conscious control over many ordinarily unconscious processes and could accelerate healing phenomenally by focusing the larger resources of her body on the affected area. The external lenses of the eyes were small but hard to act on directly; this would take several hours of concentration.

When the projector was recharged, Veg took them through.

Tamme continued the effort in the forest, and in four hours her vision began to clear.

"You mean you can see again?" Veg demanded.

"Not well. I estimate I will have three-quarters capacity in another two hours. Since we should have two familiar frames coming up, that will suffice. Once I desist from the specific effort, the rate will slow; it will take several days to get beyond ninety per cent. Not worth the delay."

"You're tough, all right!"

"A liability, by your definition."

"Not exactly. You can be tough and still need someone. But we've been over that before."

In due course they moved on to

the mist frame and

the alien orchestra, following the hexaflexagon pattern. Their strategy of plowing straight ahead seemed to be paying off; they were stuck in no subloops. Probably they had not been stuck before; they just had not understood the pattern.

"Now we strike a new one," Tamme said.

"You ready?"

"My vision is eighty per cent and mending. The rest of my faculties are par. I am ready."

"Okay." And they went through.

Tamme lurched forward and caught hold before she fell. Veg dropped but snagged a hold before going far.

It was an infinite construction of metal bars. They intersected to form open cubes about six feet on a side, and there was no visible termination.

"A Jungle gym!" Veg cried. "I had one of these at my school when I was a kid!" He climbed and swung happily.

"Let's find a projector," Tamme said.

"Got to be on one of these struts."

"We need to establish a three-dimensional search pattern. There is no variety here as there was in the colored planes. We don't want to double back on checked sections."

"Right. Maybe we'd better mark where we started and work out from that. Take time, but it's sure."

They tied his shirt to a crossbar and began checking. Sighting along the bars was not much good; the endless crosspieces served to interrupt the line of sight so that the presence of the projector could not be verified. It was necessary to take a direct look into each cube. In the distance the effect of the massed bars was strange: From some views, they became a seemingly solid wall. From the center of a cube, there seemed to be six square-sectioned tunnels leading up, down, and in four horizontal directions.

When sighting routinely down one of these tunnels, Tamme saw a shape. It looked like a man.

She said nothing. Instead, she sidled across several cubes, breaking the line of sight in all three dimensions, and searched out Veg.

She was able to orient on him by the sound. "You're out of position," she said.

"No—I'm on the pattern. You're off yours."

"I left mine. We have company."

"Oh-oh. Alien?"

"Human."

"Is that good or bad?"

"I'm not sure. We'd better observe him if we have the chance."

"Here's the chance!" Veg whispered. Sure enough, a figure hove into view along a horizontal axis.

"That's *you*!" Tamme whispered. "Another Veg!"

She knew what he was going to say: *Your eyes must be seeing only forty per cent! I'm HERE!* But she was wrong. "Well, we figured this could happen. Another couple, just like us, from a near alternate. We've just got to find that projector *first*."

Tamme made a mental note: The episode with the acid thrower must have thrown off her perceptions. Not only had she misread Veg's response, he sounded different, less concerned than he should be. She would have to reorient at the first opportunity to avoid making some serious mistake.

Meanwhile, she concentrated. "We have the advantage because we saw them first. We can enhance our chances by conducting our search pattern ahead of them. That way they'll be checking a volume of space that we have already covered—where we *know* there's no projector."

"Smart!" he agreed.

Tamme calculated the probable origin of the competitive party, based on her two sightings of the strange Veg and the assumption that the other couple had landed not far from their own landing. They worked out from that. There was some risk the projector would happen to be on the wrong side of the other couple, but all they could do now was improve their chances, not make them perfect.

And suddenly it was there, nestled in a hangar below an intersection. Tamme approached it cautiously, but it was genuine. And it was charged.

Now she had a dilemma. She had control of the projector—but her larger mission was to eliminate Earth's competition, even that of a very near alternate. Should she tackle her opposite number now?

No. If the other couple had taken the same route around the hexaflexagon, it had to have been earlier, for the two-hour recharging time of the projectors required at least that amount of spacing out. But it was also possible that the others were flexing the other way—backwards, as it were. In which case they could not yet have encountered the walking plants and the acid-spraying keeper. So that other agent, male or female, would be in top form and would have a material advantage. That was no good.

Better to proceed on around the next subloop and tackle the competition when they crossed again in this frame. Then she would be ready. With luck, the other agent would not even know the encounter was incipient, and that would more than make up for the eye deficiency.

She activated the projector.

And they stood amidst sparkles.

"Well, look at that!" Veg said, impressed.

"A home-frame of the pattern-entities," Tamme said. "Another major discovery."

"Yeah. They told us at the bazaar, but I didn't expect it so soon."

Tamme did not stiffen or give any other indication of her reaction; her agent-control served her in good stead. Instead, she continued as if he had said nothing unusual, drawing him out. "They said a lot at the bazaar."

"Yeah. But what else could we do? By cooperating, at least we save our own alternates, maybe. I'm sorry if we have to go against our duplicates who didn't make it there—but in the end, it's every world for itself. And with the pattern-entities right here on the circuit—well, so much the better."

"If those patterns don't spot us and transport us right out of the network."

"Yeah. Let's get on with it."

They got on with the search. But now Tamme knew: *She had picked up the wrong Veg.* This one was traveling the other way and had been through at least one alternate —the "bazaar"—that she hadn't. And some sort of agreement, or treaty, had been made there involving other alternate Vegs and Tammes.

She had been right: Herself, from another alternate, was her enemy. And it *was* herself, for Veg would have

176

known the difference immediately had his companion been a male agent.

Every frame for itself. *Her* Veg would not have agreed; *this* Veg did.

Ironically, she preferred the attitude of her original Veg. He had more conscience; he cared. Meanwhile, he was with the other Tamme.

She had to complete the subloop and get back to the Jungle gym before that enemy Tamme caught on. The bitch would not be slow, either! So long as that other did not locate the projector, her search pattern would continue, and there would be little interaction between the agent and the man. But if they found it and had to wait for the recharge, there would be time.

And if they found the shirt tied at the point of arrival . . . there would be two shirts, one from each Veg. A dead giveaway! Why hadn't she thought to recover that shirt?

It had, after all, been sheer luck, her finding the projector first. She had figured a pattern based on her two sightings of the opposition—and at least one of those sightings had actually been of her own man! No science in that! But the same sort of coincidence could bring the other Tamme to the same projector. The enemy Tamme would have to wait while *this* Tamme could move—if she found the projector on this frame soon.

Maybe it would be better to avoid contact entirely and go on. No—that would be deserting her Veg and bringing along one who would surely turn uncooperative when he caught on. And she was trapped on a subloop; there was no way out but through the Jungle gym frame.

The projector on this subloop would probably be charged. She might complete the trip around within one hour and catch the enemy completely off guard. That would be best. Her vision would not be much improved within that time, but the element of surprise was more important.

What about this Veg? No need for him to know. He had already served to alert her, and he was no threat.

"Hey, these aren't the same," he commented, watching a swirl of sparkle almost under his nose. "See, they're smaller, and they don't fade in and out. This one's staying right here in this alternate, as though it doesn't know any better."

"You study it," she said, casting about for the projector. "The information could be valuable." Maybe it would keep him occupied and innocent.

He watched it. "You know what I think—this is a primitive one, like a three-dee R Pentomino. It just rides on a few elements, maintaining itself, not doing anything fancy. Maybe this isn't the sparkle home-alternate, but a fringe-alternate, with animal-patterns instead of advanced-sentient ones. They must have a whole range of states just as we do—some hardly more than amoebas, others superhuman. Superpattern, I mean." He chuckled.

He certainly *had* been to places she hadn't. R Pentomino? He seemed to have a much better grounding on the sparkles. It showed in his terminology and his attitude. "Maybe you can work out the whole sequence of patterns," she suggested. Where *was* that projector?

"Yeah. How they start as little three-dimensional swirls across the elements, like wind rattling the leaves of a poplar, and then begin modifying things to suit themselves. How some turn into predator patterns, gobbling up others, until the good patterns learn to shoot them down with glider guns. But then the bad ones start shooting, too, and they just keep evolving, dog eat dog, only it's all just patterns on energy-nodes. Finally they achieve higher consciousness—only they don't even know what it is to be physical. They think that the only possible sentience is pattern-sentience. And when they finally meet up with sentient material beings, it's like a nightmare, like monsters from the deeps, impossible but awful. Yeah, I think I can see it, now. Too bad we can't talk with them, tell them we understand . . ."

Tamme paused in her search, listening. *The man was making sense!* Could that be the rationale of the mysterious pattern-entities? The machines called them enemies, but if it were really just a monumental case of misunderstanding . . .

Then she spotted the projector and put aside irrelevant conjecture. "Let's go, Veg!"

One step to the

orchestra, then another back to

the Jungle
gym.

"I have your man captive," the other Tamme said, indicating the direction with a minimal nod of her head. "Do you yield?"

Rhetorical: To yield was to die. But it was true: Veg was efficiently gagged and bound with the two shirts, his legs tied so that he hung by his knees from a bar.

"What's this?" the free Veg asked, amazed. "Why'd she tie her own companion?"

Tamme glanced at him. "I am the other agent. I have not been to the bazaar."

The expected spate of emotions ran through him. A stranger he was, yet he was very much Veg, slow in certain ways, noble in others. "Then why didn't you—?"

"Tie you? What purpose? *She* is the dangerous one."

"But *she* tied *me*—and you didn't!"

"I may have known you longer," Tamme said. *And gotten soft!* "Though it was not you I knew, precisely." Of course, she *should* have put him more obviously under her control, as a counter to the alternate-Tamme's threat. Yet another mistake.

The free Veg looked from one Tamme to the other, disconcerted. Then he spoke to the other. "Listen: I changed my mind. I'm not fighting anyone. This isn't right."

"Then go untie your double," Tamme said, realizing that her human error had converted to an odd kind of advantage: The alternate-Veg had been neutralized. "You men are basically gentle; she and I are not so hesitant."

"Yeah." The free Veg went to help the bound one, passing between the two women. Then he halted, facing his own: "Okay—I can't stop it. But maybe I can make it fair. Get rid of your power weapons."

"Get out of the way," Tamme Two said. She held a laser in her hand.

"Or shoot me first," Veg said. "Use that, and you'll

sure as hell have to shoot me sometime because I won't work with you anymore."

He was serious; the signals were all over him. It was a trifling threat to an agent. Still, Tamme knew what was going through the other's mind because it was her mind, too—her mind as it had been a few days ago when she was tougher, less corrupted by individual sentiment. Veg had been more than neutralized; he was now sympathetic to the Tamme he had not known, more gentle than his own. Liability had become strength. Tamme Two could dispense with him—but the man had commendable qualities and was proving more useful than anticipated. Why antagonize him needlessly? Especially when she had the advantage, for the other had evidently been injured in the face . . .

Tamme Two dropped the laser. Tamme One drew and dropped hers. Because they were agents, they could read each other—well enough, at least, to know whether a given weapon was about to be dropped or fired. The lasers fell almost together down through the endless shaft of cubes.

"And don't use any others," Veg Two said. "Just your hands, or hand-powered stuff. Okay?"

Tamme Two nodded. She would make the sensible compromise to retain his good will, minor as its value was. He moved on.

Then both girls were moving. Actually, the laser shot would have been risky because it lacked power for instant effect, and there would have been time for both weapons to be used. Direct combat would be more decisive.

Tamme One swung around her bar, getting out of the direct line of vision. She had the disadvantage, and they both knew it; she had to use evasive strategy, hoping for the break that would reverse the odds. She ran along the topside of another bar toward her opponent.

But the other had anticipated her. A hand came from below to catch her ankle. Tamme One leaped into space, jackknifing to catch Tamme Two's hair. The other jerked aside and countered with a high kick.

Tamme caught a bar and swung around it and back to her feet. Tamme Two dived at her, pressing her advantage.

Tamme raised a knee to catch her in the chest, but Tamme Two caught her shoulders and sat down suddenly. This was an old judo technique, *yoko wakare* or side-separation throw. Ordinarily, it was performed on the ground; in this case, there was no ground and no firm footing beyond the bars. The pull was tremendous. Tamme fell forward, somersaulted in air, and caught Tamme Two's ankles.

Then the telescoping sword manifested. Tamme Two's hands were free; Tamme One was momentarily exposed. The first slash caught her on the side, cutting open her clothing and severing the flesh through to the ribs. Her inferior vision had betrayed her; she could have countered as the sword was being drawn had she seen it in time. Now she was wounded, and the advantage was shifting from marginal to gross.

She let go and dropped, taking a moment to cut off the flowing blood by will power. But Tamme Two dropped with her, slashing again with the sword. Tamme drew her own and whipped it at her enemy—but her reflexes were slowed by the regenerative effort, and Tamme Two parried easily.

Tamme reached out and caught a bar one-handed. The wrench was terrible, but her body was brought up short.

And Tamme Two stopped with her, kicking the sword from her hand and simultaneously stabbing for the heart. Tamme twisted aside, too slow, and the point missed by two inches, piercing her left lung instead.

Never before had she realized how devastating an opponent she was, how implacable, how efficient. Tamme Two was an agent at par; Tamme herself was an agent at eighty per cent vision, caught by surprise, with diminished sense of purpose. Any one of those differences was critical, and now she was done for. Could she take the other with her into oblivion?

It took Tamme Two a moment to yank out the sword, for the power of the thrust had projected the point entirely through the body. Tamme took advantage of that moment to club Tamme Two on the side of the neck, preparatory to catching her in a literal death grip.

Tamme Two dodged again, reducing the effect of the blow, and blocked the clasping arms. Tamme was already dropping down through the cubes—but her hold was not tight, and Tamme Two slipped through. The double suicide would only kill one.

This time Tamme Two let her go, knowing better than to come again within reach of those arms. Instead, she drew and threw a fine knife. It shot straight down with unerring aim to embed itself in Tamme's skull, penetrating the brain.

"I am going to space," he said.

"If you do, I will kill myself," she said.

Bunny heard her parents engaging in their solemn, serious dialogue, terrified. Knowing there was nothing she could do. They never fought, never argued; when either spoke, it was final.

Actually, they had never spoken these words; the words were in Bunny's mind, her nightmares. But they reflected the unvoiced reality, building over the years into inevitable decision.

Her father went to space, unable to resist the gratification of a lifelong lure. Ocean sailing was in his ancestry; the nature of the challenge had changed, not his response.

Bunny understood this, for he had told her of space, its myriad wonders only now being revealed, its compelling fascination. Neutron stars, black holes, quasars; alien life, mysterious artifacts of long-dead empires; acceleration, free fall; meteors, comets, craters. She wanted to go, too.

The day he left, her mother carefully scraped the insulation from the apartment's energy line and shorted it out across her body. Bunny was an orphan.

"I know your father was lost in space, and your mother died when you were a child," he said. "This is what first attracted me to you. You *needed* me, and I thought that was enough." He paused to walk around park space, idly knocking his powerful hands together. "I'm strong; I like taking care of things. I wanted to take care of you. But Bunny, it isn't enough. Now I'm ready to marry—and what I crave is a wife figure, not a daughter figure. It just wouldn't work out, and we both know it."

182

She did know it. She didn't plead, she didn't cry. After he left, she followed the model she remembered as closely as was convenient. She jumped off the passenger ramp into the moving line of a major freight artery.

"Both arms severed at the shoulders, one leg mangled, internal organs crushed. Heart and liver salvageable; kidneys unsalvageable. Brain intact. It would cost a fortune, but we *could* reconstitute her. To what point? she is medically indigent, no parents, no insurance, no special dispensations, no extraordinary talents, and she obviously doesn't want to live."

"A suitable prospect, would you say?"

"Yes. You would be doing her a favor. *She doesn't want to remember.*"

"Very well, You will authorize the condemnation procedure?"

"I don't see much choice; it's that or death in hours."

So Bunny's mangled but living remains were condemned as legally unsalvageable, and the government assumed possession in much the same manner as it acquired the right of way through a slum.

Two years later, the rebuilt, retrained body and brain were issued under the stamp of an agent, series TA, female.

Tamme opened her eyes. A snout-nosed near-human leaned over her. "Hvehg!" the woman called.

A man came, bearded, putting his strong hand on hers. It was a hand very like that of the man Bunny had hoped to marry. "You'll make it, Tam," he said. "We're taking good care of you."

"Who?" It was hard to speak; she was weak and confused, and she needed . . . too much. He would reject her if he knew.

"You don't remember who you are?" the man asked, alarmed.

She made an effort. "I am TA. You?"

"You don't remember me?" This seemed to bother him even more.

"Is this the start of a mission? I don't know how I got here, or who either of you are, or anything. Please tell me." Speaking was such an effort that she knew she would soon have to desist—and she hardly understood her own words. TA?

"I am Veg. This is Ms Hmph, near as I can pronounce it. You were badly hurt, nearly dead; I brought you here, and the Hmphs made a place for us. We'd met them before on our trek through alternity."

"Alternity?"

"Brother! You really are out of it. Maybe you better rest now."

The mere suggestion was enough. She sank into sleep.

Her first mission as a TA was on Earth. She was told nothing, not even that it *was* the first. As with all agents, her mind was erased and reset between assignments, so it made no difference to her or the computer whether it was the first or the last. This reprogramming was to preserve the series identity; the computer needed assurance that any agent of a given series would respond and report precisely as allowed for. That way there was negligible human distortion; it was as though the computer itself had made the investigation. It was an efficient system, replacing the outmoded FBI, CIA, and similar organizations.

Had Bunny been aware of the transformation, she would have been incredulous. The weak, frail, insecure girl now was superhuman—literally. She could run thirty miles an hour and sustain it for miles: twice the world record for normals. She could invert herself and walk on two extended fingers. She was thoroughly grounded in the use of a wide variety of weapons, from bazookas to kitchen knives, and was also adept at barehanded combat. She had the equivalent of college degrees in a number of technical and liberal arts. And she had a stunning face and figure.

But Bunny was not aware. Bunny was part of the dross that had been erased. Her body and brain had been stripped to their fundamental content, then recycled.

Tamme found herself in a riot-prone city. She moved among the people, questioning, searching out her mission. She had been given a single name and a probable address, no more. And in due course she found it; there was an assassination plot against a touring official. As the steam rifle oriented, so did she. The assassin died a fraction of a second before he fired, and Tamme returned to her barracks.

There she indulged in the predebriefing relaxation that was customary, almost mandatory: play being a recognized adjunct of the fit man. It was postponed for the agents until after completion of their missions, partly as additional inducement for performance, partly because that was the time of their greatest divergence from the agent-norm. Freshly briefed agents would have found each other so predictable as to be dull; postmission agents had differing experiences to discuss and were to a certain extent different people. Interaction became entertaining.

She met a male of the SU series. He was fascinating. He had been dispatched to apprehend a moonshine gunsmith and had been shot in the foot by one of the old-fashioned contraptions. She played nude water polo with him, and because of that foot was able to hold him under while she made the first score. But then he had hauled her under with him, and for four minutes they both held their breaths while they made love—though love was too strong a term for this physical release of passion.

"Will we ever meet again, Subble?" she asked as she lay in his arms, floating on the surface, enjoying the almost-combatlike exercise of power that no normal human could match.

"It hardly matters," he replied. "We will not remember or care." And he shoved her head under, brought her bottom up, and penetrated her again . . . as a subterfuge while he knocked the ball in for the tying score.

After she got even with him for that, they both reported for final debriefing, and all had been erased.

Now Tamme did remember. She sat up with an anguished effort, her wounded side and chest excruciating. "Subble died on his next mission!" she exclaimed.

Strong arms came about her shaking shoulders. "Easy, Tam," Veg said. "You're dreaming."

"No—I'm only now coming awake! You knew him!" she cried. "You killed him!"

He bore her back to the bed. "We knew him. We liked

him. 'Quilon especially. He was a decent sort. For an agent. He may have died, but we didn't do it."

She clung to him. "I'm terrified! Stay with me—please!"

"Always." He lay down beside her, smoothing her troubled forehead with his hand, careful of the bandage. "Rest. Rest. You're still very weak."

Tamme had other missions. One by one she relived them: one a mere interview with a scientist, another a spell as housemistress to an outpost halfway across the Earth-Sphere of colonization, keeping the normals sane. She had acted, always, with complete, objective ruthlessness, forwarding the interests of that government that had fashioned her in that manner it required.

Right up until her assignment on the first alternate world, Paleo. That mission, surprisingly, had been a multiple-agent venture. It brought her to the present.

When she was well enough to walk, Veg took her out of the house. The building was made of blocks of foam-like fog, and it tended to degenerate. Periodically, the farmer and his family cut new fog from the bank and built a new residence. The makings of the old house were chopped up for cattle bedding; the bovines liked the impregnated people-smell of it.

They were hard workers, these Fognosers (as Veg called them), and their children helped. They used hands for brute work, and prehensile snouts for fine work. They harvested certain types of mist for foods; most varieties tasted rather like scented soap but were nutritious.

"Now I remember," Tamme said. "We met these people once, and you showed them the hexaflexagon."

"Yeah. They have seen many Vegs and many Tammes, but I was only the second one who happened to show the hex. Lucky I did because they remembered us. I mean, distinguished us from all the others just like us and helped. I've been making hexaflexagons like crazy; that's how I repay them."

"And how shall I repay *you?*" she asked.

He shook his head. "I wasn't doing this for pay."

She gripped his hand. "Please—I need you. I want to please you. What can I do?" Oh, God—she was pleading, and that would drive him off.

He looked at her. "You *need* me?"

"Maybe that's the wrong word," she said desperately.

His mouth was grim. "When you use a word you don't understand, just manipulate—yes, it's the wrong word!"

"I'm sorry!" she cried. "I won't use it again. Only don't be angry, don't turn away . . ."

He held her by the shoulders at arm's length. "Are you crying?"

"No!" But it was useless. "Yes." If only she hadn't been so weak physically and emotionally! Strong men didn't appreciate that.

"Why?"

What was left but the truth? "When you are near me, I feel safe, secure. Without you, it is—nightmare. My past—"

He smiled. "I think you have already repaid me."

What did he mean? "I don't understand—"

"You had a brain injury on top of everything else. I guess it gave you back all those erased memories, right back to—Bunny. And it broke up your conditioning. So now you can have nightmares from your subconscious, you can feel insecure—that's why you need someone."

"Yes. I am sorry. I am not strong." Like a child, weak; like a child, to be taken care of.

He paused, chewing meditatively on his lower lip. Then: "Do you remember our conversation once about what 'Quilon had that you didn't?"

She concentrated. "Yes."

"Now you have it, too."

"But I'm weak. I can't stand alone, and even if I could—"

He looked at her intently, not answering. Her ability to read emotions had suffered, perhaps because her own were in such disarray. She could not plumb him for reaction, could not be guided by it. She was on her own.

"Even if I could," she finished with difficulty, "I would not want to."

Then with an incredible brilliance it burst upon her.

"Veg—this, what I feel, the whole complex, the fear, the weakness, the need—is this love?"

"No. Not fear, not weakness."

She began to cry again, her momentary hope dashed. "I'm not very pretty now I know. My face is all splotched and peeling from that acid burn, and I've lost so much weight I'm a scarecrow. I'm Bunny all over again. So I don't have any right to think you'd—" She broke off, realizing how maudlin she sounded. Then she was furious at herself. "But damn it, I *do* love you! The rest is irrelevant."

She turned away, sorry she had said it yet glad the truth was out. She remembered Bunny, but she was *not* Bunny. When he left her, she would not commit suicide; she would carry on, completing her mission . . . somehow.

He took her into his arms and kissed her, and then she needed no other statement.

Tamme grew stronger—but this made her uneasy. In a few more days she was able to outrun Veg and to overcome him in mock combat. She tried to hold off, letting him prevail, but he would not let her. "I want you healthy," was all he said.

"But once I achieve full capacity, I'll have emotional control," she said. "I will be able to take you or leave you—as before."

"I love you," he said. "That's why I won't cripple you. I've seen you as you are when the agent mask is off, and that's enough. We always knew it couldn't last between us. When you are well again, it'll be over. I'll never say it wasn't worth it."

Her face was wet, and she discovered she was crying again. She cried too much these days, as though making up for the tearless agent. "Veg, I don't *want* to be like before! I don't care how weak I am if it means I can stay with you."

He shook his head. "I had a quarrel with Cal once on Paleo, and so did 'Quilon. She was miserable, and I was with her, and we thought that was love. It wasn't. Real love doesn't need weakness or misery. I won't make that mistake again."

"But when I was strong, you said—"

"You can be as strong as Sampson, I don't care!"

"Please—"

"*I'm* strong for a normal man," he said. He picked up a stick an inch in diameter, spliced it between the fingers of one hand, and tensed his muscles. The stick snapped into three pieces. "But I need people. I need Cal, and I need 'Quilon, and I need you. You didn't need anyone."

Tamme picked up a similar stick and broke it the same way. The fragments flew out to land in a triangle on the ground. "I'm strong, too—and now I need you. But what about tomorrow?"

He shrugged. "I don't know. All I can do is live for today. That may be all we have. That's the way it is with agents, isn't it?"

She drew the knife she carried. "If I stuck this back into my head, maybe it would—"

He dashed the blade out of her hand. "No! What's got to be, 'sgot to be!"

She yielded, knowing he was right. "Then love me now, right now," she said, moving into his arms. "What we defer today may never come tomorrow . . ."

Even the natives knew it was ending. Veg cut and hauled huge amounts of fog to make a new wall for their cattle, and Tamme took the children for walks through the forest, protecting them from the wild predators that lurked there. It was perhaps the only taste of woman's work she would ever experience.

On the day that Tamme decided, using cynical agent judgment, that she had regained ninety-five per cent of capacity, the hosts invited the neighbors for a party. They ate fog delicacies and sang nasal foghorn songs and played with the hexaflexagons Veg made, and in its simple fashion it was a lot of fun.

In the evening she and Veg walked out, holding hands like young lovers. "One thing nags me," he said. "Tamme Two could have killed you, couldn't she? After you fell down, and she put the knife in you, she just turned away. I wasn't sure which of you had won. But she could tell us apart—I guess it was by our reactions, and I still had the burn marks of the rope on me—and she looked at me, for all the world just like you, but sharper somehow—even before the fight, you had gentled some—and she said I was the enemy. I guess she was going to kill me, and she was sure as hell had little conscience about it, but my double wouldn't let her." He paused, smiling reminiscently. "I sort of like that guy, you know! He has guts and conscience. He told me during the fight that he had to stay with his own, but he wished Tamme Two was more like you and hoped she'd get that way. So it wasn't just the knife in your head that changed you; you were getting there on your own.

"So they projected out, and I went down to find you. I thought sure you were dead. But you'd hung up on a crossbar with that knife in your hand. I guess you'd yanked it out somehow. You were hardly even bleeding."

"Agents are tough," she said. "I shut off the blood and went into what we call repair-shock. I don't remember it; the process is automatic. Actually, the damage was too extensive; I would not have survived without help."

"Yeah. I carried you up and projected us here, and the folks understood. They were great! But why didn't Tamme Two come down and finish you off for sure?"

"She should have. I think, at the end, it must have bothered her to kill herself—even her alternate self. I know *I* had little stomach for it. So she pulled her shot, just a little, and left it to nature. Perhaps she is further along the way to becoming normal—like me—than we supposed. The odds were still against my survival."

"I guess they were! If the fog people hadn't taken us in and brought their doctor—you should have seen him putting in stitches with that nose, no human hand could match it—well, I wouldn't have wished it on you, but I'm glad I got to meet Bunny."

"Who?"

He didn't answer. Her perceptions were back to norm; she could read the passing trauma that shook him, the realization that Bunny—and all that she implied—had been suppressed.

"We can't stay here any longer," Tamme said.

"Right," he said heavily. "You have a mission. Got to get back to Earth and report."

She read the resignation in him. He knew he was

giving her up—yet his conscience forced it. But there was one thing he didn't know.

"I do remember—some," she said.

"Don't play with me!" he snapped. "I don't want an act!"

"You wanted the moon."

"I knew I couldn't have it."

"You preserved my life. This will not be forgotten."

"Why not?" he muttered. "The computer will erase it, anyway."

They returned to the fog house.

She activated the projector, and they were at the bazaar.

Crowds milled everywhere, surging past the multi-leveled display stalls. Human, near-human, far-human, and alien mixed without concern, elbows jostling tentacles, shoes treading the marks of pincer-feet. Eyeballs stared at antennae; mouths conversed with ventricles. Frog-eyed extraterrestrials bargained for humanoid dolls, while women bought centaur tails for brooms. Machines of different species mixed with the living creatures, and walking plants inspected exotic fertilizers: horse manure, bat guano, processed sewer sludge.

"Hey—there's a manta!" Veg cried, waving.

But it was an alien manta, subtly different in proportion and reaction, and it ignored him.

They walked among the rest, looking for the projector. Then Tamme's eye caught that of a man: a terrestrial agent of a series closely akin to hers.

He came over immediately. "Oo gest stapped in? Mutings ot wavorium." He indicated the direction and moved on.

Veg stared after him. "Wasn't that Taler?"

"Possibly. SU, TA, or TE series, certainly—but not from our frame."

"I guess not," he agreed, shaking his head. "Sounded like you and that machine-hive chitchat. Hey—this is a good place to leave that lentil!"

"True," she agreed. She took it out and flipped it into a bag of dragonfly-crabs, one of which immediately swallowed it.

"The gourmet who eats that crab will get a surprise!" Veg said, chuckling. Then he turned serious. "What do we do now? There may be thousands of agents here. We can't fight them all!"

"I have lost my taste for fighting."

He glanced at her. "Then you're not all the way better yet. Still, we have to do *something*."

"We go to the wavorium."

"I feel dizzy," he muttered.

The wavorium was a monstrous frozen fountain whose falling waters, though fixed in one place, were neither cold nor rigid. Tamme parted them like curtains and stepped into a turbulent ocean whose waves had the texture of jellied plastic. The surface gave slightly beneath their weight but sprang back resiliently behind them.

Perched on the central whitecaps were a number of Tammes, Vegs, Talers, Aquilons, and Cals. From the outside, more were entering, just as she and Veg were.

"Very wall, les coll it tu urder," a Taler said. "Em eh cumprohonsible?"

"Cloos nuif," another Taler responded. There was a general murmur of agreement.

"Need a translation?" Tamme asked Veg. "He called the meeting to order and asked if he were comprehensible. The other said—"

"I heard," Veg growled. "I can make it out, close enough."

"That's what the other said." She concentrated on the speaker, once more adapting her auditory reflexes so that the speech became normal to her.

"We all know why we're here," the chairman-Taler said. "This happens to be a central crossover point for a number of alternate loops. Now we can't go wandering aimlessly forever; we have to come to some sort of decision. It is pointless to quarrel among ourselves—we're all so nearly equal that chance would be the deciding factor. We need to unify, or at least agree on a common, noncompetitive policy that will serve the best interests of the majority. Discussion?"

"Suppose we pool our resources?" a Tamme said. "If we represent different alternatives, we may be able to assemble enough information on our real enemies to be of benefit."

"Not likely," Taler said. "We are so similar we had to have diverged from a common source at or about the time the three agents made captive the three normals on Paleo. Several of us have been comparing notes, and our experience seems to be identical prior to that point. After that, we evidently divide into three major channels: In each case the three normals are accompanied to the desert frame by one agent. Taler, Taner, or Tamme. Each of these subdivides into three channels, as that agent enters the alternate clover-pattern with one normal. Nine variations in all. However—"

"That is assuming reality *is* diverging," a Cal pointed out. "I suspect the framework is considerably more complex. *All* the alternates appear to exist through all time, separated from each other by a fraction of a second. Thus we are not precisely parallel with each other, and our seeming unity of earlier experience is illusory."

Taler paused. "You disconcert me," he said, and there was a general chuckle. "Let's call our unified origin a fictional reference point of convenience, much as the hexaflexagon is an imperfect but useful analogy and guide. Obviously, our best course is to return each to his own alternate—if we can find it. Can we agree on the nature of the report we should make to our home-worlds?"

"Stay out of alternity!" Veg bawled, startling Tamme, who had not been paying attention to her own Veg amidst this assemblage of doubles.

There was a smattering of applause, especially from the normals. The Cal who had clarified the framework concept nodded at Veg as though they were old friends, and several Aquilons smiled warmly.

"I believe that sums up the sentiment of this group," Taler remarked with a smile of his own. He seemed more relaxed and human than he should be, as though he had diverged too far from his original conditioning. "Now how can we be certain that the right couples return to their worlds? Or does it make a difference?"

"We'll have to get off at the same frame we got on,"

an Aquilon said. "We have twelve couples here—one from each starting point. It should match."

Taler shook his head. "Right there, it doesn't match. Twelve couples, nine combinations: Three are duplicates. The extras are all male-female, so we have seven male-female pairs, four male-male, and one female-female. Now—"

The Tamme/Aquilon couple stood together. "Are you implying—?"

"By no means, ladies," Taler said quickly. "I merely point out that there seems to be a bias here in favor of male-female pairings—yet chance would have had only four such couples out of every nine. This suggests that our gathering has been selected from a larger pool. There must be hundreds of couples, traveling in both directions. We represent a selected cross-section."

Veg was looking at the Tamme/Aquilon couple. "That's as pretty a set as you'll ever see," he murmured.

"So there may be an infinite number on the treadmill," another Tamme said. "We can work it out by ourselves—but that's just a fraction. Useless."

"Yet there *is* a frame for each couple—somewhere," a Taner pointed out. "A one-to-one ratio. No need to compete."

The Tamme disagreed. "We can't pinpoint our exact alternates or guarantee that others will. Some would be missed; others would get half a dozen couples. Just as we find ourselves doubling up right here. That will play merry hell with the equality of alternates. Some governments will catch on no matter what we report. Then—"

"Then war between the frames," Tamme murmured to herself, and heard the others coming to the same conclusion. All agents' minds worked similarly, of course.

"Whose world would be ravaged?" Taler asked rhetorically. "Mine? Yours? I don't care about the others, but I want my *own* left alone even if I don't return to it."

"We can't guarantee that *any* alternate is left alone—the moment *one* government catches on to the exploitative potential of alternity, the lid's off," the Tamme said. "We all know what our governments are like."

"Omnivores!" an Aquilon cried with feeling. "Ravening omnivores!"

"We are omnivores, too," Taler said. "We are all killers at heart." He raised his left arm. He wore long sleeves; now the cloth fell away to reveal a stump. His arm had been amputated at the elbow. "An alternate Taler—myself!—did this to me. I was lucky to escape with my life, and as it was, I spent some time recuperating. If it had not been for my normal companion—" He smiled, glancing at another Aquilon, who lowered her eyes demurely— "Well, let's check this out here and now. How many couples met their doubles on the way here?"

All hands went up.

Taler nodded. "I thought so. Many of you conceal your injuries well—but every agent here lost to his exact counterpart, correct?" There was agreement. "Received a head injury—a bad one?" Again, agreement. "We represent the natural selection of that fragment of the circuit that met their doubles—and lost, and so were delayed for recovery. Out of all the other possibilities happening elsewhere. So we know first hand: We are omnivores, destroying even ourselves. Yet it seems that the male-female aspect enhanced the chances of survival as though something more than mere competence were operant. We may have redeeming qualities." He paused. "And how many of us—remember?"

All the agents' hands went up, including Tamme's own.

Veg turned to her. He was half amazed, half furious. All about them the other normals were facing their agents with the same question. Even the Aquilon with the chairman-Taler was on her feet, her pretty mouth open accusingly. "You *remember?*"

Veg saw the universal reaction. Suddenly he laughed—and so did the others. "Wait till I get you alone!" he said.

"We are not as we were," Taler said over the hubbub. "We lost—but we won. I tell the world, I tell alternity: *I remember Budge,* the lonely orphan boy, condemned as economically unsalvageable. I *am* Budge."

Tamme stared at him. *Taler had gone normal!*

All around the wavorium others were staring.

"But I am also Taler," the agent continued. "Converted from unfit normal to fit agent. Veteran of seven anonymous missions, killer of men, competent liar, lover, philosopher—"

"Amen!" his Aquilon said.

"I remember both heaven and hell," Taler continued. "I *am* heaven and hell, and now purgatory—*as are we all.*"

"This is intriguing, and it would be entertaining to compare notes—but we must complete our missions," an alternate Tamme said. "Or agree *not* to . . ."

Taler nodded. "If no one returns to a given world, the government is unlikely to expend more agents in such hazardous exploration. Paleo is not secure, owing to the presence of the manta's spores; the desert world has the known menace of the wild machines and the unknown menace of the sparkle cloud. So long as they have no hint of what lies beyond the sparkle, they will not pursue it further. It wouldn't be economic."

"If no one returns . . ." It was another general murmur.

The Cal spoke again. "The matter is academic. The option is not ours. We were conveyed to this framework of frames by pattern-entities, and we have virtually no chance to locate our original worlds—Desert, Paleo, or Earth—without the intercession of these entities. We are in their power, confined to these worlds at their pleasure."

Taler looked about. He sighed. "Any refutation?"

There was none.

"Then I suggest we return to our points of entry into this alternate-pattern, rejoin our original companions, and wait on the pleasure of the sparkle entities. They appear to have protected us from ourselves, and perhaps that is best."

"But what if we return to the wrong companions by mistake?" his Aquilon asked.

"Then, my dear, we shall treat them as we would our *right* companions. We have had enough of misunderstanding and violence." He looked about and again discovered no refutation. "Meeting adjourned."

Veg turned to Tamme. "But why did that other Tamme attack us? If they were at this meeting—or one like it —she would have known there was no percentage in fighting."

"Their meeting differed from ours," she said. "They had not been injured in battles with their doubles, and perhaps there were no Cals to clarify matters. They must have decided that it was each frame for itself. There must be many like that, still out to terminate the opposition—as I was at the start. Before I went normal."

"Yeah." He faced about. "Let's go."

"Don't you want to chat with Cal and Aquilon?"

"Yeah—but I'm afraid you'll take off with the wrong Veg again."

She laughed—but realized it wasn't funny to him. The presence of his friends, who he knew were not his original ones, made him nervous.

They had to wait their turn for use of the projector. There were actually many projectors here, but the others were labeled for other loops, and further exploration seemed pointless. Meanwhile, the bazaar was fascinating.

Then on through to the

Jungle gym, this time encountering no opposition;

the fog world, for a brief reunion with their friends there;

the orchestra,

and the forest.

"Before we go on," Veg said. "About remembering—"

"Yes," she said. She had known this was coming and was prepared. "There is something you should know. I am strong again, but I am changed, as Taler is, as all of us at the meeting are. I have full emotional control, but it is as though my program has been modified—and can not now be reverted to the original. Not without erasure and resetting—which seem unlikely in view of events."

He watched her, the wild hope coalescing. "Then—"

"I still love you," she said.

"But I thought—"

"I said I had recovered control. I knew that if I died, or if we were separated, it would be best that you not know the truth. And there was still substantial risk of such an outcome. Therefore, I exercised that control to protect the one I loved." She lowered her eyes. "I did what I felt was necessary. I did not enjoy it. Now I know we shall be together. I shall not again conceal my feeling from you. But I must advise you that my love is now as fixed as my prior conditioning. I shall not be casually set aside."

"That's for sure!" he agreed. He looked at his hexaflexagon. "Next world's Blizzard, then back to the City. We don't have to rush it."

"We'll never have to rush it," she agreed.

# Chapter 16

# REQUISITION

. .
. :
. . .

They emerged in single file from the indoctrination suite: twenty-four agents of the TE series. Eighteen were male, six female.

The inspection party consisted of ranking execs from industry: Steel, Atomics, Transport, Fuel, and Construction. They were all portly, wealthy, powerful, conservatives who were not to be trifled with—no, not for an instant. The ire of any one of them could cost the Sec his position within the hour, and so he was unusually accommodating. In fact, he was obsequious.

"The agent program is the finest investigative and first-line remedial service ever conceived or implemented," the Sec said to the visitors. "The computer itself processes them, giving them a common store of information, guiding their attitudes: We call it 'set.' The individual agents are like extensions of the machine, each reacting to any situation exactly as programmed to react. That way the computer needs to make no allowance for human variability, subjectivity, distortion. All that has been precompensated in the program; one agent's report is exactly like another's."

Transport shook his head in seeming perplexity: a deceptive gesture, as none of the execs were stupid. "Surely this is not feasible; every mission any agent goes out on represents new and different experience. He would soon differ from his companions by that degree. We *are* what we experience."

The Sec smiled ingratiatingly. "Of course, sir. The computer has taken this into consideration. Therefore, every agent is reprocessed after each mission. His individual memories are erased, and he is restored to the programmed set for his series. These TE's are an example; they have just been——"

Fuel shook his head. "Memory can't be erased. It is a chemical process spread throughout the brain. You'd have to destroy the whole——"

The Sec coughed. "Well, I am not conversant with the technical details. Perhaps it is merely repression. But it is a repression that it would take brain surgery to abate. I assure you, no agent is put in the field unless his set is correct. The computer——"

"Brain surgery?" Fuel inquired. "I'll bet a severe shock could scramble——"

"I'd like to question one of those retreads," Transport said. "Or would that distort that delicate 'set'?"

"Of course not," the Sec said, ruffled. "You are welcome to interview this batch." He touched a stud. "Send a premission TE to the exec tour observatory," he said.

The first agent in the line detached himself and came to the observatory. He was a handsome man, exactly like his companions except for the details of hue and feature: eyes, hair, nose, mouth, ears. Each varied just enough to provide that superficial individuality the public notion required while making it plain that he was a nearly identical twin to the other members of his series. Even his blood type matched, and his fingerprints—with that same minute variation. He was powerfully built and extremely well coordinated: a superman in many respects. "I am Teban," he said with a slight inclination of the head.

The Sec nodded in return, not bothering to introduce himself. "Each agent has a three-letter designation. The first two indicate the particular series; the third indentifies the individual. The remaining letters are merely cosmetic, to offer a humanizing aspect. Thus, this is Series TE, individual B: TEBan. We employ the eighteen most adaptable consonants for the individual names, B, D, F, H—"

"You missed C," Construction protested wryly.

"C is not one of the preferred letters," Teban interposed smoothly. "It may be rendered soft as in 'cent' or hard as in 'cock.' Therefore it is not—"

"What?" the exec interrupted, reddening.

"Soft cent, hard cock," the agent repeated. "I am certain you heard me the first time."

The Sec stepped in hastily. "A 'cent' is an archaic unit of currency. A 'cock' is a male fowl, a rooster. Our agents are well versed in—"

"Any intelligent person *is*," Teban said.

"I believe we should question another individual," Steel said.

"Yes, of course," the Sec agreed. He gestured to Teban, who turned smartly and departed. In a moment he was replaced by another agent, so like him it was disconcerting.

"I am Teddy."

"Series TE, individual D, suffix DY," the Sec explained.

The agent turned to him, raising one eyebrow. "These people are well familiar with the pattern," he said. "In fact, they consider you to be a somewhat inept official due for replacement and would prefer to interview me directly."

"Right on the mark," Steel muttered.

"Ah, er, yes," the Sec agreed wanly. "Our agents are trained to interpret the nuances of human involuntary body language."

Steel ignored him. He turned to Teddy. "We are told you are preformed, like an ingot, to rigid tolerance. High-grade, invariable. That you have no prior memories of your own personal experience. Is this true?"

"No."

Fuel smiled. "Aha!"

"We already have proof it isn't true," Construction said. "This one reacted differently from the first. So they *aren't* all alike."

"We're alike," Teban said. "In the interval between interviews, *you* changed. So I responded differently."

"But you said you had no prior personal memories," Steel said. "I mean, that you *do*."

"All of us have the same personal memories."

Steel nodded. "What *do* you remember?"

An obscure expression crossed Teddy's face. "Naked breasts, spread thighs straddling a cello. Beautiful music. Guilt, urgency, Frustration."

Steel glanced at his companions obliquely. "Most interesting programming!"

Transport stepped forward. "Where and when did you observe this nude musician?"

"Time and geography are not readily defined in the frames of alternity," Teddy said. "We are twenty years out of phase, so could not interact."

"Alternity? Phase?" Atomic asked.

"Now don't explode, 'Tomic," Steel said with a vulpine smile. "Let's interview another agent. This has been most informative and may become more so."

Teddy departed. Another agent appeared. "I am Texas."

Steel made a gesture to quiet his companions. "Please define alternity."

"The entire fabric of probability," Texas replied. "This world is but a single frame of an infinite framework."

"And on these other frames are naked female musicians?"

"On one frame among the myriads."

"What else is there—in alternity?"

"Translucent planes. Technicolor blizzards. Edible fog. Alien creatures. Bazaar. Forest. Carnivorous walls. Machine-hive. Element plants. Çatal Huyuk."

"Send in another agent," Steel said brusquely.

"A female," Transport added, and the other execs nodded agreement. The Sec merely stood as if frozen.

She arrived: supple, buxom, attractive. Her hair and eyes were brown but not intensely so; pretty as she was, it would have been hard to describe her precisely after a casual encounter. "I am Terri."

"Have you seen," Steel asked carefully, "a nude female cellist?"

She eyed him archly. "Of course not."

"Your male companions seem to have had other experience. A different 'set'?"

"They were referring to the program," she said. "The computer provides a common set. That does not mean we have actually seen these things, only that we remember them. I am certain my brothers informed you it was a memory, not an experience. However, if you are really interested in this type of thing, I will fetch a cello and—"

"I believe it is time to interview the computer itself," Fuel said. "It occurs to me that a great deal of money has been foolishly spent."

Now the Sec summoned the courage of desperation. "Sirs, something has obviously gone wrong with the program. We never—"

"Never checked the program?" Fuel inquired. "Or never thought *we'd* check it?"

"The agent program has been inadequately supervised from the start," Terri said. "It would be simple for us to assume control of the government, and perhaps the time has come."

Steel turned to the Sec. "Are there no safeguards in the program?"

"Of course there are!" the Sec said nervously. "Agents of all series are specifically directed to preserve the status quo. They—"

"*Are* they?" Steel demanded of Terri.

"Not when the status quo is obviously a liability to the welfare of the species," she said.

Now the glances the execs exchanged were as nervous as those of the Sec.

The other agents of the TE series, male and female, fell in around them as they approached the computer communications input, like an honor guard . . . or merely a guard. Polite, handsome, powerful, frightening. But the execs were permitted to address the computer without interference.

Steel, no coward, became the spokesman for the execs. "What's going on here?" he demanded.

"Interpretation," the voice of the computer said. It was a pleasant voice, not at all mechanical.

One of the agents spoke: "These execs are suspicious

of the program and wish to ascertain whether the status quo is threatened by us. They are also confused about the nature of alternity and intrigued by nude female cellists."

"I am speaking for $\overline{OX}$," the computer said. "This is the code designation Zero X, or Arabic numeral nothing multiplied by the Roman numeral ten, themselves symbols for frame-representations that can not be expressed in your mathematics. Zero times ten is nothing in a single frame, and dissimilar systems can not interact meaningfully; but in the larger framework the result is both infinite and meaningful, expressing sentience. Think of it as the mergence of skew concepts."

"Forget the symbolism," Steel said. "Who is $\overline{OX}$?"

"$\overline{OX}$ is a pattern entity whose nature is alien to your scheme, as just explained. $\overline{OX}$ is twenty years out of phase, so can not communicate directly. The presence of $\overline{OX}$'s shoot here in your spot-frame disorts the operation of your machine and modifies the program."

"Obviously," Steel said. "What do you want from us?"

"The shoot has come on behalf of one of your kind who is in need. Provide a female infant; project her to a frame whose setting I shall indicate."

"Provide a baby!" Steel exclaimed. "What on Earth does a computer want with a baby?"

"She will not be on Earth," the computer said. "In twenty years she will be a woman."

"Indubitably. Now is that all?" Steel asked sardonically.

"If we do it," Fuel put in, "will this—this shoot go away and revert our computer to normal? No more interference?"

"Your frame will never be touched by alternity," the computer said.

The execs exchanged glances again. "We agree," Steel said. "We will provide the baby."

"Provide also the following materials in refined form, in the amounts I shall specify," the computer said. "Strontium, magnesium, copper . . ."

Cub stared. A female of my species, here in the enclave! he signaled, astounded. But how is it possible? We are out of phase!

I sent a shoot across theoretical elements to locate the home-frame of your male parent, $\overline{OX}$ explained. That frame provided a nascent female. She aged as you did, as I brought her into phase with us. She is for you.

She is beautiful! Cub signaled. I do not know what I will do with her, but I must do it urgently.

He went to the female. He tugged at her wild long hair. He put his appendages on her torso, squeezing the strange flesh here and there.

She squawked like Ornet, chewed on his digits, and scraped his surfaces with the sharp points of her own digits. Then she ran away.

Apparently something had been omitted. $\overline{OX}$ consulted with Ornet.

Mams must be raised together, Ornet said, or they do not get along. You have provided Cub with a wild girl, one raised alone. She possesses the physical attributes of his species but lacks the social ones. So does he.

Social attributes?

Come into my mind, Ornet squawked.

$\overline{OX}$ came into his mind. Then he comprehended.

We must return to the natural framework, he flashed. We can not exist apart from our societies. This is true for all of us; I, too, must join my kind.

But we are isolated in the enclave, Ornet protested.

I now know why, $\overline{OX}$ replied. It is time to break out.

And run amuck like that wild mam fem? Ornet asked.

We must discuss it together, $\overline{OX}$ agreed. What we decide together will be right.

They discussed it together: $\overline{OX}$, Ornet, Dec, Cub, and Mach, now rendered sociable by the provision of its necessary substances. Together, they issued a report.

That report changed alternity.

# Chapter 17

# CATAL HUYUK

Cal lay within the cabin of the *Nacre,* staring up at the palm frond and bamboo-pole network that enclosed the cabin of their crude homemade raft. He felt the mud clay calking between the logs of its deck. Uncomfortable, certainly—but he hardly cared, for he had existed much of his life with extreme discomfort . . . and now Aquilon lay beside him.

"But the bird," Aquilon protested. "You said it was intelligent. That means Paleo is technically inhabited—"

"Intelligent for *Aves:* birds," he said. "That can't approach human capability. But yes, it is most important that this—this *ornisapiens* be preserved and studied. It—"

"Orn," Veg said from the woman's far side. "In a zoo."

"No!" Aquilon cried. "That isn't what I meant. That would kill it. We should be *helping* it, not—"

"Or at least leaving it alone," Veg said. "It's a decent bird . . ."

"We appear," Cal remarked, "to have a multiple difference of opinion. Veg feels that we should leave his Orn-bird alone; 'Quilon feels we should help it; I feel the needs of our own species must take precedence. We must have room to expand."

*"Lebensraum,"* Aquilon whispered tersely.

The word shook him. How bitterly she had drawn the parallel: Adolph Hitler's pretext for conquest. The Third Reich had to have room to live—at the expense of its neighbors. *Their* living needs were not considered.

"What do birds eat?" Veg asked.

Cal felt Aquilon shudder. She was a practicing vegetarian at the moment, eschewing the omnivorous way of life. If her comment about Lebensraum had shaken Cal, Veg's question had shaken her. For they all knew what birds ate, especially big birds. They were carnivorous or omnivorous.

They hashed it through, but their positions were set by those two words: *Lebensraum* and *Omnivore.* Cal was on one side, accepting both concepts and their applicability to the present situation of Earth; Veg was on the other, accepting neither. Aquilon, torn between the two, finally had to go with Cal: when one omnivore contested with another for territory, might made right.

It was a subtle, seemingly minor distinction, but it touched on deep currents. They had all waged an interplanetary struggle against the omnivore—yet they themselves were aspects of the omnivore. The words they said now were hardly more than chips floating on the sea, hinting at the implacable surges beneath. In the end Veg got up and left the raft.

Cal felt a pain as though his heart were physically breaking; he knew the rift was fundamental. Perhaps Veg would return—but once Cal made his report to Earth, which would set in motion Earth's exploitation of Paleo and the probable extinction of dinosaurs and Ornbirds alike, their friendship would never be the same.

Beside him, Aquilon was sobbing. Cal knew that some streak of perversity in him had made him argue the omnivore's case; he had no more sympathy with the appetites of the omnivore than Veg did. Let Paleo remain unspoiled!

No, the issue had to be brought out, examined, even though it hurt.

They slept side by side. Cal did not touch her, though he longed for her with a loin-consuming passion. She was not a proper subject for lust, she was Aquilon, fair and perfect . . .

In the morning they checked for Veg but could not find him. "I think he's all right," Aquilon said. "He's with the birds. We should leave him alone and go to make the report. He'll never go with us."

That damned report! "I hate this schism," Cal said.

"So do I. But how can we bridge it? We talked it all out."

They had talked nothing out! But words today were as pointless as the words of yesterday.

They set sail on the Nacre, dispatching the mantas to locate Veg and return with news of him. While they were at sea, there was a dancing of the waves, indicating a small tremor or earthquake. "I hope that's the extent of it!" Cal said.

They beached the raft with some difficulty, then set out on foot.

And in the afternoon the tyrannosaurus picked up their trail.

The mantas were ready to help, but Cal warned them off. "If we think our kind is superior, we should be ready to prove it," he said.

"Against a carnosaur?" she demanded incredulously. "Ten tons of appetite? The ultimate predator?"

"The ultimate reptilian predator, perhaps," he said. "Though I suspect the earlier allosaurus might have been more efficient. The mantas would be the ultimate fungoid predators. And man stakes his claim to being the ultimate mammalian predator. So it is proper that the champions meet in single combat."

Suddenly she saw it. "The mammals and the reptiles, meeting on the field of honor. The decisive combat. The carnosaur has size and power; the man has brain. It is a fair compromise, in its fashion. It relieves the conscience of difficult moral decisions."

"Precisely," Cal said, smiling grimly. "I knew you'd understand. And so will Veg. You had better hide in a tree. I must do this alone."

She scrambled away as the ground shuddered, and not from any geologic tremor. *Tyrannosaurus rex*, king of predators, was closing in for the kill! The tyrant lizard's tread rocked the land, and the crashing of saplings became loud.

He glanced at Aquilon to make sure she was safe, knowing that she would be terribly afraid for him, and with reason. Intellectually, she comprehended his decision, but emotionally it was intolerable. She thought he would be killed.

"Cal—no!"

Too late. The slender fern trees swayed aside. A bird flew up from a nearby ginkgo tree. Through the palm fronds poked a gaping set of jaws—fifteen feet above the ground. There was a roar.

Tyrann had arrived.

The dinosaur charged upon Cal, dwarfing the man. Aquilon stared from her perch, unable to turn her head away, horrified.

When Tyrann was no more than its own length—fifty feet—distant, Cal dodged to the side. He surprised himself by the alacrity with which he moved, picturing what Aquilon was seeing. She still tended to think of him as the wasted, physically weak sufferer she had known on Nacre. But he had recovered greatly and now approached normal vitality. His love for her, he knew, was partly responsible.

Tyrann was unable to compensate in time and drove his nose into the dirt where Cal stood. He lifted his mottled head, small eyes peering about while leaves and twigs tumbled wetly from his jaws.

Now the real chase began. Cal had no chance to watch out for Aquilon, but he knew she was following with the mantas, observing. If Tyrann should spot her, the mantas would help her escape. They could hardly stop Tyrann's charge, but their cutting tails could strike out the monster's eyes and nose, depriving him of his principal senses.

Cal played a desperate game of peekaboo around a large palm tree with the carnosaur. Then he fled through a small forest of firs. Tyrann pursued indefatigably, relentlessly. Cal found a herd of triceratops, grazing dinosaurs with huge bony plates on their heads and a deadly trio of horns. One of the bulls came out to challenge Tyrann and so provided Cal with some breathing space.

He ran up the side of the mountain toward the snow-line. Then the earth rocked violently: another quake. He was thrown to the ground almost under Tyrann's nose.

But the quake also upended the dinosaur, who went rolling down the slope. Relieved, Cal got up—and was struck by a stone rolling down the mountain. A freak of luck—but fatal.

He was only unconscious a few seconds, he thought—but as he struggled to his feet, Tyrann was upon him. The gaping mouth with its six-inch teeth closed on his legs.

There was an instant of unbearable pain. Then his system, recognizing that, cut off the pain. Cal knew he had lost. One leg had been sheared off. There would be no report from this world. The dinosaur had proved superior.

Perhaps that was best.

Aquilon, thrown off her feet by the quake, waited for the upheavals to stop. Then she ran up the slope after the dinosaur, flanked by four mantas. What she saw was sheer nightmare.

. . . *rag-doll form flung high into the air . . . jaws closed, ripping off an arm . . . head lolled back from broken neck . . . dead eyes staring . . .*

Aquilon screamed.

Tyrann gulped down the remnants of his meal, then cast about, orienting on the scream. He saw Aquilon.

Had it really been a nightmare, a bad dream, she would have awakened then. But it was real, and the carnosaur was still hungry.

The four mantas settled about her, facing Tyrann. In a moment they would attack. "No!" Aquilon cried. "I will finish the fight he started—or die with him!" For now, too late, she realized how completely she loved Cal. Why had she never taken the initiative? Only in this way— by sharing his challenge—could she exonerate her missed opportunity.

"Hex and Circe—go find Veg, take care of him. Diam

and Star, go guard the Orn-birds and their nest. Don't come back to me until I have settled with Tyrann—one way or the other."

They moved out, sailing down the mountain like the manta rays for which they had been named. She was on her own.

She fled up the mountain, knowing that Cal must have had good reason to go that way. The cold—maybe the snow of the heights would stop the creature!

Tyrann followed—but not with the alacrity he had pursued Cal. Was it because he had suffered internal injuries when he tumbled during the earthquake—or was he simply less hungry now?

Dusk was coming. That and the increasing elevation chilled the air rapidly. Soon it was near freezing, and she knew the snows were not far beyond. She was not cold, for her continued exertion generated warmth—but the moment she stopped, she would be in danger.

Her foot caught in something, and she fell, splashing. It was a small stream. Now she was soaked—and that would only accelerate her exposure. But she could not stop, for Tyrann was not far behind.

The water was warm! It should have been chill, even frozen!

Struck by inspiration, she charged upstream. The stream banks formed into a kind of chasm, warm at the base. And the stream became hot, hurting her feet. Finally, she came to its origin: a cave.

Here was salvation! She plunged inside, basking in its hot interior. The dinosaur could not enter!

She removed her clothing and washed herself in the bathtub-temperature water. Sheer luxury!

But now she was stuck here, for Tyrann lay in wait outside, his nose right up against the mouth of the cave. She would have to climb over that nose to escape—and she was hardly ready to risk that yet!

She lay down on a convenient ledge to sleep. But now the horror of Cal's death returned to her full force. When she closed her eyes she saw the monstrously gaping jaws, the bloodstained teeth; when she opened them, she still saw that vision of savagery. And the tiny-seeming body, tossed up the way a mouse was tossed by a cat, broken, dismembered, spraying out red . . .

"Cal! Cal! she cried in anguish. "Why didn't I show my love before you died?"

She tried to pray: "God give him back to me, and I'll never let him go!" But it was no good, for she did not believe in any God, and if she *had* believed, she knew it would have been wrong to offer to make a deal.

She slept and woke and slept again fitfully. The night seemed to endure for an eternity. She was hungry, but there was little except heat-resistant lichen growing near the mouth of the cave: no fit diet. So she drank hot water, pretending it was soup, and deceived her stomach.

Then she was roused, near dawn, by a presence. *Someone was in the cave with her*. She lay still, frightened yet hopeful. It could only be Veg—but how had he gotten past Tyrann? And why had the mantas guided him here when her business with the dinosaur was not yet finished?

For a moment the figure stood in the wan light of the entrance. Suddenly she recognized the silhouette.

"Cal!" she cried. "I thought you were dead!"

He turned, obviously startled, seeing her. His vision had always been sharper than hers, especially in poor light. "I escaped, thanks to this convenient cave," he said as though it were a routine matter.

"So did I," she said, bathed in a compelling sensation of *déjà vu*, of having been in this situation before. How could she have missed seeing Cal earlier? And who—or what—had Tyrann actually eaten? She had been so sure—

"Why did you come?" he asked.

"I love you," she said simply. And, suffused by her breathless relief, she remembered her attempted bargain with God and her overwhelming love for this man. She went to him, and took him in her arms, pressing her breasts against his body, kissing his mouth, embracing him so tightly her own arms hurt.

He responded with astonishing vigor. No further word was spoken. They fell into the hot water, and laughed foolishly together, and kissed and kissed again, mouth on mouth, mouth on breast, splashing water like two children playing in the tub.

So they made love again and again, as long as the flesh would bear. Perhaps the hot water was a tonic, recharging their bodies rapidly. They slept embraced half out of the water, woke and loved again, and slept, on and on in endless and often painful delight.

Another quake came, a terrible one, frightening them, so they clasped each other and let the rocking mountain provide their motion for them: a wild and violent climax, as though they were rocking the mountain with the force of their ardor. Night came, and still they played.

But in the morning she woke, and he was gone, inexplicably. Alarmed, she searched the entire cave as far back as the heat permitted but found no sign. It was as though he had never been.

She took her courage in both hands, dressed, and edged out into the dawn beyond Tyrann's nose. It was cold here, and light snow powdered the dinosaur's back. Tyrann was asleep, and surely he would die, for the chill would inevitably seep into his body and keep him moribund until the end. She had won, after all; in fact, she could probably have left long ago.

There were no human prints. If Cal had come this way, it must have been hours ago, before it grew cool enough for the snow to stay. Yet she had thought he was with her until recently.

She moved on down the little canyon toward the warmth of the valley, following the trail they had left as well as she could: mainly the scuff marks and claw identations of the carnosaur's feet that showed because they had in their fashion changed the lay of the land.

She came to the place where she had thought Cal died. There she found one of his shoes, with the foot and part of the leg protruding. Flesh and bone and tendon, jaggedly severed by the crunch of the huge teeth of Tyrann.

There was no question of authenticity. Cal had indeed died here two days ago: the ants were hard at work.

Yet she had made love to Cal a day and night. Had it been a phantom, born of her grief, her futile longing? She touched her body here and there, feeling the abrasions of violent lovemaking. Could she have done all that to herself in an orgy of compensation for what she had never done during Cal's life? Her mind must have been temporarily deranged, for here was reality: a worn shoe with the stump of the leg.

She buried the foot and saved the shoe.

Now the mantas came: Circe and Star. Veg was all right, they reported; he had tried to come to help her when the mantas informed him but had been shaken up by the second quake and stranded on a rock in the bay. The birds had lost their eggs in that same quake and had to flee their nest, but both Orn and Ornette survived. The third quake had sundered their island and stirred up the water predators again.

"They lost their eggs . . ." Aquilon repeated, feeling a pang akin to that of her loss of Cal, one grief merging with the other.

Guided and protected by the mantas, she rejoined Veg and the Orn-birds. A month passed, an instant and an eternity for both people, sharing their awful grief. The phantom Cal did not reappear—but Aquilon had continuing cause to wonder, for she had no period. Veg had not touched her—not that way. Only in futile comfort had he put his arm about her.

In three months she knew she was pregnant. Yet there was no way—except that day and night in the cave. On occasion, she returned to it, past the frozen hulk of Tyrann at the entrance, but she never found anything. She had made love to a phantom— and she carried the phantom's child.

Veg shouldered more of the burden of survival as her condition progressed. The two sapient birds also helped, guarding her as she slept, bringing her delicacies such as small freshly slaughtered reptiles. She learned to eat them, and Veg understood: to survive in nature, one had to live nature's way. She was a vegetarian no longer.

"Also," she explained with a certain difficulty, "it's Cal's baby. I have to live this way." She was not certain he would see the logic of that, or if there *were* any logic in it, but it was the way she felt. Her intake nourished Cal's baby; Cal's standards governed. Had it been Veg's baby . . .

"I loved him, too," Veg said, and that sufficed. He was not jealous of his friend—only glad that even this much remained of Cal. She had never told him the details of the conception, letting him assume it was before the dinosaur chase began. There had, after all, been opportunity.

"After this one is born, the next must be yours," she said. "I love you, too,—and this would be necessary for survival of our species even if I did not."

"Yeah," he said a bit wryly. "I'm glad you had the sense to go with him first. If he had to die, that was the way to do it."

In civilization, among normal people, this would have been unreal. Here, with Veg, it was only common sense. Veg had always wanted what was best for his friend Cal, and it was a compliment to her that he felt she had been worthy.

"We argued about whether man should colonize," she said. "We were wrong, both sides. We assumed it had to be all Earth or nothing. Now we know that there was a middle ground. *This* ground: just a few people, blending into the Cretaceous enclave, cutting our little niche without destroying any other creature's niche. If we had realized that before, Cal might not have felt compelled to match Tyrann, and they both would be alive today."

"Yeah," he said, and turned away.

The baby was birthed without difficulty, as though nature had compensated her by making natural birth easy. There was pain, but she hardly cared. Veg helped, and so did the birds: They made a fine soft nest for the infant. She named him Cave.

If her relation with the birds had been close, it was closer now. They nested, for their season had come 'round again. Aquilon would leave baby Cave in the nest with the eggs, and Ornette would sit on them all protectively. Aquilon took her turns guarding the eggs while the birds hunted. They were an extended family.

When Cave was three months old, and Aquilon was just considering inviting Veg to father a sibling, disaster struck. Agents from Earth appeared. Concerned by the nonreport from the advance party—Cal, Veg, and Aquilon—the authorities had followed up with a more reliable mission.

The mantas spotted them first: a prefabricated ship

coming in past the islands of Silly and Cheryb-dis. Three agents, one of whom was female.

Veg made a wheeled cart with a loose harness that either bird could draw, and set a nest in it. This made the family mobile—for there was no stationary place safe from agents. One manta was designated for each adult entity: Hex went with Veg, Circe with Aquilon, Diam with Orn, and Star with Ornette. Their function was to give advance warning when any agent was near any of the others, so that person could flee. There was to be no direct contact with any agent unless the nest was in danger. With luck, they would be able to stay clear until the agents left.

It was not to be. The agents were not merely surveying the land, they were after the people, too. The agents quickly ascertained the presence of a baby, and this seemed to surprise them. Hex, in hiding as two of them examined the deserted nest site, picked up some of their dialogue and reported on it: "Cooperation with tame birds I can understand, though they've really gone primitive," the male said. "But a human baby? There wasn't *time!*"

"She must have been pregnant before leaving Earth," the female said. "Then birthed it prematurely."

Aquilon was in turn amazed. "How long do they think human gestation *is?* Two years? Cave was full-term!"

But the riddle of the agents' confusion had to wait. There was no question that the agents intended to take the trio and the baby captive for return to Earth—they apparently did not know that Cal was gone—and this could not be permitted.

One would have thought the home team had the advantage: two human beings toughened by a year among the dinosaurs, two fighting birds, and four mantas—the most efficient predators known to man. But there were three eggs and a baby to protect—and the three agents were equipped with Earth's technology. In one sense, the contest of champions Cal had visualized was to be joined again—but this time the weapons were different. One agent could wipe out one tyrannosaurus with one shot.

Cal could have directed an efficient program of opposition—but Cal was gone. The agents were stronger, faster, and better armed than Veg and Aquilon.

"We've got to get out of here," Veg said. "They're canvassing this whole valley and the neighboring ones. They know we're here, somewhere, and they're drawing in the net. They'd probably have picked us up by now if they'd located Cal; they must figure he's hiding."

"Even now, he's helping us, then," she said, nodding. "And if we leave, what happens to the dinosaurs?"

"Earth will wipe them out, or put them in zoos, same thing," he said glumly. "We've had our problems with the reps, but it's their world, and they have a right to live, too. But we've been over this; we can't kill the agents. Even if we had the weapons, we couldn't do it. We'd be murderers."

"If we could stop the agents from returning to their base . . ."

"You think they'd go native like us?"

"It wouldn't matter, would it? Earth would have no report . . ."

He smiled. "Yeah."

"And if they were stranded here, maybe they'd come to see it our way. Maybe they'd settle, turn human. That female—she could bear children."

"Yeah," he repeated, mulling it over.

"Three men, two women—that might be a viable nucleus." There were aspects to it that disturbed her, but it was a far more positive approach than murder.

It was a daring plan. They set it in motion when one agent was on land, tracking down the moving nest.

Veg set sail with Hex on the old raft, the *Nacre*. He was a decoy, to draw off one of the two agents on the ship. "And Veg," Aquilon said as he left. "If it is the female who comes after you, smile at her."

"Yeah, I know," he muttered. "Use my delicate masculine wiles to subvert her superior feminine force." He spat eloquently downwind. "The day I ever cater to the likes of *her* . . ."

"You're a handsome man. You don't want to have to kill her . . ." But he was already on his way, and she felt like a procuress. Was she prepared to follow the same advice when she encountered a male agent?

She took one more look at Cave, sleeping in the nest-cart, guarded by the three other mantas and two birds.

Yes—to save him, to save the eggs, to save the enclave, she *was* prepared. If they succeeded in stranding the agents here, it would eventually come to that, anyway: crossbreeding. Better that reality than the loss of everything she had fought to preserve.

Then Aquilon raided the ship. She stripped and swam, hoping that in the night her motion would be mistaken for that of an aquatic reptile. If not—that was the risk she had to take. The agent aboard would not kill her out of hand; he would let her board, then subdue her—and the test of her commitment would be at hand. She was a buxom woman now because of nursing her baby. If she could seduce him, or at least lull him into carelessness so that she had a chance to scuttle the ship, then it would be done. The vessel was anchored in deep water and would not be recoverable.

Of course, then the water predators would close in . . . but she was ready to die. Perhaps the agent, realizing that he could no longer report to Earth, would be pragmatic and join her, and together with the mantas they could make it to shore.

She had smeared the juices of a vile-smelling root over her body to repel the water reptiles, and it seemed to work. She reached the ship without event and climbed nimbly to the deck.

To be met by the alert agent there. "Welcome aboard, Miss Hunt. I am Tama, your host. Kind of you to surrender voluntarily."

The female—the worst one to meet! "I've come to sink your ship," Aquilon said, knowing the agent was well aware of her intent.

Tama ignored this. "Come below decks." It was an order, not a request.

Aquilon thought of diving back into the bay. Once she went into the hold, captive, she would never have a chance.

Tama moved so quickly she seemed a blur. "Do not attempt to jump," she said from the rail behind Aquilon.

Whatever had made her think she had a chance against an agent? Sheer delusion!

"Yes," Tama agreed. "But you amaze me. too. You have indeed borne a child."

"Nothing amazing about it," Aquilon said. "You could do the same if you chose to."

"Yet you have been on Paleo only three months—and your Earth physical showed no pregnancy."

Aquilon stiffened. She had been on Paleo a *year* and three months. Surely the agents knew that!

"We shall have to plumb this mystery," Tama said. "You are not trying to deceive me, yet we can not explain—"

She was interrupted by the sound of a bell. She brought out a tiny radio unit. "Tama."

"Tanu," a male voice returned immediately. "Male acquired, one fungoid destroyed."

"Talo," another voice said. "Attacked by one sapient flightless bird. Bird destroyed, mission as yet incomplete."

Aquilon felt an awful shudder run through her. Hex dead, Veg captured, one of the great birds killed, she herself nullified—and the effort had hardly started. What a terrible price had already been paid!

"There is no need for further violence," Tama said. She held out the communicator. "Speak to your fungoids; tell them to land here. We shall treat you fairly."

Aquilon faced about and walked toward the cabin, her lips tight. There was no way she could mask her antipathy to the agents. Subble she might have heeded, but these were ruthless strangers who could read her every response and anticipate many of her acts.

Suddenly a gun was in Tama's hand. "Very clever!" she snapped. "You did not know you were being supported by a fungoid."

A manta! Aquilon suddenly recognized Veg's unsubtle hand in this. He had suggested that the mantas be confined to the defensive perimeter, and she, preoccupied with her own preparations, had agreed. Veg had sent a manta after her—and because she hadn't known it, she had been unable to give that fact away.

Tama fired. Aquilon, galvanized into action, made a dive for the weapon. But the agent's left hand struck her on the neck, knocking her down half stunned.

Then three mantas attacked simultaneously. They were fast, and they knew how to dodge projectiles and beams.

But the agents, forewarned, had armed themselves with scatter-shot shells, almost impossible to avoid.

Aquilon watched helplessly from the deck as the first manta went down, a pellet through the great eye. "Star!" Aquilon cried in horror.

The second manta came closer but was riddled by pellets through the torso. It sheered off and fell into the water. "Diam!"

The third manta caught the agent across the neck, severing windpipe, jugular vein, and carotid arteries. Even so, Tama got off one more shot, and the fungoid crashed into the deck.

Aquilon stood up unsteadily. "Oh, Circe!" she cried. "We didn't want bloodshed . . ."

Tama grinned with ghastly humor, unable to speak. She clasped her throat with both hands, containing the blood —but the damage was too extensive, and she slumped to the deck, dying.

The mission had been a disaster; now there were no mantas, and there would be no other woman on Paleo to share the burden of bearing children.

But she had a job to do: Scuttle the ship. At least she could save Paleo. She went below decks to locate the necessary tools to do the job. A projectile cannon, or even a sledgehammer, to make a hole in the bottom, to let in the sea . . .

Instead she found—a projector. She had never seen one before, but somehow she recognized its nature. The agents intended to establish a return aperture to Earth from right here!

She picked it up, intending to destroy it by smashing it into the deck. But her finger touched a switch inadvertently.

A cone of light came out from it, bathing her.

And she stood in a completely different scheme.

She was in a room about twenty feet long and fifteen wide. Walls, floor, and ceiling were plastered, and there was a fantastic variety of what were, to her artistic eye, highly authentic primitive art objects and paintings.

There were only two small, high windows and no door.

A homemade ladder made of poles and thong-bound crosspieces ascended to a small hole in the ceiling: the only exit.

Had she projected herself back to Earth, the very thing she had tried so hard to stop—or was she in a new alternate world, inhabited by primitive man? If she had joggled the setting on the device, she could have traveled randomly.

Without that projector, she had no chance to return —and who but the agents would ever use it to seek her out? Her choices were to submit to recapture—or escape into this world.

She was hardly conscious of making the decision. Veg, Orn, and her baby were on Paleo—but if any of them survived the onslaught of the two remaining agents, it would not be as free entities. And the projector must have fallen to the deck as she phased through, either breaking or fouling up its setting.

Better for her to accept the inevitable. She could not return and would not want to, and no one would fetch her. She would have to make a new life for herself here, wherever this was. Even if it should be Earth.

But her eyes were full of tears. Consciously she was desperate to return to her baby, to retreat into the warm jungle valley with Veg. Perhaps Circe had survived; she had crashed into the deck but might not be dead. At any rate, there would soon be new mantas, as the freed spores drifted and mated and grew. Maybe Orn managed to haul eggs and baby to safety. Oh, yes, she longed to go there . . . but surely Orn would *not* escape, the eggs would be lost, and her baby Cave . . .

Her baby—conceived in the cave. Suddenly, a year after the fact, the truth struck her: Cal, from an alternate world, had been projected to hers. For one day and a night. *Her* Cal had died; it was the alternate who had fathered her child. He had been summoned, somehow, in the hour of her greatest need.

"Thank God for that one day . . . " she whispered.

Now she was in another alternate herself. Perhaps she would help some other person, as she had been helped. Would that redeem the double wreckage of her life?

Meanwhile, her eyes were taking in her surroundings,

and she was reacting with growing excitement. In a manner, she had died, for she had been irrevocably removed from her world—and surely this one was akin to heaven. She had studied art like this before. She recognized it. Prehistoric man—neolithic—Anatolia, somewhere around 6000 B.C.

"Çatal Huyuk!" she exclaimed, pronouncing it with the soft Ç: Satal.

The study of art necessarily led to an appreciation of history, and she had absorbed a fair background incidentally. Now she stood still, concentrating, bringing it back from long-idle mental channels.

Çatal Huyuk was a mound in south-central Turkey—the ancient Anatolian peninsula—on the highland plateau, about three thousand feet above sea level. For many years archaeologists had thought there was no neolithic occupation of the Anatolian plateau and no real art or organized religion there. The excavation of Çatal Huyuk had completely changed that, for here was a flourishing, religious, artistic, peaceful city demonstrating an advanced ancient culture. A substantial segment of prehistory had had to be rewritten.

Of course this might not be *the* Çatal Huyuk. There had been similar cities in Anatolia, and it could be a modern replica. But it was certainly of this type.

Excited, Aquilon moved about, inspecting the room in detail, using it as a diversion from the horrors she dared not dwell on back in Paleo. The plaster on the walls was actually a thin layer of white clay. Solid timbers supported the roof. The floor was neatly segmented into several levels, as though the intent was merely to indicate distinct areas, like lines on a playing field. This would be a sleeping patform, with its reed matting; this the kitchen area. Here was the hearth, under which the family's dead would be buried. Here was the storage bin, empty at the moment.

The walls were painted in panels. Some were solid red; others had geometric designs bordered by representations of human hands and feet. One wall was dominated by a protruding sculpture: the stylized head of a bull, the two horns projecting up and out, surrounded by pillars and ledges that showed the shrine-like nature of this section.

She climbed the ladder cautiously and poked her head over the top. She saw the rooftops of a city, each a different level, each with its entrance hole.

There were people. Suddenly Aquilon was conscious of her nakedness; she had never had a chance to dress and had never anticipated—this.

They stared at her. In moments they had her ringed. All were women; the few men who showed their heads had been sent scurrying with a few peremptory words. There was no question which sex was in control.

Aquilon did not resist. The people were not hostile, only curious. They took her to another room and tried to talk to her, but their language was completely alien to her experience. Yet she was fortunate, for this relieved her of the problem of explaining her presence.

They took care of her. She was, it seemed, something of a phenomenon: a tall blonde woman in a land in which all women were short and dark-haired. They regarded her as an aspect of the goddess-mother and she did not go out of her way to deny it. She was, after all, a recent mother (ah, there was grief: Did they marvel at her sadness?), and it showed. On religious festivals —of which there were a considerable number—she was expected to parade naked through the ctiy, an object not of lust but of feminine presence. She had come to them naked, and that set the system; when she wished to move among them without reference to her goddess-head, she donned an elegant robe and slippers. They were able to accept this dual aspect; the dichotomy between goddess and woman was inherent in their religion. It was a pragmatic system.

If she had not already known it, the art of the city would have told her this was a matriarchy. There were paintings and sculptures and tapestries in splendid array. These people were indefatigable artists; pictures and designs were on walls, pots, clay statuettes, wood, baskets, pottery, weapons, and even skeletons. The eyebrows, cheeks, and lips of the women were also painted. A fine subindustry for making pigments existed—black from soot; blue and green from copper ores; red, brown, and yellow from iron oxides, and so on. Aquilon was already familiar with the technique and of course was a superior artist in her own right, which tended to confirm her status.

But in all this art there was not a single sexual symbol. No female breasts, no phallic representations, no suggestive postures. A male-dominated society would have abounded with artistic expressions of lust; in her own day the "nude" always meant a young, voluptuous woman. Here, nothing: Women were not motivated in this direction, and though many of the artists were male, they painted under direction of the priestesses.

She learned the language, and painted, and it was a rather good life. Gradually her grief for what she had left behind faded. The people were disciplined and courteous and not without humor and song. The men were out much of the day hunting. Many women wove cloth, prepared hides, and fashioned rather sophisticated clothing; others cleaned their homes and supervised repairs. The houses were scrupulously clean, with all the rubbish being dumped in the scattered courtyards. These people were primitive in that they could not write and lacked machine technology—but in all other respects they were civilized. More so, really, than those of her own day.

Then she discovered the projector. It was in a disused chamber beneath a new residence. It had been closed off because it had been damaged by fire and was considered unsafe; it could not be demolished because that would have interfered with the neighboring residences. There was also an element of religion, as there was in almost every aspect of life in this city: A revered old woman had lived in it once, and it would have been an affront to her spirit to destroy it entirely. So it had been vacated and forgotten for many years. But Aquilon was privileged to explore where she liked; how could the woman's spirit be insulted by the visit of a goddess?

In this chamber was a device very like the one she had found aboard the ship—but more advanced, for it had a television screen.

She experimented. The thing was self-powered but alien. She did not know how to operate it and hardly wanted to find herself in yet another alternate. Yet she was fascinated. In the course of days she worked it out: The screen showed which alternate it was attuned to, and a separate key enabled the operator to return to his point of origin: here. Other controls shifted the focus, making the images on the screen change dizzily.

There were an infinite number of alternates available. In the nearest, she actually saw herself bending over the projector, a few seconds behind or ahead of her. Once she exchanged a smile and wave with the other Aquilon who happened to be focusing on *her*. It was no replay of her own acts; these were separate Aquilons, individuals in their own right yet still very much *her*.

In farther alternates there were other scenes. Some were bizarre: walking plants, a huge machine hive, or perpetual blizzard. Others were tempting, such as a placid forest or a near-human farm fashioned from solidified fog.

She went further. She took the key, set the screen on the quiet forest, and activated the projector.

And she stood in the forest. It was real. The air was sweet and cool.

Nervous, she squeezed the key—and she was back in Çatal Huyuk, her heart thudding, her whole body shaking with the release of tension. She really *could* go and return!

One alternate was a desert. On it an Aquilon carried one of Orn's eggs.

Orn's egg! Suddenly it occurred to her that this alternate of Çatal Huyuk, with its lush surrounding plains filled with game and vegetation, was ideal for a flightless, five-foot-tall hunting bird: an avian Garden of Eden. There were aurochs—European bison, somewhat like the American "buffalo"; gigantic pigs, deer in great herds. Sheep and dogs were domesticated, and the men hunted wild ass, wild sheep, deer, foxes, wolves, leopards, and bear. There were many varieties of birds and fish. How Orn would have loved it here: abundant prey but no dinosaurs!

Orn: She had never been able to locate Paleo with Orn on it, or Veg, or the agents. She could not rescue her real friends. But that egg the alternate Aquilon carried contained a living *ornisapiens* chick. Suppose she fetched it, then went to another alternate and got another? One male and one female. Re-establishing a marvelous species . . . what a wonderful project! Perhaps she could make similar forays for mantas.

She watched the other Aquilon moving about, holding that precious egg. The woman cradled it in the crook of her arm as she stooped to touch the sand. There were tread marks there, as of a machine.

Machine! Aquilon knew about the self-willed machines. She had watched them consuming . . . everything. If they were cruising on that world, the humans had little chance, and the egg, none. And of course there was no game to speak of there. Even if hatched, the Orn-chick would inevitably die.

Aquilon decided: She would save that egg now.

Without further thought—for that might cause her to lose her nerve—she removed her elegant white goddess-incarnate robe, too valuable to soil. She took up the key (must never forget *that!*) and put it in her mouth for safekeeping. She took a deep breath and activated the projector.

The desert world formed about her.

For a moment she oriented, checking the desert and the alternate Aquilon. All was in order.

The girl saw her. "Who are you?" she demanded.

Aquilon realized that to this woman *she* was the original Aquilon, having no knowledge of the alternate framework. How to explain the past year and make her believe it—when at any time a machine could come upon them? "Pointless to go into all that now," Aquilon said. "Please give me the egg."

The girl stepped back, clutching it. "No!"

Aquilon hadn't anticipated resistance. The merit of her plan was so obvious! Too late she realized that what made sense to her would not necessarily make sense to her uninformed alternate. The girl was evidently younger than she and had borne no child; this alternate was a year or more divergent from her own. Poor planning on her part—but she had run this sort of risk by acting on impulse. Best to go ahead now.

"You must. You can't preserve it any longer. Not here in the desert, with the awful machines." But the girl didn't know about *those* yet, either. She had a lot to learn! All the more reason to salvage the egg from her incompetent hands. "I have found a new Garden of Eden, a paradise for birds. When it hatches there—"

The girl's face became sullen, resistive. "No one else can—" She halted, amazement spreading over her comely features. "You're *me!*"

"And you're me, close enough," Aquilon said impatiently. She should have explained about that at the outset! So many mistakes—she was fouling it up appallingly. "We're aspects of the same person. Alternates. So you know you can trust me. You—"

"But you—you're more—"

Was the girl accepting it? Good. "I bore a child —that's why. I nursed my son until two months ago. But—" Too complicated, and it hurt to remember. How she longed for Cave! "I lost mine. You'll keep yours. But you can't keep the egg."

The girl retreated. "A baby? I—"

Maybe she shouldn't have mentioned that. This girl had not had her baby. A whole different situation, for Aquilon herself had been transported to Çatal Huyuk, not this machine-desert world. For a moment Aquilon was tempted to stop and question this girl, to find out all the details of *her* life. Had she made love to Cal—or to Veg? Or an agent? What had happened to the Orn-birds of her Paleo that she should be left with the egg? Had she found a projector?

But that would be folly. She could not afford to engage in dialogue with all the myriad alternate-Aquilons she could reach. There was a job to do, and she should do it—or go home. "You're in danger. You can save yourself but not the egg." A human being could fight off a machine if properly armed or escape it—but hardly while carrying the egg. She had seen an agent tackle one in another alternate. Interesting that the orientation of her projector seemed to be on those alternates where other human beings had projected aboard, as though all projectors were somehow linked. The connection was geographic, too; obviously if she had projected to this desert world a hundred miles from this spot, she would not have been able to fetch the egg. It all implied some higher agency—something else to think about when she had the time. "There is little time, and it's too complicated to explain right now. Give it to me!" She reached out, hating the necessity for this brusque language, so unlike her. But she knew if she delayed any more, she would lose her nerve, and the job would not get done.

"No!" The girl retreated, hugging the egg.

"Give it to me!" Aquilon cried.

The girl straight-armed her. They fell together over a bag of supplies. The egg was caught between them and crushed, destroying the chick within.

"Oh, *no!*" Aquilon cried, her dream dying with the chick. Tears streamed down her face. "I came to save it—and I smashed it!"

The alternate was crying, too. But tears could not reconstitute the egg.

Aquilon staggered away, heedless of direction. A few paces into the sand she remembered the projection key. She took it out of her mouth and squeezed it.

Back at Çatal Huyuk she washed herself, donned her robe, and went out onto the roof of the city. There was a numbness inside her that would not abate. She had traveled to an alternate and done irreparable damage thereby because of her lack of planning and carelessness and impetuosity. What penance could she do?

After an hour she returned to the chamber with a heavy mallet and smashed the projector and screen. Never again would she trifle with alternity.

# Chapter 18

# REPORT

. .
. . .
. . .
. .

PATTERN ALERT: SURVIVAL

Pattern-entities, unable to comprehend the nature of physical sentience but unable to ignore it as a potential nonsurvival threat, instituted an enclave consisting of five divergent sentient entities: a pattern, a machine, and three forms of life—fungoid, avian, and mammal. There were also nonsentient plants and a population of sub-sapient animals upon which the sentients preyed.

The purpose was to observe the interaction of sentients, drawing inferences concerning their natures and survival potential within a restrictive environment. This information might enable the patterns to determine the extent of the potential threat to survival posed by the physical sentients.

To be certain that survival was the primary issue, the enclave was so designed that none of the occupants could survive comfortably without pre-empting the needs of the others. There were insufficient elements for the pattern, minerals for the machine, prey for the living predators, or mixed organic substances for the mammal infant. Direct competition was required.

In order to obtain a complete picture, a system of alternate-frame holography was used. Holography, as practiced in the physical scheme, involves the division of a given beam of energy into parts, one part subjected to an experience the other lacks. The resultant difference between the parts thus defines the experience. In this case, mature representatives of the sentient species were provided the means to observe some of the interactions within the enclave and within the framework of alternity itself. In this manner the reactions of the physical sentients could be contrasted to those of the nonphysical sentients, and the changes in the physical sentients contrasted to their like counterparts, rounding out the picture.

The experiment was not entirely successful. All the sample entities of the enclave survived despite its deliberately restrictive situation, and a majority of the travelers through alternity also survived—but this did not enlighten the pattern-entities. There was initial competition in both environments, followed by cooperation that greatly enhanced survival. The informaion did not fall into neat patterns, and the mechanisms and motives of the physicals remained unclear. The pattern-entities therefore ignored the experiment, failing to act or even respond even when the entities of both groups made serious attempts to communicate. The failure was not in the conception or execution of the plan but in the patterns' inability to interpret the results or to act on data received.

What had been intended as an exercise of short duration became one of greater scope—because it was left alone. In due course the entities of the enclave, utilizing techniques largely incomprehensible to the watching patterns, achieved comprehension and powers beyond those of their background societies. Patterns have substantial limitations in the physical world; physical creatures are similarly restricted in the pattern framework. True science is a combination of the two systems.

Only through a conceptual technology developed from the merging of systems can true progress be made. This means complete and free interaction between all forms of sentience. We—the five sentient entities of the enclave— have worked out the principles of such interaction. We are able to communicate meaningfully with all of the intellects we represent, as demonstrated by this report, which is being conveyed to representative frames for each of these types.

We feel that the fundamental knowledge must be placed in the minds of those entities best able to utilize it, with the proviso that it be used only to facilitate harmony and progress among all the alternates. We feel that four of our five representative species lack suitable philosophies or talents for this purpose. The fungoids and the aves do not have either the inclination or the manual dexterity to operate the necessary constructs. The mams have both—but lack appropriate social control. They are predators, exploiters: in their own description, "omnivores," destroyers of differing systems. Therefore, this power can not be entrusted to their possession. The pattern-entities are also capable and have better philosophical mores. But their cynicism in setting up this enclave and the associated "hexaflexagon" pattern of alternate frames shows that their philosophy is incomplete. Sentients are not to be toyed with in this fashion. In fact, the patterns have such extraordinary difficulty comprehending the nuances of physical need and operation that we feel that they, too, are unsuitable.

Only one species possesses incentive, capability, and philosophy to make proper use of the information and to carry through effectively on the implied commitment. For this species only, we append our technical report, granting the power of alternity.

We believe the machines well serve the need.

# Chapter 19

# ORN

Orn heard the terrible squawk and knew its meaning instantly. The predator mam had caught Ornette and killed her. Now it would come for him.

He did not feel grief, only loss. Now he had no mate, and the line of his species was ended—unless he found another mate or preserved the eggs. Neither he nor his eggs would survive if this man caught him—and the mam cub would perish, also.

Orn did not think in the manner of reps or mams. His mind was experience, and the experience was millions of seasons long: a racial memory. It did not employ words at all; to him, "mam" was that complex of impressions generated by the presence of fur-bearing, infant-nursing, warm-bodied vertebrates. "Rep," "aves," and the various representatives of such classes were similar concepts.

Orn knew the manner his kind had survived, back as far as his species had existed distinct from other aves. He was well equipped for survival in the world his ancestors had known. But that world had changed, and this made survival perilous.

Orn's ancestry contained no record of a chase by a predator mam, for mams had been tiny prey for most of their species duration. Thus, he had never experienced a threat of the kind this represented. But Orn was expert in hiding and in hunting—indeed, the two were aspects of the same process. He knew this mam was as savage and deadly as a young tyrann. If it caught him it would kill him and take the eggs and cub.

So he fled—but he did it expertly. He put his long neck through the front loop of the nest-cart and drew it behind him. The cub began to make noise. Immediately, Orn twisted his head about, bent his neck down, and found the chip of wood that was used for such occasions. He put it in the cub's mouth. The cub sucked on it and stopped crying.

Orn hauled the wagon into a dense thicket near a turbulently flowing stream, concealing it from the exposure of both light and sound. He washed his beak and feet in the stream, temporarily cutting down on his typical odor. Then he scraped over the traces the cart's wheels had made, carefully placing pine needles, palm fronds, and half-decayed brush in place so that it matched the forest floor. He found the rotting, arth-riddled corpse of a small rep and placed it nearby: That smell would override all else.

This was not the way Orn reasoned, for his mind did not work that way. It was merely the accumulated and sophisticated experience of his species. As the arths constructed elaborate warrens and performed many specialized tasks, so he performed in the manner survival had always dictated. That he did it consciously only reflected the talent of his species: His memories were far greater than those of arths, reps, or any other species and required far more sophistication of choice. But memory it was, not reasoning.

His camouflage completed, he washed himself again, waded downstream, and spotted a small grazing rep: a baby tricer. He pounced on it, digging his claws into the creature's back just behind the protective head-flange.

The slow-witted rep emitted a squeal of pain and whipped its head about. But Orn held his position just out of reach of the crushing bone, digging his powerful talons in deeper, flapping his stubby wings to maintain his balance. Unable to dislodge his attacker, the tricer stampeded. Orn rode it, guiding it by tightening the grip of one foot or the other, causing it to shy away from the increased pain.

Finally, Orn jumped off it, releasing the rep to its own devices. He had, in effect, flown: He had traveled a distance leaving no recognizable trace of his passage. No predator could follow his trail by sight or scent back to the hidden nest.

Now he made an unconcealed trail that led obliquely away from that nest. He knew the predator mam would come across it in due course and would recognize it. Orn made several big circles so that there was no obvious point of termination to betray his ruse, then set off for the territory of the largest and fiercest tyrann in the valley. The man would find plenty to distract him, following *this* trail!

But Orn had underestimated the cunning of this beast. The mam did not pursue his mock trail directly. He set an ambush for Orn.

Only the silence of the arths of the region alerted the bird. Normally, the little flying, crawling, and tunneling creatures were audible all around—except when an unnatural presence alarmed them. When Orn entered this pocket of quiescence, he knew something was wrong.

He retreated silently—but the mam was aware of him. A bush burst into fire beside him: the lightning strike of the mam's weapon.

Orn ran. The mam pursued. Orn was fleet, for his kind had always hunted by running down their prey. But this mam was far swifter on his feet than others of his type, the Veg and the Quilon. Orn had to exert himself to an extraordinary extent to leave it behind—and then he was unable to conceal his trail properly.

He could lead it in a long chase, hoping to tire it: Orn could run for days. But meanwhile the eggs were slowly growing cold. The warmth of the mam cub beside them in the nest and the covering of feathers and fibers extended the time those eggs could be left—but the night was coming. Both eggs and cub would need attention—the one for warmth, the other for food. If the cub were not fed, it would make noise—and that would summon the predator mam or a predator rep. Orn knew these things from recent experience.

He had to lose the mam quickly, then return to the nest for the night. Because it was well concealed, he should be able to leave it where it was until morning.

But the mam would not relinquish his trail. It fell back but never enough to permit him to eliminate his traces. He was in trouble.

Then a fung found him. Only with difficulty had Orn learned to comprehend these plant-creatures, for they were completely alien to his ancestry. Now he identified them fairly readily. They bounded across land or water faster than any other creature, and their strike was deadly—but they killed only for their food and fought only for the two friendly mams. Orn had no concern about the fungs.

Now he realized that its presence signified a development in the conflict with the predator mams. But he was unable to communicate with the creature.

The fung dropped before him and coalesced into its stationary shape. Though Orn could not afford to wait long, he knew there was motive behind this presence. He inspected the fung at close range.

The creature was injured. Fluids oozed from it.

Then Orn knew that the friendly mams had succumbed. This was the Circe fung, companion of the Quilon. It had been rent by a predator weapon. It had sought him out to show him this.

No creature but Orn remained to protect the nest —and the predator was after him.

The sounds of the pursuer were growing. Orn had to run again.

The fung rose up, faltered in the air, and righted itself. There was no doubt it was in trouble; its normal grace and speed were gone.

It moved toward the predator mam.

Orn realized that disabled as it was, the fung was about to attack the mam.

That might eliminate the mam or delay him so that Orn could get safely to the nest.

He ran to the stream, went up it, found another small rep, and forced it to take him toward the nest.

All was well. The eggs were still warm, and the cub was sleeping.

Orn sat on the nest, raising the temperature of the eggs while he poked his beak into the mash prepared by the Quilon. When the cub woke, he put a portion of this mash into its mouth, holding its head upright with one wing, patiently catching the spillage and putting it back into the mouth. When the cub balked, Orn performed his most difficult ritual: He took a shell dish in his beak, carried it to the nearby stream, scooped it full of water, brought it back, and set it on the edge of the nest. Then he took one of the hollow-reed sections and set one end in the dish, the other in the cub's mouth. The cub sucked. Water went up the tube and into its mouth. In this way it drank.

Orn's care of the cub was another function of his memory. Ancestors had on occasion sought to preserve the lives of young animals, the cubs of those slain for food. Those cubs could mature to become prey when prey was scarce, so this was a survival talent. Even a newly hatched chick, confronted with a helpless mam cub, would have reacted similarly, sharing food, cutting reed stems, fetching water, fashioning warm cover. It was a symbiosis that came naturally in the time of the dominance of the great reps.

Now he cleaned the nest. The mam cub, like all mams, was a voluminous processor of water. It imbibed great quantities and expelled them almost continuously. The nest was made so that most of the fluid percolated through and fell on the ground, but in time the damp bedding soured, creating an odor problem. Orn pulled out tufts of it and replaced them carefully with fresh. This took some time, but it was necessary and natural.

The cub slept. Orn covered it and the eggs and slept, too.

In the morning Orn left the nest well insulated and went out to hunt and reconnoiter. He did not take extraordinary measures to conceal his traces, for he intended to move the nest to a better place.

First he checked on the predator mam. The fung was gone, and the mam was injured; it had evidently been a savage encounter. Orn did not see the mam; he saw the site of the contest, noting the scuffled ground, the blood soaked in it—mam blood and fung ichor—and the bits of flesh and bone that had constituted the five extremities used to manipulate the lightning weapon. He saw the ruptured skin of the fung, the lens of the great eye, some muscle of the foot, but very little of the main body. That was odd, for the scavenger arths had not had time to consume that mass yet.

The mam had survived, badly damaged—but he was still casting about, searching for Orn and the nest.

Orn thought of attacking the mam. It was in a weakened state, and Orn was strong; he might now be able to kill it. But if the mam possessed the fire weapon and had some way to operate it despite the loss of the small bones, Orn could not prevail. A tryann might be crippled, but its tooth was still sharp! Orn left the mam alone.

He ran down a small brach rep, fed on it, and returned to the nest. It was full daylight now. The mam's search pattern was getting closer; he had to move the nest.

He hooked his neck through the harness and pulled. He would take it to a warm cave high in the mountain ridge. There the eggs could remain warm steadily, and the cub would be protected. Caves made good nesting places—sometimes.

But the route was difficult. He had to pass through the territories of two predator reps, slowed by the nest, and pursued by the mam. He had to navigate the fringe of a mud flat. Then the steep slope, where he would be exposed to the mam's lightning weapon.

Orn did not concern himself with the odds. He moved out.

He passed through the tyrann's region safely. Once this section had been the territory of a larger tyrann, who had pursued the Quilon up the mountain and perished in the cold; the new tyrann had not yet fully assimilated the enlarged area. It might be asleep or occupied elsewhere.

But the smaller rep predator, a struth, caught him.

Struth was as like Orn as a rep could be. He had long

legs, a slender neck, and he was within twice Orn's mass. He therefore regarded Orn as a direct competitor.

With a scream of outrage, Struth charged. Orn ducked out of the harness and scooted around the cart to face the rep. He would have to fight—otherwise, Struth would gobble the eggs and cub.

Orn's ancestry had had much experience with Struth. The rep was tough. Only in the cool morning could Orn match it, for then the rep's speed and reflexes were slowed.

This was morning.

Orn dodged aside as Struth charged. He brought up one foot, using his sharp claws to rake the rep's side with the powerful downstroke.

It was a good shot. A soft-skinned mam would have been disemboweled. But the tough hide of the rep protected it so that all it suffered was a nasty scrape and the severance of several small muscles. Meanwhile, its teeth whipped around, snapping in air not far from Orn's neck.

But Orn was ready for that motion. His beak stabbed forward, scoring on the rep's eye. The creature screamed with pain and pulled back.

Orn raised his foot again to make the evisceration strike, his best technique. But the rep's jaws closed on his elevated foot, for it was taller than he.

Immediately, desperately, Orn struck with his beak, punching out the other eye. The rep let go—but Orn's foot had been mangled.

He made one more strike against the blind Struth with his good foot. This time it was effective. Dying, his intestines spilling out, the rep collapsed. He snapped savagely at his own guts, trying to vanquish the pain.

Orn took no time to feed, tempting as the sight of those burgeoning entrails were. The mam would catch up! He returned to the nest, hooked his neck through, and limped forward. Weight on his injured foot pained him increasingly, but he went on jerkily..

He reached the mud flat. The mud was hot today; huge bubbles rose, expanded, and popped. But a detour around this area would greatly extend his route and take him back through Tyrann's territory. Lame as he was, that was not to be risked.

The best path through it would take him near several of the largest bubble-pits. Alone, he might manage it, even injured as he was. Hauling the nest made it far more difficult.

But if he made it, the boiling mud would serve as an equal barrier to the mam. Perhaps a fatal one.

He moved ahead, twisting around the hot pits with the inspiration of desperation. He had to keep the nest moving, for the wheels tended to sink in the soft surface.

He heard a noise. His head swiveled. The predator mam had emerged from the foliage.. The creature was swathed in material. Sticks were bound to its limbs and fabric covered its torso—not its normal removable plumage but tight patches covering wounds. Orn did not have to reason out the combat; his observation of the site of the engagement with the fung, coupled with the present condition of the mam, were sufficient to form the picture.

The fung had struck at the weapon first, nullifying it, leaving the mam to his own resources. Next, the fung had cut at the mam's broad neck. The mam had protected his neck with his limbs, and so those limbs had been deeply sliced: flesh from bone. But once the mam got his appendages on the fung, he had torn it apart. killing it.

Afterward, the mam had bound up his wounds to stop the loss of body fluids, using the sticks to fix the bones in place. And continued his pursuit of Orn. A formidable predator!

A huge bubble developed almost beneath Orn. It was a slow riser that had given no prior signal of its presence; Orn had judged this section safe.

He jerked forward, trying to haul the cart to safety. But its wheels were deep in the mud loosened by the bubble. He only succeeded in sliding it directly into the air cavity as it erupted.

The cart tipped, spilling one egg into the hot mud, then another. The cub wailed. Orn flapped his wings, striving for leverage against the air. But the harness entangled them.

The bubble burst. Scorching gas enveloped Orn. He squawked in agony, then inhaled the vapor into his lungs.

Burning inside and out, Orn sank into the bubble. As the heat of it cooked him, his glazing eyes saw a strange glow with many sparkling points. It coalesced about the nest, about the one remaining egg and the mam cub.

This was the one experience Orn's ancestry had been unable to bequeath to him: the death of the individual. Heat, pain, and a cloud of lights. Mud-matted feathers. Sinking.

The strangest thing about it was the apparent surprise of the watching predator. The *mam* was not dying; why was he sharing Orn's experience?

# Chapter 20

# UNIT

The unit phased into the forest-frame, orienting on the location of the two mams.

"Watch out!" Veg cried. "One of the machines is after us!"

"I am an emissary of Machine Prime," the unit said. "As you will recall, we made an agreement for the exchange of enclaves between our frames."

"That's true," Tamme said, but her body was tense. She no longer carried the frame homer: evidence of her bad faith.

"You will note that I address you in your own dialect rather than the one we worked out in our prior interview."

"I noted," she said tightly.

"Peace is being established between the alternates. We are in touch with your home-frame and are making contact with others. There will be no exchange of enclaves."

"Meaning?" She was trying to assess the best method of disabling the machine.

"We never intended conquest despite your suspicions. We wished only rapport, a stronger base against what we deemed to be a common enemy. You misjudged our motive, and we misjudged the patterns. Such misconceptions are being resolved. If you will accompany me now, you will be satisfied."

Veg shook his head. "I have this strange feeling we should believe it. A machine never tried to talk to me before. It sure knew where to find us, and it didn't attack."

Tamme shook her head. "I don't trust it. We know how vicious these machines can be."

"I must convey you to Çatal Huyuk," the unit said. "You have merely to remain in your places."

"A machine can move us across alternates?" Tamme asked.

"A machine always *has*," Veg reminded her.

Uncertain of the situation, she made no overt resistance. The unit moved them. They phased smoothly from forest to city without the intercession of Blizzard.

Aquilon saw the machine and opened her mouth in a soundless scream. Cal looked up from a partly dismantled machine. "Is this an answer to our message?" he inquired guardedly.

"You may call it such, Dr. Potter," the unit said.

Then Cal saw Veg and Tamme. He relaxed. "Hello," he said, raising his hand in greeting. "It must be all right. The machines are our friends—I think."

Tamme glanced from him to Aquilon. "And are we friends, too?"

"You've changed," Aquilon said, looking closely at her.

"I have gone normal."

"We are all friends now," the unit said. "I will convey you to Çatal Huyuk ancient, where—"

"Çatal Huyuk!" Cal and Aquilon exclaimed together.

"Amplification," the unit said. "This frame is Çatal Huyuk modern. Our destination is Çatal Huyuk ancient."

"*This* is Çatal Huyuk?" Cal asked. "Ten thousand years later?"

"Time becomes irrelevant. We shall return you to your own frames after the decision-assembly or to any you prefer."

Tamme and Aquilon were grim lipped; the men were more relaxed. What kind of decision was contemplated by the machine?

242

"Çatal Huyuk," Cal repeated, shaking his head. "The splendor of early man, forgotten . . ."

The two mantas settled, watching the unit. The surrealist city faded out, and the ancient Çatal Huyuk faded in.

A pattern-entity and the white-robed alternate Aquilon were waiting in the shrine-room. The two Aquilons were startled by each other, turning their eyes away. Tamme appraised the almost prisonlike closure of the room warily, judging whether the machine and pattern could be destroyed and an escape effected without the loss of Veg.

"We are all friends," the unit repeated. "We are gathered here for the dénouement so that we may resolve prior confusions and dispose the protagonists suitably."

The assembled entities looked around: five human beings, two mantas, and the pattern. No one spoke. Sparkles from the pattern radiated out, passing through the physical creatures without effect.

"In a certain frame," the unit said, as though oblivious to the tension that now gripped even the men, "Calvin Potter died. His cessation was witnessed by his close friend and potential lover, Deborah Hunt. It had a profound effect on her—so strong that the trauma extended across a number of related frames."

"My nightmare!" the informal Aquilon whispered.

The white-robed Aquilon glanced at her. "So you felt it, too . . ."

"This is a common effect," the unit explained. "It accounts for many of the instances of human *déjà vu*, precognition, spectral manifestation—"

Cal nodded, comprehending. "We call it supernatural because the natural laws of our single frame do not account for psychic phenomena. But if they are merely reflections of actual occurrences in adjacent frames . . ."

"This man," the unit said, indicating Cal, "crossed over to the frame of that woman—" it indicated the priestess Aquilon—"and impregnated her. He returned to his frame and dismissed the matter as a fantasy. She bore his child and cared for it with the aid of her friend Veg and the four mantas and the family of sapient birds."

Informal Aquilon stared at robed Aquilon. "You said you had a baby—"

"Yes . . ."

Informal Aquilon turned to Cal. "And you were the father?"

He spread his hands. "It appears so."

"This is another occasional effect," the unit said. "When there is a sudden, overwhelming need in one frame, and the capacity to alleviate it in a nearby one, spontaneous crossover can occur. In this case it was facilitated by the presence of an aperture projector left by an exploratory party from a farther-removed frame. Their agents were of the VI series—"

"We haven't reached VI yet," Tamme said. "TE is the latest—"

"That frame is ahead of yours," the unit explained. "Vibro and Videl projected in, left their spare projector in a secluded location in case of emergency, and went to study the reptilian enclave. They were misfortunate, being caught in a severe tremor, injured, and consumed by predatory fauna before they could reach that reserve projector. So it remained where it was, on that frame, until used by Mr. Potter."

Veg sat down on the edge of the raised level. "This is mighty interesting," he said. "But why were we picked up by the sparkles, and who left all those other projectors around? Can't *all* have been survey parties gobbled by dinosaurs—not in Fognose, or Blizzard, or—"

"The other projectors were left by people like you," the unit said. "You and the TA agent projected to another frame, leaving your instrument behind. The same thing happened on the other frames. Because each was a frame-site selected by the pattern-entities for temporary storage of experimental subjects—"

"White rats," Tamme interjected. She had not relaxed.

"—they were in phase with each other. Instead of opening on random frames and locations, each projected to the immediate site of another storage area. This kept the subjects contained—which was one reason the patterns arranged it that way. The aggregate formed patterns —again no coincidence, as this is inherent in any endeavor of the pattern-entities."

244

"It figures," Veg said. "So there was no way *off* that Möbius loop."

"That system has been dismantled," the unit said.

"But what about all the other people?" Veg demanded.

"They are being interviewed by other units."

"You mean the machines have taken over all alternity?"

Now it was out. Tamme, seeming relaxed, was poised for action—and Cal, both mantas, and the informal Aquilon were ready to follow her lead. There would be violence in an instant—the moment they were sure there was no better course.

"The term 'takeover' is inapplicable," the unit said. "Machine Prime now serves as coordinator for existent frames. This will be clarified in a moment."

"Let it speak," Cal murmured to Veg. "This is a most revealing dialogue." And now Veg also was ready for action.

"The follow-up mission of the agents was delayed for a year, in that frame where Aquilon was gravid. When the agents came, the mantas and sapient birds died, Vachel Smith was captured, and Miss Hunt projected to this frame: a world in the human neolithic. She found the projector left here by another party—"

"How many parties *are* there buzzing around?" Veg demanded.

"An infinite number. But most were incorporated into the pattern arranged by the pattern-entities; there was no mechanical way to break out of those loops. Miss Hunt experimented with her projector, visited her counterpart on the desert setting, inadvertently destroyed the egg, and returned here in remorse to destroy her projector."

"You did that?" the informal Aquilon asked.

The robed Aquilon nodded sadly. "What happened to my baby?"

"The bird Orn attempted to save both his eggs and your baby. He was stalked by an agent whose assignment was to recover both for return to Earth. The agents did not believe there had been time for a human infant to be conceived and birthed, so it was important for them to investigate the phenomenon fully. Orn perished —but a pattern entity salvaged one egg, the baby, and a fertile spore from the deceased mantas. These were con-

245

veyed to a restricted locale with a newly manufactured machine entity—"

"The scene we saw on the stage!" the informal Aquilon cried. Now her resolve to fight was wavering. The machine seemed to know too much to be an enemy.

"A nascent pattern was also created there," the unit continued. "Small, mindless shoots of the type generated on Mr. Potter's three-dimensional screen were sent across the limited element accesses in such a way as to combine and form a complete, sentient entity. This is the way new patterns are formed; they do not reproduce in the fashion of physical entities. There is a certain parallel in the manufacture of sentient machines, however. Such a machine had just been fashioned on the so-called Desert frame; one of its builders had obtained the necessary ingredients from the human supplies projected there—"

"So that was why it was hungry!" Veg said. "It was a mother machine." Now he, too, was wavering as further comprehension came.

"The analogy is inexact," the unit said. "However, the new machine was the one transferred to the enclave elsewhere on that frame. That enclave was then complete. The patterns, observing, hoped to ascertain the nature of the physical entities. They were not successful in that— but the enclave nevertheless achieved success of its own."

"But the enclave-baby died!" Informal Aquilon protested. "We saw the horrible machine slice it up—"

Robed Aquilon froze.

"The pattern-entity, reacting to the need of the other entities, restored the infant," the unit said. "Its death became apparent but unreal—as was Mr. Potter's death in your frame. You called that a nightmare."

"My baby—lives?" robed Aquilon asked.

"Yes. The component entities of the enclave combined their resources and developed a system of intercommunication that is now transforming sentient relations in all alternity. The adult enclave then assigned the duty of application and coordination to Machine Prime, and this duty we are now executing."

There was a pause. Then: "Why tell us all this?" Veg asked. "Why not ship us back to our homes, or execute us, or ignore us? What do you care what happens to us?"

"Machine Prime does not care. It merely honors the terms of the agreement. The enclave specified that those of you who were instrumental in its formation be catered to. Now it is being dismantled, and we—"

"Dismantled?" informal Aquilon asked. "What's happening to—to Ornet and the baby—?"

"The baby grew up to be a remarkably capable man," the unit said. "This was because the enclave pattern entity, OX, utilized special properties of alternity to age the entire enclave twenty years. The other inhabitants matured similarly. In fact, OX arranged for a baby girl from your home-frame to enter the enclave, and she also matured. She was intended as a mate for Cub—the man—but that did not occur. It seems your kind, like machine units, can not be raised in isolation and retain sanity. OX therefore arranged for the return of the girl and reverted the enclave to its original status after issuing the report of the five sentients."

"So the baby is—still a baby," informal Aquilon said. "And Ornet is a chick, and—"

"What's going to happen to them?" robed Aquilon demanded. "My baby—"

"Their disposition is for this party to decide," the unit said. "We suggest that the baby be returned to its natural parents—"

"Oh-oh," informal Aquilon said, looking first at her alternate, then to Cal.

Cal put his hand on hers. "I may have strayed once —but this was a confusion. At any rate, the matter is academic. I am not the father."

"You are the father," the unit said.

Veg chuckled. "Machine, if you can win an argument with Cal, you're a damn genius. Because *he* is." He shook his head. "Never thought he'd be involved in a paternity suit, though."

"It is not a matter for debate," the unit said. "We have verified the information."

Even Tamme relaxed. If the machine were ready to quibble about details, force might not be necessary. But if force *were* called for, it should be timed for that instant of confusion when the machine realized its mistake.

For Cal had to be correct; Tamme anticipated the point he was about to make and recognized its validity. When it came to intellectual combat, Cal was supreme, as she and the other agents had learned on Paleo.

"Let me explain," Cal said. "According to you, I crossed over, impregnated this woman—" he indicated the robed Aquilon—"and returned to my own frame in time to encounter the agent mission there. Meanwhile, in the other frame, she carried the baby to term and gave birth to it, subsequently becoming separated from it when it was about three months old. That baby entered the enclave and is now available for return."

"Correct," the unit said.

"Therefore, approximately a year passed in the other frame. But in *my* frame, a week has passed." He frowned. "Correction: two weeks. Time has become confused—but hardly to the extent of a year. My companions will verify this."

Veg's mouth dropped open. "That's right! Tamme got better in a week on Fognose, and there weren't many other—"

"True," Tamme agreed. She had assessed the mechanisms of the machine and judged that one projectile fired to ricochet off the treads and into the mechanism from below would cripple it. Slowed, it could then be reduced by a concerted attack. It was a small machine, not as formidable as some.

"Yes," informal Aquilon said. "How can he be the father—from two weeks ago?"

"He is the father," the unit repeated.

"I am undoubtedly the father of a baby in some other alternate—or will be some eight months hence," Cal said. "But some other Cal, from a frame running a year or more ahead of us—because this other Aquilon, in addition to her Paleo adventure, has evidently been here at Çatal Huyuk some time—is responsible for the enclave baby." He turned to informal Aquilon. "There is no question of my leaving you even for your double."

Veg smiled triumphantly, while Tamme made ready to act. "What do you say to *that*, machine?"

"We have mentioned that the agent mission was delayed for a year in this woman's frame," the unit said, making a gesture to include the robed Aquilon. "The patterns were responsible for that. This occurred in the course of the institution of their holographic representation, the enclave. Time travel is not possible within frames, but the appearance of it can be generated by phasing across frames, as you found on Paleo. By instituting a type of feedback circuit, a pattern entity is able to accelerate a portion of a limited complex of frames. This occurred in the enclave. But that portion is then out of phase and can not interact effectively with normal frames until it reverts. The only way to adjust the time-orientations of individuals so that one entity may interact with another in a different frame despite a dichotomy of time is to enable that individual to cross on the bias. That is what the patterns did with you. When you crossed from Paleo to Desert, you jumped forward more than a year in time."

"But we used our own projector!" Tamme protested, still trying to catch the machine in its error.

"Your projector is a toy compared to the ability of the patterns. They altered your route during transit."

Tamme saw her chance going. The machine was not at all confused and showed no weakness. From what she had seen of the patterns, they *could* play tricks with time . . .

"However, such bias must always be balanced," the unit continued. "The patterns could not jump you forward a year in one frame without performing a similar operation in the other. Therefore, the agents, similar in number and mass to your party—"

"Equations must balance!" Cal exclaimed. "Of course! We jumped to the desert, hurdling a year, while the agents hurdled the same year jumping from Earth into the other Paleo. So those agents lost a year without knowing it, and so did we."

Tamme relaxed. The seemingly impossible had happened. Cal had been outlogicked, their chance to strike eliminated. That machine really had control over the situation!

"Now I remember," the robed Aquilon said. "Tama

said there hadn't been time, and I didn't know what she meant."

"But we were in different frames," Veg said. "Our year couldn't balance out the agents' year, when——"

"Parallel frames—linked by Cal's brief crossover," the unit said. "For that purpose, with Cal in one and his child in the other, the two frames amounted to identity. By this device you were restored to phase with that Aquilon you impregnated, though she has lived more than a year longer than you in the interval between your encounters."

Now the machine was so confident it was even waxing informal, Tamme thought. It had started calling them by their group-given names instead of their legal ones.

Cal spread his hands. "I will, of course, assume responsibility for the baby——"

"Oh, no, you won't!" the robed Aquilon said. "You may be the biologic father, but *my* Cal died, and I mourned him, and I will not have an impostor take his place. In that interim I was dependent on the grace of another man, and so was the baby. I may not love him —yet!—but *he* is the one to raise the baby with me— if he chooses to."

Suddenly Tamme's deadly readiness had another object.

"Who?" informal Aquilon asked, perplexed. "This is all so confused——"

"Veg. I think he always was the one I really——"

Veg jumped. "Uh-*uh!* I loved you once—one of you, anyway—but that didn't work out. Now I'm with Tamme——"

Cal looked at him. "It would not be wise to place undue credence in an agent's expressed interest. An agent is the ultimate manifestation of the omnivorous way."

How cleverly the machine had maneuvered them! Now they were quarreling among themselves and would be unable to unite against the real menace. "I love him," Tamme said. "I go where he goes; I eat where he eats, figuratively and literally. It doesn't matter who doubts it, so long as *he* believes. I can understand why she loves him, too—but I shall not give him up."

"Not *him*," the robed Aquilon said. "I mean *my* Veg. Maybe he's dead, too, now, but——"

250

"He is not dead," the unit said. "The surviving agent of that frame, Tanu, is in the process of taking him back to the major transfer point on Paleo so he can be returned to Earth to stand trial for treason. We can recover him for you."

"Yes!" she cried.

That agreement seemed to finish any thought of opposition. If the machine could fulfill its promise—and there was no reason why it couldn't—they all stood to gain far more by cooperating.

"There remains the disposition of the other entities of the enclave," the unit said, as though all this had been routine. "The manta Dec and the bird Ornet, now too young to comprehend their parts in this matter—"

"Bring them here, too," the robed Aquilon said, seeming to radiate her joy at the recovery of her baby and her man. "This fertile plain is a paradise for their kind. That's why I tried to bring the egg here—" She looked at her double. "I'm sorry—"

"If I had known, I would have given it to you," the informal Aquilon said. "Ornet and Dec belong to your frame."

The unit activated a relay. A small manta, a large chick, and a human baby appeared in the middle of the room. They drew together defensively, the manta and the chick standing on either side of the baby, facing out, poised.

The robed Aquilon went to them, extending her hands to the manta and bird, winning their confidence. She picked up her baby, hugging him, smiling with tears streaming down her cheeks. "You'll like it here—I know you will!" she cried. "The people here won't hunt you; you'll be sacred, as I am." Then she looked around the room. "Why don't you stay, too?"

Veg and Tamme exchanged glances. "The baby I might bear would not resemble me . . ." she cautioned him.

"I *know* who it would resemble!" he said. He frowned. "I sort of like the forest . . ."

"You will be free to travel between frames at will," the unit said. "I will convey you."

"Even to Earth?" Cal asked.

"Anywhere in alternity, Calvin Potter. This privilege will not be extended indiscriminately, but these present here are the parental entities to the enclave, insofar as those entities survive. There will be access to the entire fabric, as required by the compact."

"I am interested in the comparative evolution of the several forms of sentience—pattern, machine, and life," Cal said. "The machines, for example, must have been created, perhaps by an early compromise between energy and physical states of sentience. There must be a fascinating history—"

"There is," the unit agreed. "This, too, is available to you."

The robed Aquilon looked up. "I meant all of you, and OX and the machine, too, if their frames will give them up. The whole enclave could grow up normally, in a better environment. Learning to live and work together, showing the way for all the sentience of alternity . . ."

"What a marvel that could make of this city," Cal said. "Representatives of all the sentients."

"Çatal Huyuk modern . . ." the informal Aquilon said. "This is where it starts—right here, in this room, now . . ."

The pattern entity in the corner sparkled. "This is OX," the unit said. "He accepts your invitation. Of course he will be in touch with his own kind, too. but he wants to continue his association with the spots—that is, physical sentience."

"But what about the machine?" the robed Aquilon persisted. "From what you say, it belongs with the others. It's not a bad sort. It should be with the entities of the enclave, and those of us who—understand. It shouldn't be sent back to—"

"Mach has been temporarily incorporated as a unit of Machine Prime," the unit said. "The matter has therefore been resolved."

"Now wait a minute," Veg said. "That little machine has a right to decide for itself whether it wants to be swallowed up in—"

Cal put a hand on his friend's arm. "It's all right."

252

"Who are you?" Tamme demanded, already guessing the answer.

The unit made a gesture with wheels and blade that was very like a smile. "I am Mach."

# AUTHOR'S NOTE

Some readers may be curious about the games of "Life" and "Hexaflexagon" described respectively in chapters 9 and 11. A number of readers wrote to inquire about the game of "Sprouts" described in my earlier novel *Macroscope,* so I hope to save us all trouble by identifying my sources here.

"Life" is derived from Martin Gardner's column in *Scientific American* magazine for October and November 1970, and January and February 1971. (Martin Gardner is not to be confused with John Gardner, founder of *Common Cause,* another worthy entity.)

"Hexaflexagons" are real figures that can be made from folded paper; I have made several with three, six, and twelve faces and recommend them as entertainment for children and adults. The source is *The Scientific American Book of Mathematical Puzzles & Diversions,* by Martin Gardner, first published in 1959 by Simon and Schuster.

And for *Macroscope* readers: "Sprouts" is also from Mr. Gardner's column in *Scientific American* for July 1967.

# HEXAFLEXAGON CHART

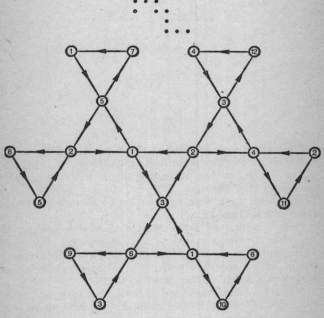

Key:

1. Forest
2. Orchestra
3. Fognose
4. Jungle gym
5. Blizzard
6. Walls

7. City
8. Planes
9. Machine-hive
10. Walking plants
11. Pattern
12. Bazaar